STONE KINGDOM

VOLUME 6

THE GREAT FORGET FANTASY SERIES

TERRY IRONWOOD

All rights reserved. No part of this publication may be reproduced, stored or transmitted in any form or by any means, electronic, mechanical, photocopying, recording, scanning, or otherwise without written permission from the publisher. It is illegal to copy this book, post it to a website, or distribute it by any other means without permission.

Copyright © 2024 by Terry Ironwood

This novel is entirely a work of fiction. The names, characters and incidents portrayed in it are the work of the author's imagination. Any resemblance to actual persons, living or dead, events or localities is entirely coincidental.

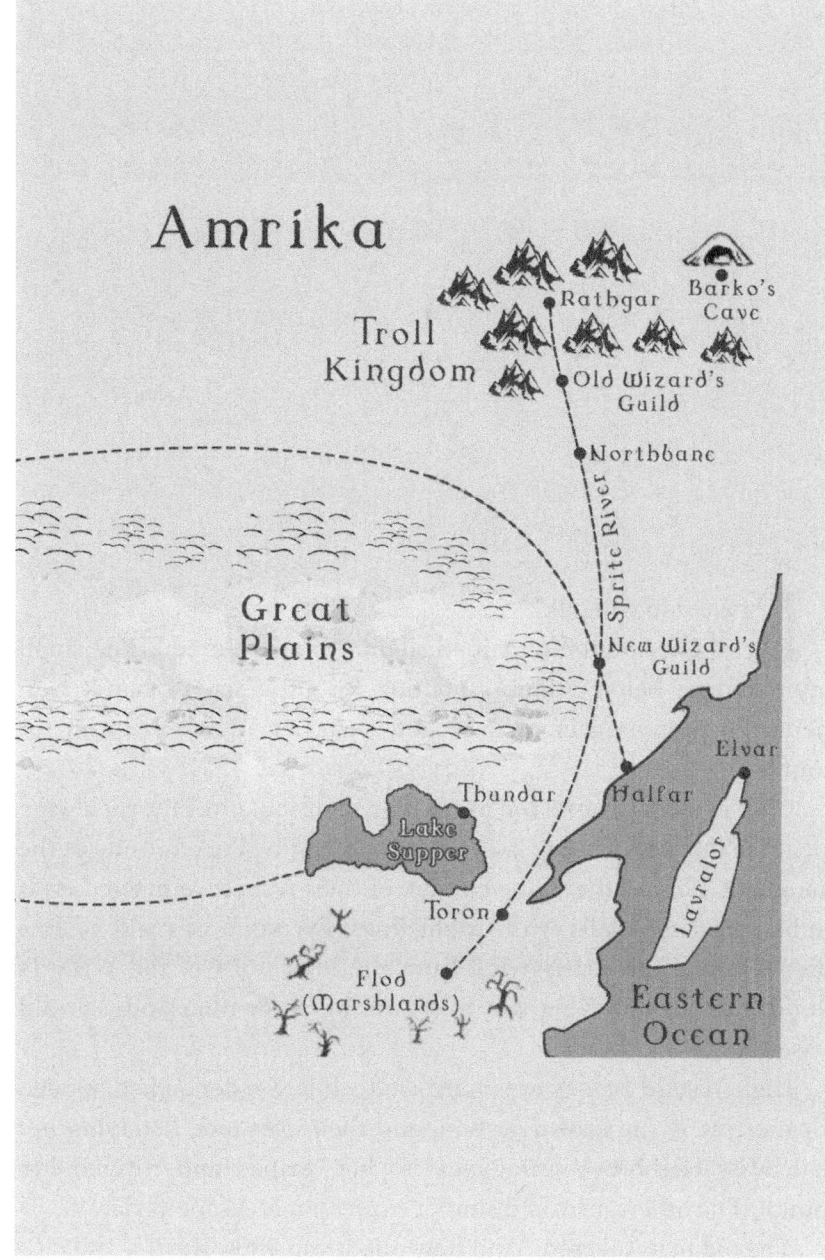

1

"The Guild will fall."

The council remained silent. All eyes stared at the small boy standing before them, clutching his little sister's hand. Han made the pronouncement loud and clear, leaving scant room for doubt.

Chip glanced around the room. The representatives for each wing sat at the immense hexagonal oak table, digesting the enormity of the statement. Behind them, the colours of their respective magic Levels emblazoned the walls with bright hues. Everyone was still reeling after watching the barrier fall from the high walls of the Wizard's Guild. The Demon King was free from his three-thousand-year-old prison.

High Wizard Balor's eyes narrowed while Xander sighed. Queen Eleanor sat in the brown section, and their eyes met, betraying her fear. Miss Highbrow, sitting next to her, gasped and covered her mouth. The others mirrored similar expressions, except Skylar.

The old man sneered. "And how might you know this?"

Han looked at him with his pale-blue eyes. "I have seen it in my dreams."

"Then that is what it likely is, boy. A dream." He did not bother to hide his contempt. "There are no Seers your age. I see no benefit in wasting more of the council's time, so I vote to—"

"There is more." Han cut him off, looking at the High Wizard.

Skylar made a choking sound. "How dare you..."

Balor raised his hand. "Carry on." The old Seer sat back in the blue section with a dark expression but remained silent.

"You must find the Light Elves."

"We have scoured all the histories. There is no mention of their disappearance or location." The High Wizard spread his hands, letting the white embroidery on his blue cuffs slip below his wrists. He sat alone in the raised white section. Chip surmised that given his status as the most powerful human Blue Level magic wielder in the world, coupled with his reputation for ostentatiousness, the High Wizard felt he deserved his own section. Why it was white still puzzled the boy.

"You have not searched them all," Han stated.

Auntie Clare stood behind the children, looking bewildered. Chip felt sympathy for the confused midwife, who looked out of place. The two soldiers, Neb and Jon, stood to the side with stoic expressions. After entering the Wizard's Guild earlier in the afternoon, the small party had exchanged hasty greetings with everyone before the Cleric ushered them into the council room to escape the approaching storm.

"Yes, we have," Balor said evenly, his face beginning to betray impatience.

"My goodness, the boy is right." Xander let out an explosive breath and turned to his older brother. "We emptied what we could before the troll army reached the gates three millennia ago, but we left the archives. They describe Earth's history before the Breaking, located deep in the lower levels above the dungeons. We had no time to extract them."

The High Wizard shook his head. "Those books and scrolls are dusty tomes written after the Great Forget and end at the Breaking. That is only the first thousand years of our history. How could they predict the current location of the Light Elves four millennia later?"

Xander sighed. "I do not know, but they still form part of the histories."

Skylar looked at them as if they were mad. "May I remind you that the old Wizard's Guild is now King Jaggar's fortress, and we have been at war with the trolls for a thousand years? It would take a mighty army to retake the fortress, and the casualties would be too many to count. This would play exactly into the Demon King's hands. Such a plan would require a vast number of magic wielders, which would weaken the Guild. We would be self-fulfilling this boy's supposed prophecy."

Xander turned to the old man, his face darkening. "The child has been right about everything so far. The Seer Linduk spoke of his ability to See in Thundar. The Galad prophecy speaks of a young Seer holding the key and revealing the last prophecy. Surely you are not disputing the veracity of our most revered telling?"

"Yes, but is he the one? How can you be sure?" Skylar scrutinized Han. "Perhaps we should find out." He waited a moment to see if the High Wizard would object, but Balor remained impassive. The old Seer took his indifference as permission, and his eyes blazed bright blue. "Let's see what you are hiding in there, boy."

Han turned to him without fear.

Chip knew the old man was entering the little boy's mind, delving into his memories. Xander sat up to intervene, but Han's casual defiance seemed to give him pause.

"Ah, now I see..." Skylar smiled. "I will interpret this myself..." The old man suddenly stopped talking, and a look of shock crossed his features, then horror. "It cannot be..." He seized up, eyes bulging, then he screamed. "Make it stop...please... Help!"

"I have only shown you what will likely be. You wanted the truth," Han stated calmly. Something seemed to pass over the little boy's eyes, almost a flash of white. Chip leaned forward, unsure. Skylar wrenched his head away, causing his chair to topple backwards. His feet stuck out straight in the air as he struggled to right himself. Garth Stone stood a few feet to the side but remained motionless, except for a tiny smile that only Chip could likely discern. The skinny blond boy, Ethrang, laughed out loud in the green section, causing Wing Leader Pete to frown.

Gasping, the old Seer struggled to his feet and repositioned his chair. His eyes had returned to normal, and his hair looked dishevelled. He smoothed the front of his robes and sat rigidly back down. At least he had stopped screaming.

The amusement in Xander's eyes was unmistakable. "Did you get the answers you were looking for?" the wizard asked mildly.

The old Seer glared at him and then turned to Han. "Is that our future?"

"Most Paths lead to it. Yet not all," the boy replied.

"What did you see?" asked Balor, giving the man time to collect himself.

Skylar coughed and then began to speak, his voice trembling. "I tried to see his memories... He somehow blocked me then chose a select few. I saw the Guild, the gates smashed apart like paper, and watched one of the great statues fall on the students. Then the demons came, clawing and tearing them to shreds as they tried to flee. The next memory showed the Last Battle. The great city of Toron was in ruins, bodies strewn everywhere, fire and smoke..." The old man's face turned stark white. "There were so many of them, all shapes and sizes, led by the Demon King. Red power shielded his body as he walked across the corpses with a long black cape. He wore a horned helmet with slits for his shining red eyes. His Power was unimaginable. They trapped us in a dark place. We were exhausted, and then they came, tearing us apart." He shuddered, looking up at the small boy with haunted eyes. "How can you stand it?"

The young Seer's face softened. "Because I know it is not real, at least not yet. It is foolish to worry about things that haven't happened, especially the scary things. I focus on the moment...the now."

Balor studied the child. "Why did you show him this?"

"So he sees what is at stake if the Demon King wins." Han scrutinized Skylar, his eyes boring into the old man. A look of sadness or possibly disappointment crossed his features before he continued. "There has been a...shift."

"Shift?" the High Wizard asked.

"Yes. The Balance has responded. Or perhaps it is the natural course of things."

"Responded to what?"

"Him." Han pointed at Chip.

"And how has it responded?"

"The white-eyed demons now have magic." He stated it as if talking about the weather. Balor's eyes raised. "I saw it in my dreams."

Skylar's head snapped up. "I knew it. The boy never should have saved her. Now, do you see?" He glowered at the Guardian. Queen Eleanor looked down.

Chip's anger flared, but before he could retort, Han responded. "He creates his own Path."

The old Seer grumbled but said nothing.

"So then there is free will?" Chip said, letting his anger subside. Han gave him an impish smile and shrugged.

"I think it's important we believe we have free will," Miss Highbrow said quietly. "Or else no one would feel responsible for their actions."

"Thank you, Brown Wing Leader," Balor interjected, "but that is a subject for another day. My concern is this added level of complexity. This news is disquieting, to say the least. White-eyed demons with magical abilities running through the countryside will terrify the people. The Unnamed One could be at the gates of Toron in a month. How can we possibly go to the old Wizard's Guild, find out where the missing Light Elves are, retrieve the Orb and return in time?"

"You have longer than you think," Han said. "The Unnamed One will not attack in the winter. The demons cannot survive the cold. They don't give off much heat, even if clothed. They will hide in their caves. He also wants to ride a dragon."

Skylar scoffed. "And if you are wrong? We are sitting ducks."

"I am not wrong. All Paths lead to this."

Xander nodded. "Young Han has a point. Winter is a demon's weakness, even in the old days. If they were caught on the Great Plains during a snowstorm, much of the Demon King's army would perish. Winter arrives early there. However, I suspect his ego will have more to do with his decision. The Unnamed One prefers to ride his black dragon up to the gates of Toron and set it aflame. A few extra months will give him time to birth the creature and grow it to adulthood. He likely has ways to speed up its development. I know that, near the end, before the dragons supposedly went extinct, the Light Elves could coax a dragon's growth with magic. Very well, this is finally a stroke of good fortune. Finding the elves may not be easy, but we have a starting point."

The High Wizard agreed, "Good. Who should we send? King Jaggar bears ill will towards me, so I will remain here."

"I wonder why," Xander muttered, causing Skylar to gasp. "Very well. I will go with the Guardian, Queen Eleanor, Wing Leader Mary..." He paused, turning to the green section. "And Ethrang. I have a feeling our young shapeshifter may come in handy."

Eleanor's eyes widened at the mention of the Blue Wing Leader. Chip remembered their wizard's duel not ending well. The queen's magic had overpowered Mary, the former advisor to High King Dominor, causing open resentment. She considered Eleanor a barbarian for living in the small, backwards town of Vanalon. Mary reacted to her selection with a grimace.

"I do not wish to be around...trolls," the Blue Wing Leader stammered and glanced at Eleanor. The double meaning was clear. "I think I am better suited at the Guild or in Toron."

Chip turned to see Chase gawking at her beauty and rolled his eyes.

"It is not a request," Balor said then turned as Kristan and Thomas raised their hands at the same time.

"We would like to go too, High Wizard," the blond twins said as one.

Balor glanced at Xander, who nodded. "Kristan won the Wizard's Duel, making him a powerful ally, with Thomas not far behind. I cannot think of a more important mission." The twins nodded vigorously in agreement. "I also think a dozen or so Protectors should accompany us in case things get out of hand. Maxim can choose."

Balor turned to his Protector, who nodded.

Another hand shot into the air. "Can I go?" Jordy asked with a hopeful look.

"No, you will stay and administer the Trials. I can't send everybody." The young man's face looked glum, but he nodded.

"It is settled then. You will leave in two days hence. Make preparations," Balor ordered. "Your mission is of the utmost importance. Without the orb, we are lost. Find the Light Elves and bring it to me. The High Council meeting in Toron will be delayed until your arrival. We need all the races with us to stand a chance. Remember, King Jaggar is cunning. I never trusted him. Be on alert." He paused to look at young Han. "Is there anything else?"

The little boy scrunched his eyes, looking inward. Then he blinked, pointing at Chip. "Two darknesses will descend on you. One you cannot defeat. The other you will lose yourself in unless you see life." His face took on a look of sadness. "You will be all alone."

Chip groaned. "Is nothing ever easy?"

"Nothing worthwhile," Xander chimed, offering a supportive but weak smile.

"That concludes—" Balor began.

"Wait!" Ethrang exclaimed with a smile. Skylar's mouth dropped open at the interruption, but nothing came out. The breach of protocol was apparently too much for him to lend a voice to. Chip smirked.

"Yes?" Balor regarded the skinny blond boy with a mild look of disapproval.

"There is a certain magic wielder who did not respond to the summons to train at the Guild. His name is Siz. Or at least we think it is. His father is a fisherman, and they live on Lake Supper in Thundar. The Dark Elf named Murk impersonated him. I'm curious to see what he is really like."

"I agree. Refusing a summons is grounds for punishment," the High Wizard said. Ethrang beamed, displaying a broad smile. The twins looked at each other and hid grins. It was obvious the green-robed boy was causing mischief. "I will send a couple of Protectors to retrieve him."

"No need," Ethrang piped up again. "I can fly there as a Giant Eagle in a couple of hours and return with him before nightfall on Redmane. Well, at least my version of Redmane."

"High Wizard," Balor corrected.

"Sorry, High Wizard," Ethrang added.

"Very well. Fetch the boy. Introduce him to the Wing Leader for his appropriate Level tonight. He can be Assessed tomorrow."

"Will do…High Wizard," Ethrang said with a straight face.

Balor glanced around the room. "Make preparations for this important journey. Follow my brother's lead when dealing with the trolls. He and King Jaggar had at least a civil relationship. Han, thank you for giving us this valuable information. I have much to think about. The soldiers accompanying you can stay with the Protectors. The rest of you are welcome to the guest suites."

"I want to stay with Chip. Along with Auntie Clare and my sister, Beth." Han looked down at her and smiled. She beamed back at him.

"I think I can grant that request. Miss Highbrow?"

The Brown Wing Leader looked bewildered as she digested another breach of protocol then recovered. "Why not? The more the merrier, High Wizard." She offered him a strained smile.

"Good. I would like to speak with Chip in private. The rest of you may go." Han's face drooped. "Don't worry, he will rejoin you later in the Brown Wing." The little boy broke into a smile and nodded.

Everyone filed out except the Guardian and High Wizard.

Balor stood up. "Follow me."

Chip watched him pick up a dark staff leaning on the back wall. Tiny runes covered its full length.

"Can I ask what the purpose of the staff is, High Wizard?" the boy inquired.

Balor turned to study him for a moment as if debating whether he should answer. Then he smiled and held it out for him to look at. "This is from a rare ironwood tree that grows only in the barbarian forests far to the southwest. They have many types, but only a few come from this species. It is the hardest wood in the world. Like stone but much lighter." He handed it to Chip, who picked it up easily with one hand, marvelling at the smooth texture. As he did, a jolt of energy ran into him, and he sensed a tremendous magic stored within. There was something else too, a...darkness.

"How is this possible?" Chip breathed in wonder.

Balor laughed. "Power can infuse objects, but the effect is short-lived and usually ineffective. This special wood holds the Power in it for much longer and can store vast quantities of magic. I have been feeding it Power for millennia. It might even stop a blast or two from you."

The boy's eyes widened. "What are those symbols?"

"They are runes." The High Wizard grimaced. "I may have obtained the staff from a...questionable source."

Chip raised an eyebrow.

Balor rolled his eyes. "Fine. A witch inscribed them. And not just any witch. Her name is Morgeth, High Witch of the Secret Caves." He paused, again deciding what he should disclose. "After erecting the barrier, the witches rose to prominence and founded Banfar, awaiting the Demon King's return. They were an ancient sect formed soon after the Great Forget. Rumour has it they descended from the north, in the Darkwood area, though nobody knows. The witches created trinkets for people to ward off evil, yet a pattern developed where those with such talismans experienced terrible luck and ill fortune. Runes were discovered on these small pendants and charms, and finally people realized the witches were evil. The people shunned them, and some became nomadic. On their journeys, they discovered a special ironwood tree and made three of these staffs.

"Their holy book, the Book of Seeing, spoke of a return of the Unnamed One, who would return to rule the world. They waited in Banfar and prepared for him. Two centuries passed. The Guild discovered what they were doing, and I led a group of magic wielders to investigate the rumours. I was the newly appointed High Wizard and had completed the construction of the Guild. I wanted to show the monarchs I could dispose of any threat. We tried to capture the witches, but they blocked our magic with these talismans and fled north. I was able to trap their leader, Morgeth, before she could escape Banfar. She offered me the staff for her life, explaining the Power it could hold and the protection it offered. She promised to leave Banfar and never return. I was a young man then, and she was incredibly beautiful. I found myself agreeing. Perhaps, she bewitched me." He smirked and took the staff back.

"So runes can attract evil?" Chip asked.

"It is possible, yes. Runes can contain things or trap them, yet also invite them. It is a form of magic that should not be used. It is dark magic. I would not have made the trade, but it felt right then. The staff may prove useful one day, though I sense darkness deep within."

"I felt it too."

Balor nodded and turned. "Come. I have something else to discuss." He gripped the staff and led them to a door at the back of the council room. He opened it to a short hall that led to a gold door. Grasping the polished knob, the High Wizard opened the door to reveal a massive room that took the boy's breath away.

The vaulted ceiling looked to be a hundred feet high. Sculpted pillars ran up walls covered in rich paintings with gold or silver frames. Various tables and chairs were arranged on the gleaming white marble floors. Soft lanterns surrounded by glass emitted a warm glow around each sitting area. Everything shimmered and sparkled with light and beauty.

"Is this...the Blue Wing common room?" Chip asked in awe.

"What? Of course not. These are my private chambers." The boy looked at him with wide eyes. Balor appeared sheepish for once. "I suppose it is a bit much for one person, but it is important to let people know where they stand. Kings and queens sit here and must be suitably impressed. Do you know how many important documents have been signed in this room? How would it look if their living quarters looked nicer than mine? No, appearance is very important. If you want to impress someone, begin by dressing nice. It will change the way you perceive yourself as well. Pretend until it becomes a reality. Don't simply want to be a certain way, be that way."

Chip thought it over and nodded. "I suppose it makes sense, but... I feel that if you have this much, others are forced to have less."

"Yes, greed is a powerful urge. It can never be eliminated, only controlled. Nothing we do is unselfish. My father, Arkan, always reminded me to serve the people." Balor looked down, likely remembering the ball of light that arced across the sky earlier in the day after the barrier fell. It was the spirit essence of his father, disappearing forever into the cosmos. The High Wizard sighed. "Come, let me show you something."

He drew the boy to a beautiful wood table in the center of the room. On it rested a long, jewelled dagger. The hilt shimmered with colour from slivers of multi-coloured stones masterfully set into the metal hilt. Chip had never seen anything like it. Balor shifted the staff into his left hand, keeping it between them, and picked up the dagger.

The High Wizard turned quickly and stabbed at the boy's midsection. Chip didn't react in time, and it sliced him open. Blood spattered the ground as he stumbled back. Balor stood in front of him, gripping the staff and dagger.

"Never trust anyone."

2

Chip gasped as his blood spilled on the ground. Luckily, he had blocked the attack with his bare hand, which sliced open. The blade had not entered his stomach. The boy's rage exploded, and his eyes blazed a bright red. He glared at the High Wizard of Amrika, shocked and disappointed.

"Why?" he asked, drawing in his Power to retaliate.

"Now, now. It was a test. More importantly, I needed your blood." Balor leaned the staff against the desk, ignoring the boy, and used the jewelled dagger to slice open his own left hand, creating a similar wound. Chip's rage changed to confusion. "I knew you would block it, and if you didn't, I would recommend you train more. The lesson is still valid. Don't trust anyone, especially near a weapon. Believe me, I have learned the hard way."

Balor put the dagger on the polished table. "Now, the blade already had your blood on it, which is now in me, but feel free to spare a little more. Hold your hand over mine." Chip did not move. "For goodness sake, I want you to heal me. First, I need more of your blood. I am trying to replicate what happened in the cornfields."

Chip finally understood. His blood mixed with Eleanor and Chase's when he healed them in the cornfields. They now had red chips in their eyes, giving them increased powers. Balor wanted the same. He felt a wave of fear for a moment, picturing Balor with red chips in his intense blue eyes holding the staff. Finally, he said, "You could have asked."

"What would be the fun in that? It taught you a lesson and allowed me to gauge how much control you have over your Power. You showed good restraint." He let out a rare laugh. "Now, be so kind to spare a little of your blood. I apologize for cutting so deep."

The boy looked at him for a moment longer then sighed and held his dripping hand over Balor's wound. Their blood mixed.

"That should do it," the High wizard said. "Now, please be kind enough to heal me. Try to replicate what you were feeling in the cornfields."

Chip surrounded the wound with his Power, mending the split tissue. He forced himself to care about the wizard's well-being. He looked up when the wound had fully healed.

Balor's eyes were the same bright blue. The boy looked closer, but there were no red chips in them.

"Well?"

"Nothing, I'm afraid. I tried," Chip confessed.

Balor scowled. "Nothing is ever easy," he muttered. "Think back. What were you feeling when you healed them?"

The boy thought of the tremendous pain he felt watching Eleanor bleed out. His blood had fallen into hers as he repaired her grievous wounds. He remembered how desperate he was to save her. "I was willing to do anything to heal her."

"Even giving your own life?" Balor pressed.

"Yes. Same for Chase. Xander asked if I had spare blood to give, and it didn't matter if I gave all of it. I only cared about them."

The High Wizard let out a frustrated sigh. "That's it then. Somehow, your willingness to die for them created a special kind of magic. A bond, if you will." He looked skyward. "The chances of you feeling the same thing for me, or anybody else really, is nearly impossible. Very well, I tried." He touched Chip's hand and healed the wound. The speed at which he did it was impressive.

"No hard feelings?" Balor winked. Chip gave him a reluctant nod. "Do you know the Protectors do that to each other all the time? It keeps them sharp. Heed the warning. That will be all for today. Show yourself out." He began walking towards a door at the side of the room. "Oh, and keep the dagger. It was a gift from King Luminor a long time ago. It is a rare elven blade. The sheath is in the drawer. Perhaps you can find some use for it one day." He left the room.

Chip could not help but smile as he shook his head. He pulled open the drawer below the table and found a supple black sheath. He grasped the dagger's hilt, which had an excellent grip due to the slight ridges created from the polished stones and slid it into the sheath. The boy crossed the cavernous room and exited through the gold door.

When Chip returned to the Brown Wing, Miss Highbrow was sitting at her desk, cutting bread into small pieces on the plate before her. Before he could acknowledge the Wing Leader, Han ran across the common room and leapt into his arms. The others gathered around.

"This place is so wonderful," the small boy laughed. "They have games and activities. The students are very nice." Beth nodded in agreement. Chip knelt and hugged her. Auntie Clare came over, and they embraced.

"I heard what you did to save Eleanor." The midwife held him at arm's length. "You are very brave."

"And foolish," Eleanor laughed. "Of course, I'm not complaining."

Chip smiled. "I am happy everyone is here."

"What did Balor want to talk to you about?" the queen asked. "Unless it's private, of course."

"Oh, nothing much. He told me about a staff he carries and then stabbed me. In hindsight, it was kind of funny."

Eleanor's eyes widened. "Oh dear."

"I'll explain later. For now, who wants to play a game?" Han and Beth raised their hands, jumping up and down.

They spent the remainder of the afternoon playing games and then enjoyed a stunning dinner in the dining hall. Chip smiled as he watched the children sample all kinds of food. Han and Beth had grown up with good parents in a small village on the outskirts of Vanalon living a simple life. He felt a pang of sympathy for them as the memory of the black dragon killing their parents surfaced. Chip pushed it aside and watched Auntie Clare help them eat. He was grateful they had her. He allowed himself to revel in the moment and felt at peace for the first time in a long while.

Halfway through the meal, Ethrang arrived accompanied by a terrified overweight boy. Miss Highbrow tried to stop them, but the skinny blond orphan ran up to them with a laugh, dragging the teenager with him. Chip stood up and introduced himself.

"Hi, I'm Chip. You must be Siz." He extended his hand.

The flustered boy took a deep breath and then shook it. "I'm Ciz with a 'C.' Not that it matters. Oh gosh. So many people. Wow, that's a lot of food. Sorry, I'm still jumpy from the flight."

"The flight?" Eleanor asked, shaking his hand.

"Ya, Ethrang turned into a giant bird, wrapped me in a blanket, and flew me here. Well, first, he told my parents a crazy story about someone impersonating me. He said it was a Dark Elf who can shapeshift. Anyways, we didn't believe him until he turned into a tiger, then a charging buffalo, then a wolf, and a bunch of other things. He said we could leave on a unicorn but then changed his mind, saying it would take too long. I wasn't going to go until he said the High Wizard demanded it and would turn me into a frog if I didn't. I'm not even sure that's possible because I'm not a shapeshifter, so how could my body morph into a frog…anyways, the magistrate in Thundar ordered magic wielders to go to the Guild, and I'm pretty powerful, you know…so here I am." He took in a deep breath and puffed his chest out.

Nobody said a word.

Then, unable to contain themselves, everyone broke out laughing. Even Miss Highbrow, standing behind Ethrang with fists on her hips, emitted a strange laugh that sounded like a pig. This made everyone howl even harder. Ciz looked wide-eyed around the room as if they were all insane, but each of them gave him a welcome hug.

"He acts exactly the same."

"The Dark Elf played him perfectly."

"He's identical."

Mina, the pretty brown-haired girl who initially arrived with the imposter Siz, looked him up and down. "I've never met anyone for the first time twice before. I will show you around."

"Wait," Chip said, turning to the new arrival. "Do you remember meeting someone by your house one day when you were cleaning your boat? It happened a few weeks ago."

The boy began to shake his head and then raised a pudgy finger. "Yes, I remember. I met a soldier behind the store and sat on a picnic table with him. He asked a lot of questions and seemed nice."

"Did he shake your hand?"

"Why yes, as a matter of fact, he did. Why?" The large boy looked perplexed.

"Shapeshifters have to touch a living being before they can shapeshift into them. He impersonated you for weeks before we figured out it was the Dark Elf, Murk. I'm so sorry to laugh at you, but he did it well. Now, we want to get to know the real you. And don't worry about getting bullied. I will take care of that." Chip turned to see Gob and Bart sitting at the other end of the table. He waved them over. The two big boys walked up.

"Ciz, meet Gob and Bart. They will make sure no one bullies you. I'm asking them as a favour."

"No problem, Guardian," Gob said, cracking his knuckles.

"We've got him covered," added Bart with a lopsided grin.

"I have to leave in a couple of days, but I will be back to see how he's doing. Thanks, Gob, Bart." He nodded to them, and they moved back to their seats. He turned to Ciz. "Mina and Ethrang can show you around."

"Thank you so much. I never thought I would feel so...welcome. Do you think I could eat first?" Ciz rubbed his belly. Everyone smiled.

Ethrang put his arm around the boy's shoulders. "You know what, you ain't so bad." The blond boy smiled and sauntered over to Mina.

"I have to leave soon," he said, turning serious.

"I know." Mina looked down, trying to hide her disappointment.

He lifted her chin. "But not for two days. So do you wanna have some fun? I won't be gone that long anyway. All we have to do is find a whole race of Light Elves who have been missing for three thousand years. Sounds pretty easy, right?" She couldn't help but laugh, and they wandered away.

Chip looked at Eleanor. "Are we ready for this? I think it's going to be quite a journey."

"As long as I'm with you, it won't be a journey. It will be an adventure." She smiled and kissed him. Miss Highbrow made a muffled, high-pitched sound and walked away, muttering about the new generation.

The following two days flew by. Siz was Assessed as a strong Brown. No silver tinge appeared in his Power, which was a relief. Chip spent his free time playing with Han and Beth. Auntie Clare said she wanted to stay with the children in the Brown Wing until his return. Miss Highbrow instructed Han to inform the High Wizard immediately if he received any new Tellings. She said Skylar had asked her to inform him first, but Balor clarified that he would receive the news before anyone. The students mobbed Han and Beth, pinching their cheeks and playing various games with them. Auntie Clare watched it all with a smile.

Everyone met on the morning of the second day in front of the gates. Work had already commenced to reinforce them. Skylar began sketching an escape plan for the students, working closely with Maxim. The master trainer had selected twelve Protectors, including Garth and Chase, to guard the wizards. The twins arrived in good spirits, excited to begin what they called "the adventure of a lifetime." Horses awaited them, loaded with all manner of supplies.

Balor stood in front of the group. "The Guild wishes you find fortune in your travels. Send word back when you can. Jordy will accompany you to the forest's edge. Make for the city of Northbane, the last outpost before the front lines. The commander there is Gunnar. He will update you on the situation. At least one thousand trolls stand between you and the old Wizard's Guild. Remember, everything rests on this mission. Keep your wits and fare you well. May the Creator shine on you." The High Wizard stepped back. Xander walked over to confer with his brother before saddling up.

"Only a thousand trolls? No big deal." Chase whispered from Chip's right. He looked over at his best friend and stifled a laugh. Garth stood on his other side and raised an eyebrow.

Ethrang appeared beside Chip and grinned. The orphan always seemed to pop out of nowhere. "Don't worry, we've got this, Guardian."

The companions said goodbye to Mina and Ciz. The brown-haired girl had slowly come out of her shell in the last few weeks. She had befriended Ciz for the second time and he was thankful for the attention. Chip was happy they were both adjusting so well. Before he could say farewell to Auntie Clare, a ball of energy leapt into his arms.

Han hugged him tightly and whispered a final message, "You will be betrayed. Do not lose hope. The Light cannot be dimmed." The small boy's face turned solemn. "There is one more thing. I cannot tell you yet. You are not ready. You will know when I see you again, maybe."

Chip set him down and kneeled in front of the boy. "Don't you ever have anything nice to say?" He ruffled his hair. Han let out an infectious giggle and stepped back, revealing his sister Beth.

Chip had never seen the little girl so happy. "You are safe here. I will be back as soon as I can." She nodded, smiling. After giving her a tight hug, the boy stood up and looked at Auntie Clare.

"Please be careful. Come back safe." She cupped his cheeks and kissed his forehead. For a moment, he was back in Vanalon, sitting on her lap by the fire while she read a soothing tale.

"I will. You have been through a lot yourself. Rest here now." She nodded and stepped back.

A growing crowd of students had gathered in the immense courtyard to see them off. Many yelled a final message.

"Go get them, Guardian!"

"Don't forget about us!"

"May the Creator shine on you!"

The companions mounted and rode across the Guild's front lawn. Chip looked back to see everyone waving from the open gates. Loud cheers erupted from students gathered on top of the wall. A pang of sadness ran through him as he realized how much the school meant to him. He vowed to return victorious.

They reached the bridge that spanned the dangerous river that surrounded the grounds. At its arc, he turned and waved a final farewell to the Wizard's Guild, before they all rode down into the Ancient Forest.

The towering trees immediately enveloped him in a cocoon of peace and serenity. A soothing calm imbued the air, and he breathed in the intoxicating forest scents. At the fountain, the party turned right. Chip looked at the stone figure of a young Balor pointing towards the Guild. He shook his head. The man was arrogant, selfish, and entitled, but he had his good qualities. The boy hoped the High Wizard would figure out a way to save the Guild or at least minimize losses.

Grand Wizard Xander turned to the group. "We ride west to the Frontier Road that borders the Ancient Forest then turn north. Let's enjoy this forest while we can. If Han's Telling is true, there will not be much left of it when the Demon King arrives." His expression turned grim as he took the lead.

There were nineteen of them, plus Jordy, who was the chaperone. Chip recognized several of the Protectors from the challenges when Chase became Certified. There was Sheldor, Hunter, Carvor, and towering over them all, Bulch. The giant carried a large club and rode a burly horse that sagged from the man's weight. He did not know the other Protectors. Several looked like they would be handy in a fight.

The boy closed his eyes and let the forest sounds cradle him. He had been through a lot at the Guild and welcomed the respite. Even as he rested, Chip felt a pull from a distant source ahead of him. He knew instantly who it was—Redmane! He sent his presence out, and for a moment they connected. The boy could feel a surge of joy from the magnificent red unicorn. A need to run and explore filled the horse's mind. It spoke of wind and trees, rivers and grasslands, and a breathtaking wildness. The boy's heart quickened with excitement, remembering his first ride with the great beast. The feeling of running with reckless abandon energized his soul. It made him forget the heavy weight of the world's troubles, freeing him momentarily from the mantle of responsibility.

He called ahead to Xander. "The unicorns are on the other side of the forest. They are coming to see us."

The twins, Kristan and Thomas, looked at him with open mouths and then let out a whoop of laughter.

"Can I ride the red one this time?" Kristan asked excitedly.

"No, it's my turn," Thomas said, pushing his horse ahead of his twin.

Mary, the Blue Wing Leader, looked at them as if they were mad. She had remained silent during the preparations, maintaining a stoic expression. The woman sniffed then moved away from the twins.

"I don't control who rides him. They are free spirits. All I know is their leader, Redmane, wants to see me," Chip said. "And I'm pretty sure that means me, not you two." He smiled as their expressions turned to disappointment.

"There are still the white ones. I could settle for that," Thomas said after a moment, his face brightening.

"I suppose a white one will have to do," Kristan added, pretending to be glum.

"May I remind you we have a mission," Xander called from the front. "There is no time to watch you two take a joy ride on unicorns."

"I would like to see the Chaircats," Eleanor said, sidling her mount beside Chip. "They are so soft."

"I second that." Jordy grinned from the side.

"I think we should feed the Cuddly Bears," Chase turned around. "Carvor, why don't you try it?" The former Silver Sword champion looked at him with a sour expression but said nothing. Garth and Chase rode at the front while the rest of the Protectors formed a loose circle around them. Even though the forest was safe, their eyes constantly scanned the area for threats. They were trained well.

The companions continued on the meandering path, absorbing the sights and smells. The soft brown earth dampened the sound of the horses' hooves as they guided their mounts between the giant trunks. Multi-coloured butterflies flew high in the canopy of the three-thousand-year-old trees. Smells of clean earth and wood infused the morning air. Chip noticed most of the leaves had turned from bright green to orange and red, creating a dazzling visage. Winter was coming.

"There's Chirps," Jordy exclaimed, pointing up ahead as they rounded a massive bole. A large bird with stripes sat on a broad tree limb staring at them balefully. "Hi, Chirps, how are you today?"

It cocked its head at the brown-robed wizard. "Little man. Nice day."

"That's not nice. We are on a mission. Wish us luck."

The bird peered at the group before settling its gaze on Chip. "Darkness. No luck." It leapt into the air and sailed over them, wings beating strong, then disappeared around a large trunk.

"That was ominous," Kristan remarked.

"Quite," Thomas agreed.

"I hope the bird was talking about the weather. I did notice a storm brewing far to the west this morning," Chase said. "In fact, it's been there ever since…" No one needed reminding of what was coming from that direction.

They were approaching the first resting station, which had a gazebo and hammocks, when a low rumble grew in volume. The Protectors tightened the circle, hands going to their sword hilts.

"It's alright," Chip said. "The unicorns are here." The boy marvelled at how quickly they had reached the small group from the other side of the forest.

Unicorns began appearing around them from all sides, forming a wide circle. In front, Redmane broke through the trees. His coat shone a beautiful crimson as he cantered up with stunning elegance. The horse embodied pure energy, muscles rippling in the morning light, white horn gleaming. He stopped in front of Chip and reared up on his hind legs, emitting a musical whinny. The other unicorns joined him, creating a melodious symphony the boy could feel in his bones. A joy infused him from head to toe.

He nodded in deference to the magnificent creature, dismounted, and walked up to Redmane. The horse pointed his white horn earthward at the boy's feet. Chip ran a hand down the smooth mane and patted his elegant neck.

"I miss you too," he whispered. The unicorn whinnied softly and nuzzled his cheek. The others looked on in awe. Even Carvor seemed impressed. Bulch broke into a lopsided grin and grunted in contentment.

Redmane raised his head and surveyed the group. He then took a knee in front of the boy.

"Yes!" Kristan shouted. "We can ride them!"

Chip shook his head. "Xander is right. We don't have time for this. We would have to wait for the horses to catch up anyway. Thank you, Redmane, but we are on a mission and must leave the Ancient Forest. You cannot follow. I wish you could…" The horse reared backwards and neighed again, more insistent this time. The boy shook his head and broke through his Wall. He sent his presence into the unicorn's mind, showing the animal the task in images. The horse settled down but stayed where he was.

Chip finished and waited. Suddenly, a powerful presence pushed back into his. Redmane showed him images of running across a sea of green grass at dizzying speeds. He leapt over streams and ran up low hills, creating his own wind. Different terrains whizzed by as the wild animal revelled in complete freedom. The horse sent an image of the confines of the Ancient Forest and, despite the beauty of his surroundings, Redmane wanted to be truly free. The unicorn was accepting of the risks involved and wanted to help the boy. The horse then withdrew his presence and took another knee.

Chip turned around in wonder.

"He wants us to ride them. He understands the dangers. It is better to be free and live than to be confined and die. He speaks for them all. They want to come with us."

"My goodness," the wizard said softly.

"Yes!" shouted the twins as one.

"Sounds good to me," Chase laughed.

"Cool," Ethrang said, nodding.

"What? These are wild animals!" Mary looked mollified.

"Yes, but I assure you they are safe," Chip said. "The unicorns will shorten our journey considerably. "But I'm not sure if they will agree to a saddle. We need them to carry the packs." Redmane did not move. "Only one way to find out."

Chip removed his saddle and carried it over to Redmane. He gently placed it over the unicorn's back and tied it down. The horse did not move. With relief, the boy leapt onto the saddle. Redmane stood tall and whinnied.

The rest of the unicorns took a knee.

"What are we waiting for?" Kristan yelled then looked at Xander and waited for approval.

The old wizard paused for a moment, spreading his hands. "As they say, don't look a gift horse in the mouth. Let's ride." The twins whooped as everyone began untying their saddles and placing them on the willing unicorns. Mary grumbled but followed suit. There were two more unicorns than riders, which allowed extra gear to be placed on them.

Jordy watched it all in disbelief. "Wow, that would have been fun. How am I going to herd nineteen unsaddled horses back to the Guild?"

"Um, use magic," Ethrang offered, staring at the diminutive wizard from atop a shiny white unicorn.

"I suppose that makes sense. Well, it seems there is no need to guide you any further. I could not keep up anyway." Jordy gave them a fond look. "May you find fortune in your travels. It would have been fun to go with you, but Chirp's comment about darkness has given me second thoughts. Good luck." He shook hands with everyone and stepped back, herding the regular horses out of the way.

Chip looked at Xander sitting astride a beautiful white unicorn with a gleaming brown horn. "Would you mind if I lead the way? Redmane likes to be at the front."

"By all means," the wizard answered, "but make sure we can keep up."

The Guardian laughed and pulled on the left side of the unicorn's mane. The horse responded instantly, facing west. With a final wave to Jordy, Chip squeezed Redmane's ribs with his knees, and the animal sprang into action, galloping down the path in a blur of motion. The other unicorns followed their leader, running free and wild, excited to leave the Ancient Forest and explore the world.

They passed other animals that looked like sloths compared to their speed. A group of deer scattered in panic, and a family of Cuddly Bears had to scamper out of the way. Chip managed to catch a few wood sprites in the middle of eating a berry or pulling bark from a tree, likely to make clothes. They looked up in surprise then scrunched their wizened faces in a scowl at the intrusion. One laughed madly and jumped into a tree hollow before peeking out with bright green eyes. The boy spied a familiar group of orange felines and pulled up on the reigns to take a brief break, indulging his queen.

Eleanor squealed in delight and leapt off her still-moving unicorn. The queen plopped herself onto the lap of her favourite Chaircat, which she had named Tigger. Immediately, the creature started purring, all the while looking skyward. Mary gawked then shook her head in disgust. Several of the others, including the twins, took a short break, letting their bodies sink into the orange beasts. Ethrang snuggled into an extra furry one, grinning from ear to ear. The skinny, green-robed boy nearly disappeared inside the cat.

The weapons master gave Chip a mild look of disapproval for the loss of time, causing the boy to shrug. The queen would never forgive him if they rode past. Chase let out a whoop as he leapt off his unicorn before choosing a large white-bellied Chaircat to sink into. The other Protectors looked on with stoic expressions. Xander watched it all with amusement.

After a short while, Chip jumped back onto Redmane, and the others followed suit. The unicorn was anxious to be off, so they sped towards the western edge of the forest. The party arrived at the entrance with the two statues and halted. The unicorns neighed, sensing the ward.

Xander's eyes shone a bright blue, and he removed the barrier. Chip watched in fascination, beginning to understand how it worked. The ward was only a magic wall rooted into the ground, unseeable to the naked eye. He could tell it needed constant maintenance, as it would eventually dissipate. The wizard waved his hand, and it vanished. The unicorns, sensing its disappearance, surged through, whinnying with joy.

Chip turned to look at the towering stone statues of the High Wizard on either side of the entrance while Xander reestablished the wards. He shook his head. Balor certainly had an ego.

When finished, the wizard turned, pointing to the right. "It's a week's ride to Northbane, but I suspect we will get there much faster on unicorns. It is the last town before the front lines. The trolls have taken it over many times over the years. For now, we hold it. They will not welcome magic wielders there. Long ago, at the beginning of the war, I brokered a partial peace deal between the trolls and humans. Wizards and mages were dying in increasing numbers when the war began, so I asked King Jaggar for a truce. He refused, saying he deserved both the New Wizard's Guild and the old one since my brother stole the position of High Wizard from him after the Great Battle. I could not get him to lay down arms, but I did get Jaggar, Balor, and the High King of Toron to agree on banning magic wielders from the war. Only soldiers could fight. Our arrival at the front lines will likely be considered a breach of the treaty. Especially if we use magic."

"Why do the trolls hate us so much?" Chip asked. "I understand King Jaggar's enmity towards High Wizard Balor, but do they all despise humans?"

Xander sighed. "After this many years, I believe most do. When there are different races in the world, some people paint everyone with the actions of a few. It is worse that they have been at war for so long. For a thousand years, trolls fought humans and, before that, the elves. They joined us to erect the barrier in the Great Battle, but the relationship deteriorated quickly afterwards. My brother felt, due to Arkan's sacrifice, that he deserved the position of High Wizard. King Jaggar believed he was the right choice, since he was older and more experienced. King Luminor was also a strong contender, but he picked up the orb and disappeared, believing the Light Elves deserved it after the losses sustained over the millennia fighting the Dark Elves. It didn't help that Luminor slew Jaggar's father, King Malkor, long ago. Wounds run deep."

"Imagine if humans hated each other for their different cultures or how they looked?" Eleanor observed.

"That's ridiculous," Chase laughed. "Would never happen."

"What if only humans existed?" the queen pressed. "Maybe then they would attack each other based on differences."

The tall boy thought about it. "Hmm, I still don't think so."

Everyone stared at him.

"It has happened," Xander said. "The Barbarian Wars lasted many years before I brokered a peace treaty. I will say that most wars are between different races, and the trolls tend to be involved. I am not called Peacemaker of the Races for nothing."

Ethrang chimed in. "There are all kinds of different people in Banfar, and everyone is treated equally until they prove otherwise... which I have to admit happens a lot, but that's because of their actions, not their looks or customs."

"The point is peace should always be the goal," Xander explained. "Leaders can make a group of people believe and do almost anything. The Troll King has honed them into a war-like culture over many millennia. They were not always like that. I will try to convince Jaggar to end this war and join us in the Last Battle, but it will not be easy."

The wizard indicated that Chip should take the lead. Under Garth's instruction, the Protectors lined the sides and back of the group. The midday sun shone brightly overhead. They had made excellent time getting through the Ancient Forest.

The boy looked far to the west, where dark clouds were gathering on the horizon like a portent of doom. He knew the Demon King was coming. The barrier was gone. Winter might slow him down, but it was only a reprieve. A cold wind sprang up as if on cue, and a smattering of dead leaves landed on the road.

The Guardian lightly urged Redmane forward. The unicorn leapt into action, maintaining a torrid pace as they headed towards Northbane.

3

The companions passed several groups of soldiers and sporadic travellers as they journeyed north at great speed on the Frontier Road. The expressions on the people were ones of fear and shock. Thankfully, the sounds of the unicorns' hooves allowed the people enough time to get out of the way. An old woman with two small children could not move in time, so the herd split in two to avoid them and rejoined soon after. Chip glanced back to see the woman's mouth agape and the small children jumping up and down.

Any breaks they took were for themselves, as the unicorns seemed to need no rest.

"This is quite the way to travel," Xander called from behind. The boy could barely hear him above the rushing wind.

"It definitely saves time!" he shouted back.

That night, they camped in a farmer's field. The unicorns spread out to munch on small bushes and hay. The farmer came out with hands raised in anger but dropped them as he stared at the animals grazing. His mouth worked with no sound, and then he returned to his home and slammed the door. Ethrang couldn't stop laughing.

They set up tents and retired early. Chip noticed that though it had been a long day, he wasn't as saddle-sore as he would be on a regular horse. Something about the fluidity of the unicorn's movement created minimal tension in his muscles.

He shared a tent with Chase, who began to snore almost immediately. The Protectors had a rigid schedule, forcing them to get up early and retire early. Chip remembered the weapons master's lectures vividly during training. "Good habits are the key to success, which breeds happiness. If you are not succeeding, change your habits. Small changes over time make a big difference." He had followed that advice, training before and after school, and the changes, small at first, became huge. The Protectors followed a similar regimen, honing themselves into outstanding fighters. He was glad they were here. Eleanor had her own tent, but the Protectors kept a vigilant watch.

Chip allowed himself to relax and slipped into a fitful sleep.

Over the next two days they made excellent progress. The unicorns ate up the leagues easily, running at breathtaking speed with unbridled energy. They camped in fields each night and woke at dawn to continue. On their third day, it looked like they would reach Northbane by early evening.

After a full morning of riding, the group was about to stop for lunch.

As the sun passed its zenith, a brief shadow crossed Chip's vision on the ground. Redmane suddenly spun completely around, sliding on his hooves to a complete stop. The boy watched in amazement as the magnificent animal's horn shone brighter, and a strange magic he had never felt before sizzled around him. The red unicorn crouched and leapt straight into the air, horn pointed to the sky.

That was when he saw them.

At least a dozen wasp demons were free-falling from above, diving straight down, claws extended. The boy had no time to respond and frantically tried to seize his magic.

It would have been too late.

Redmane launched straight up at the winged demon nosediving towards them, his horn going effortlessly through its tough chest armour, right through the creature's black heart. The red horse landed heavily, casting off the dead body before launching at another. Unfortunately, some of the others did not fare so well.

A wasp landed with devastating force on a Protector riding in the back, crushing him against his horse. The winged demon seized the unicorn around its body by impaling massive claws into the poor animal's sides then lifted them both high in the air, wings beating madly. Squeals of pain rang out. The wasps were insect-like creatures bred over millennia by the Dark Elves to develop thick armour and wings. They had long jaws and sharp fangs below almond-shaped black eyes. Their front forelegs dangled below them as they flew, ending in sharp talons.

Ethrang leapt off his mount, eyes flashing green, and shapeshifted into a massive Giant Eagle. With several beats of his monstrous wings, the boy flew directly at a diving wasp, wrapping his immense talons around its insect-like skull. Turning in a circle, he wrenched violently and tore the thing's head clean off. The Protector's swords rang out as they thrust upward. The largest man, Bulch, swung a massive club like a maniac, knocking the creatures to the ground. Others even stood on their saddle to fight the diving demons.

The Guardian filled himself with magic, about to fling a cushion of air at the falling unicorn and Protector as they plummeted from high in the sky. Before he could release, three more wasps came at him. It was clear he was their intended target. In frustration, Chip turned to them with splayed hands and shot a blistering stream of red fire in a broad swath. Such was his Power that, upon contact, the giant insects burst into flames, shooting backwards to land in shrivelled husks. When he turned back, Xander had, at the last moment, thrown a cushion of air to slow the falling Protector, but the unicorn struck the ground with full force. The sound of its bones breaking was almost unbearable.

With a shout of rage, Chip shot a red ball of fire clean through a demon harassing Carvor, melting it into oblivion. Eleanor and the twins sent out wizard fire in all directions with deadly accuracy. The queen's eyes shone a wicked brown with glints of red. To her right, Mary was protecting their backs, shooting streaking blue daggers of magic. Those that didn't land a death blow still rocked the wasps, knocking them down and leaving their skin smoking. The Blue Wing Leader's back was straight, her face frozen in indignation at being attacked. Chase was a whirlwind of motion, hacking off wings and talons. The chips in his eyes burned bright.

"There's more!" cried Xander, pointing down the road. His eyes blazed bright blue as he turned to deal death. The flock was coming from the north to take them by surprise, hoping they were too distracted to notice.

"Ethrang, watch out!" screamed Kristan. After disposing of several wasps, the Giant Eagle turned too late as a demon flew up from below and raked his right wing. Losing several feathers, the bird faltered. As the shapeshifter fell, his eyes flashed a brighter green, and he shot a ball of fire from his talons into the wasp's face, melting its features. Before he landed the short distance to the ground, Ethrang shifted into a ferocious brown tiger, spinning to land on his feet. Blood leaked from a large gash in his front foreleg and shoulder, but he leapt up to slash the throat of another low-flying wasp.

The other unicorns were jumping high into the air with shimmering horns, impaling anything foolish enough to come close. Some of the horses turned and kicked with their back legs, sending demons hurtling to the ground, where they stood on wobbly legs, only to be gored by another charging unicorn.

Chip turned to face the low-flying ones coming down the road. Redmane sprang forward to meet them head-on, white horn glowing. Thick red ropes of fire shot from the boy's hands, creating a tunnel of death. A few of the wasps managed to evade his attack, but then the twins were there, one on either side, setting the fleeing creatures ablaze with powerful blue magic. Their faces, usually laughing and jovial, were deadly serious as they cut down the enemy with ruthless precision.

After they killed everything before them, the three turned, looking for more enemies. Xander shot fire at one that landed on the ground, while Ethrang hung on the back of the last airborne creature, maniacally slashing at its neck with his razor-sharp claws, roaring with glee. As the demon died and fell to Earth, the tiger shapeshifted into a butterfly to slow his descent before reappearing in human form, landing lightly on his feet. The blond boy had a light sheen of sweat on his face but grinned from ear to ear. His right arm leaked blood.

"Takes more than that," the green-robed boy said, striding up.

"Good work," Chip responded as he surveyed the others. Everyone was breathing hard, and the unicorns were wild-eyed, but the threat was over. Several Protectors had various gashes across their bodies from talons, but none seemed life-threatening. The twins immediately began healing the injured men.

"One has escaped," Chase said, pointing at a diminishing black speck heading west.

"It will report back to its Master," Xander said grimly. He hurried over to the Protector who had fallen to the ground. The others rushed up.

Sadly, despite the cushion of air, the young man's head was hanging at an odd angle. The Protector's neck was broken, and his ribcage looked concave. The wasp had crushed him on impact when landing on the horse. They turned to look at the unicorn, which had landed a short distance away. The once-glorious animal was on its side, unmoving. Strangely, the unicorn's brown horn had fallen off, resting beside it. Bright red blood streaked across the animal's beautiful white coat. Several bones protruded from its body.

Rage and sadness filled Chip, and he clenched his hands. "How could they have found us?"

Xander stepped forward. "Somebody told them."

"But we only decided on this mission five days ago. That is not enough time for someone to travel to the Demon King."

The wizard sighed. "I do not know. They likely used a pigeon. Even so, it would be difficult for the bird to deliver the message and the wasps to fly back in time. What I do know is they knew we were on this road, and you were the target."

Eleanor sidled up to him, putting a hand on his back. "Someone has betrayed you...all of us. There is a source in the Guild. I know it is difficult to believe, but with that many people, there will be spies. There always are."

Mary, her beautiful hair somehow still neatly combed, nodded. "The queen is right. Every court has spies. The Wizard's Guild is no different." Eleanor showed a hint of surprise that the woman agreed with her but quickly masked it.

"When we reach Northbane, I will have a message delivered to my brother informing him that the Guild harbours a traitor." Xander looked off in the distance. "Sadly, betrayal is a part of life. It is an aspect of the human condition. The most painful ones are the betrayals that come from someone close to us. It is in times of strife and desperation that the trait emerges. Most people would never steal a loaf of bread in good times, but the opposite is true when your family is starving. Self-preservation can be a powerful motivator. For others, simple greed is enough. Be wary, for times will get worse, and the head of betrayal will rear itself."

Garth Stone waited until he finished before stepping forward. "Grand Wizard, can we pause to give our fallen Protector a proper burial? His name was Jon. He was a good fighter."

Xander assented. "Of course. Today taught us how fragile life is and how quickly it can be snatched away. The Demon King knows our mission and where we are headed. We must take extra care to look not only around us but up as well. The enemy can attack from any direction. And attack us, he will. The Unnamed One sacrificed many demon wasps today, but I have a feeling there are worse things coming. Beware the white-eyed ones. They now have magic."

"The unicorns have magic too," Chip whispered. "There is always a balance. I thank the Creator that they are here. Redmane saved me."

"I felt their magic, too," Eleanor agreed. "It is different from ours. Their horns shine brighter and become weapons but something else too."

Xander studied the beautiful creatures. "King Luminor once told me long ago that unicorns can link. We never witnessed it in the Ancient Forest, but now there is a red one. Perhaps he unites them.

They are as rare as dragons. I do not understand their magic, but I know they are special. The Demon King rode one once." Chip blinked in surprise.

Kristan nodded. "I read about it in the histories. The red-eyed elf rode a unicorn when he was young before removing his Wall."

"What happened to the unicorn?" Chip asked.

Thomas spoke up before his brother could respond, "He found it dead one day, lying in the forest. The Dark Elf prince could not find the cause of death, but the loss made him sad and angry. He began to withdraw from others. Morgo arrived on the scene right about then."

"Hey, look!" Ethrang pointed at the unicorns as they formed a tight circle around the dead animal. Everyone stopped talking and watched. The horse's eyes glistened as they stared with great sadness at their fallen member. At the same time, the magnificent beasts lifted their heads and emitted a long, mournful whinny that carried aching sorrow. Chip's eyes brimmed as a lump formed in his throat. The sound was timeless and carried on the wind for long moments.

Then, as one, the great animals dipped their heads, pointing their great horns at the dead unicorn. Everyone remained silent, not daring to move, knowing they were witnessing something profound. The unicorns remained motionless for a long moment before lifting their heads and backing away. They gathered again by the road.

The weapons master turned to the Protectors. "Gather wood to make a pyre. Let's give our brother a proper send to the afterlife." They nodded as one, spreading out.

"Are you alright?" Chase asked Mary, who looked at him with a cold expression and did not answer.

Eleanor moved closer to her. "Thank you for protecting our backs," the queen said in a level voice.

Mary looked at her, eyes tightening. "Members of the Guild protect each other, despite who you are. It is the way." She walked away.

Chase looked bewildered. "Was that a compliment?"

Eleanor looked at him, rolled her eyes, and then stalked off, shaking her head.

"What? Did I say something wrong?"

Chip gave him a look of sympathy and followed the queen. Ethrang snickered.

Kristan walked up to the green-robed boy. "Are you going to just bleed to death?" Before he could grab his arm, Thomas put his hand on the orphan's shoulder, and his eyes blazed blue, mending the wound.

When finished, Ethrang moved his shoulder in a circle. "Much better. Thanks." He turned to Kristan. "I didn't see it coming up beneath me. Thanks for the warning. I was able to avoid getting my face torn off."

"No worries. That Giant Eagle is something. What else can you turn into?"

The blond boy laughed. "You'll see."

A short while later, they completed the funeral pyre, and six Protectors placed the body of their fallen comrade on the mound. They laid the dead unicorn to rest beside him.

Bulch, over seven feet tall, bent to pick up the unicorn horn. "Can Bulch keep?" he asked the weapons master. Garth shrugged. The big man slid it inside his rope belt and joined the others.

The Protectors formed a ring around the wood, crossing one fist over their hearts.

"May the Creator protect you forevermore," Garth intoned then lit the base of the mound. Within moments, flames danced among the branches to surround the body. Chip watched as Protector Jon took his final journey. The boy sighed, wondering how many more they would lose. He could not help feeling angry that someone in the Guild had caused this. One day, he would find out.

The Guardian strode up to Redmane and stopped, looking into his brown eyes. The boy gently sent his presence into the horse's mind. He immediately sensed other entities. With a start, he realized all the unicorns were now in some way connected to their leader's mind. Redmane showed him an array of images, with the last one indicating they were now bonded. If the red horse died, they all died. The bonding allowed them to use magic, but there was a steep cost.

Chip gasped, turning to the others.

"If Redmane dies, they all die. It is the price of using their magic."

"My goodness," Xander breathed.

"Are you saying this is the first time they bonded?" Eleanor asked.

"Yes. They never needed to before. They were safe in the Ancient Forest. When a red unicorn is born, it can choose to unite the others if threatened. They are the last herd in Amrika." Chip was unsure if the unicorns wanted to continue the journey after their loss. He would understand if they did not. The red horse's eyes showed sadness, but he saw something else underneath.

There was a simmering rage.

As if in response to his unspoken question, Redmane took a knee. Chip breathed a sigh of relief and mounted. The others followed suit. The Protectors climbed up last, saying their final farewells. Xander turned to the group.

"We have suffered a heavy loss today. Let's learn from it and move on. If we maintain our current speed, we will reach Northbane this evening. We have saved a lot of time. Keep your eyes open. I fear this is only the beginning." He indicated that Chip should take the lead.

The Guardian took one last look at the funeral pyre blazing in the distance, said a silent prayer to the Creator, and turned to the north. This time, he did not have to urge Redmane forward. The leader of the unicorns sprang into a fast gallop down the Frontier Road with the others close behind.

The land gave way to low hills and streams. The number of farms began to diminish, likely due to the proximity of the front lines. It made no sense to grow fields of crops that could be overrun by trolls pushing south. So far, Northbane held, but nothing was certain.

As evening approached, the sporadic homes they passed were mostly abandoned. Unshuttered windows gaped at them like empty eye sockets warning them to stay away. Weeds and vines crawled over the homes as nature reclaimed the land. The fields, once containing rows of carefully planted crops, were overtaken by all manner of shrubbery, finally free from bondage. Many of the houses had been badly burned, and some only showed basements full of charred wood.

Xander rode up beside him, following his gaze. "Every few years, Northbane changes hands," he yelled above the wind. "Over the centuries, the trolls have burned it down countless times and pushed south, setting the homes on fire. The High King then sends reinforcements to retake it, and the men rebuild it to their liking. It took them a while to figure out not to use wood. Stone is far more durable, though not impervious. You won't find any wood structures in Northbane. There is a road up ahead. Turn left. It will lead us to the fortress and town, which backs onto the Sprite River." Chip nodded.

As the road approached, the boy tugged on the left side of the red unicorn's mane. The horse barely slowed to turn, forcing him to lean low. They did not have to travel far before short stone walls surrounding a small town appeared. A wide moat surrounded the city, with one wooden bridge leading to the main gates.

Chip surmised it was intentional to keep the only access point made of wood so the men defending the town could burn the bridge themselves, preventing the trolls from entering. In the back, a large square fortress overlooked the walls. Men stood at even intervals on the crenellated top.

Redmane slowed to a halt a hundred feet from the bridge. Chip urged him forward, but he refused to budge. The boy connected to his mind and was immediately shown that the unicorns refused to enter man-made cities. The walls of a city felt like prison cells to them despite their size. They would graze in the fields until they returned. The boy did not argue. He suspected it would do no good anyway. Redmane knew precisely what he wanted.

"Gather your packs," he instructed. "The unicorns will wait for us here when we depart. They will not enter the city."

Nobody argued, though he thought he had heard Mary sniff. She gave him a cold look and then dismounted to retrieve her packs, of which she had several.

"Can I have a Protector carry these?" she directed more than asked. Garth Stone looked around and asked Bulch to take the woman's bags. The big man nodded and lumbered forward. He picked them all up in one hand as if they were full of feathers. Mary looked at him in disgust and moved away. Chip glanced at Eleanor, and they both stifled a laugh. Ethrang elbowed the twins, all three grinning.

In short order, everybody carried their belongings towards the town.

The weapons master took the lead. He was the natural leader in a town full of soldiers.

"Stop where you are." A man in a crisp green uniform shouted atop the gates when they reached the bridge. "State your business."

"I am Garth Stone, Honorary High Commander of Toron and Protector to Grand Wizard Xandrostrika. We seek counsel with General Gunnar."

"Who accompanies you, High Commander?"

"Eleven Protectors and seven wizards. Their names are confidential."

The man paused for a moment. "Very well, sir. I will send a runner. Bear with me."

Garth nodded and turned to the others. "These are hard men here. If you are not strong, you don't last against the trolls. They are disciplined and organized but quick to anger. Some will not like the idea of wizards being this close to the front lines. The treaty prohibits magic wielders from entering the battlefield. If the trolls feel there has been a breach, there could be a full-scale assault. The men don't wish to die before reinforcements arrive. Stay close together. We will sleep here tonight, then ride to the front lines tomorrow."

Everyone acknowledged the instructions. Chip realized how close he was to coming face-to-face with trolls. The stories he heard as a child were terrible tales of lumbering monsters with gnashing teeth who tore humans apart using their bare hands. The veterans from Vanalon who fought on the front lines usually had missing ears, teeth, or misshapen heads from a troll club. Almost all were severely scarred. Their stories were often worse than the children's tales. The idea of the trolls amicably switching sides to fight the Demon King, a common enemy, seemed wishful at best and foolish at worst. By all accounts, they were brutish creatures that only knew war. A thousand years of enmity would not be easy to dispel. Their arrival on the front lines might be most unwelcome.

A short while later, the gates opened, revealing a barrel-chested man with a commanding presence. He was clean-shaven, with gray hair at his temples. Unlike the soldiers in Banfar, he wore a clean, pressed uniform. A Giant Eagle insignia adorned his chest, and stitched into each shoulder were four yellow embroidered lines.

"Ah, there you are, Garth. It's been a long time." The man strode forward with a grin, hand extended. He was wider than the weapons master and as tall.

Garth took his hand in a firm shake. The man spun around cat-like, launching the weapons master over his back. Garth twirled in mid-air, landing on both feet, then pulled the man towards him, not letting go of his hand. The man's momentum allowed the weapons master to slide beside him and wrap his free arm around his neck, forming a tight chokehold. Garth began to squeeze.

The guards at the gates pulled out their weapons, and the Protectors responded in kind.

"Ha!" the man gurgled. "You've only gotten better!"

The weapons master released him. Both men made placating gestures, so everyone lowered their weapons.

"Meet General Gunnar," Garth said with a rare grin. "We trained together as Protectors."

"Yes, we did," the general said, rubbing his neck. "I could not beat him then and certainly not now. I was hoping your time in Vanalon had made you soft." He slapped the weapons master on the back. He turned and waved the others forward. "Grand Wizard Xandrostika," he said, bowing low. "Come, I hear you wish to discuss something."

"Yes, we have urgent business." The wizard moved forward as the general led the way.

The rest of the group looked at each other, shrugged, and followed.

4

Northbane was a soldier's town. The buildings were made of rough-hewn stone with few decorative markings. Everything was geared for war. They passed armories, forges, dining halls, and barracks for the men. There was a constant din as smiths hammered out weapons, farriers' re-shod hooves, and cooks clanged kitchen items. The street led them past large training yards where men fenced with wooden swords or practiced archery against targets made to look like trolls.

The soldiers gave disapproving looks after seeing their wizard's robes before recognizing the general and returning to their business. Their grim faces were more often scarred than not.

"Wizards are mistrusted in Toron, more so here," Gunnar commented, seeing the expressions. Chip walked closer to listen. "High King Dominor would break ties with the Guild if he could but acknowledges the usefulness of the treaty. He pays a hefty tithe to be advised and protected by the wizards. In return, it allows him to ship magic wielders out of his city. He weathers the occasional advisor and values the Protectors but sends them back frequently. If he could have his way, the High King would ban all magic. Anyone who does use unauthorized magic in Toron is severely punished. I think he feels it's a threat to his rule. The man likes control, and wizards are loyal to the Guild. He feels no person should have that much power. Other than himself, of course."

"Sounds seditious," Garth observed with a hint of a smile.

"Ha, my loyalty is unwavering. I swore an oath. I could have returned to the Guild, but Dominor beseeched Balor to have me train his soldiers, and now I am a general. Pretty good for a farm boy from Calgar. You did a stint yourself in Toron before returning to the Guild. How you became an Honorary High Commander in two years is beyond me." Gunnar grinned.

"I trained the Torons to change their archaic war tactics and sloppy swordsmanship. I did win the Silver Sword, after all. If I recall, I defeated you in the first round. You only scored one point." Gunnar grimaced.

"No need to bring up the past. I'm sure I could now score two." He coughed as Garth arched an eyebrow. "Fine. Your title is well deserved. Since then, the Torons have changed their antiquated weaponry and techniques to embrace modern warfare. Who uses lances in a battle? More often than not, the impact sends the rider off his horse to be mauled by the enemy. Your insistence on switching from short to long swords has saved many a man from a troll's reach. I'm surprised Dominor didn't try to keep you."

"He did. Xander was adamant I return as his Protector. He had to come in person and remind Dominor that the Protectors were on loan from the Guild to train soldiers. They are not his property. A monarch can request a gifted Protector to stay on, but it is up to the Guild to agree. I, unlike you, was such a rare commodity and made such a profound impact that Xander had to stare down the High King." Garth winked at Xander.

The wizard smiled. "Indeed, I would have asked for your return as well Gunnar, but we had enough troublemakers at the Guild." The general feigned injury.

"I can assure you if I had known I would be sent to Northbane to fight the trolls, I would have run back to the Guild with my bare feet. It is not called 'Bane of the North' for nothing. Most men don't return." His expression turned grim. "The trolls are up to something. We will talk more in the keep."

Ahead of them sat a squat stone fortress with iron doors. Another smaller moat ran around the perimeter of the structure. Chip could see the Sprite River, full of moored boats off to the sides. Northbane's strategic significance made sense. If the men were ever forced to abandon the city, they could flee on the river.

They crossed a short bridge to enter the fortress. Two guards in clean uniforms saluted and opened the doors. The general led them into a large hall with an immense wood table. It contained sparse furnishings and bare stone walls.

"Just in time for dinner." He called several soldiers over to set the table. "Make arrangements for eighteen more guests. A small roast pig and some fowl should do the trick." The men saluted and hurried off. The general turned to his guests. "Have a seat. We can speak before dinner, if that suits you."

"It does," Xander said, pulling up a chair. Everyone sat at the stone table, with the general sitting in the middle so all could hear.

"What brings seven wizards and eleven Protectors to Northbane on unicorns?" the man asked without preamble.

"There were twelve Protectors," Xander declared grimly. "A flock of winged demons attacked us on the Frontier Road earlier today. We lost a man and a unicorn."

The general sat back, eyes widening. "My condolences." He crossed his right fist over his heart. "The Demon King's reach has grown long indeed. It makes this war with the trolls even more foolish. We should be fighting the common enemy."

"We are here to see King Jaggar. First and foremost, we need access to the old wizard's guild by any means necessary. Then we must try to convince him to join our cause."

Gunnar raised his eyebrows. "There are a thousand trolls standing in your way, indoctrinated into hating humankind by a ruthless leader with a vendetta against the High Wizard. Otherwise, it shouldn't be a problem." He sat back. "What is so important in the old guild?"

Xander sighed. "In our haste to escape a troll army led by a vengeful King Jaggar three millennia ago, we overlooked a room containing our early writings. They form part of the histories. In them, we believe there is a key to the location of the missing Light Elves. Without them and the Orb of Power, all may be lost."

The general nodded. "I see—threads of hope, one piled on another. Our training taught us that the impossible is achievable if you attack it one piece at a time. I daresay you have your work cut out for you, but I will assist you in any way I can. To start, I will prepare the entire city for an attack. If Jaggar refuses, he will throw everything at us. We will be prepared. Tomorrow, I can escort you to the front lines, but you must ride forth alone. If my men join you, it will be considered an attack. They need little provocation at the best of times. The trolls are built for war, both men and women. It's all they do."

"The women fight too?" Chase blurted in disbelief.

Gunnar looked over. "Yes, they are nearly as strong as the men and quicker. They only get a reprieve for child-bearing and breast-feeding then return to the front lines. The older trolls who can no longer fight begin training the children as soon as they can walk. When the trolls are so old they can no longer train the children, they are sent back to the front with a club to take down one more enemy before they die."

Chip's eyes widened. Even the Protectors showed surprise.

"So how do we convince them?" Chase asked.

"You don't," Mary answered. All eyes turned to the Blue Wing leader. "You dangle a carrot or threaten their self-perceived honour. I advised King Dominor for several years. He's a paranoid, stubborn control freak, but if he sees a benefit for himself, he can be swayed. He will also act if he feels his honour is being attacked, as long as it is public."

"In private, many powerful people lack honour," Eleanor agreed. "I was privy to nobles and royalty behind the scenes. Many act or defend honour before the people but are not so virtuous behind closed doors. We need to force their hand publicly first."

The two women glanced at each other and then looked away.

"True honour is what you do when no one is watching." Garth murmured.

"Is there anything a troll's honour forces them to do?" Eleanor asked.

"Yes," Gunnar answered. "Accept a challenge. They will not refuse physical combat."

"That's easy then," Ethrang piped up. "I can turn into a brown tiger and tear them apart. Or now I can now be a wasp demon." The general looked at the skinny blonde boy as if he had three heads. The twins hid their grins.

"No time for jokes," Xander admonished. "People with certain abilities should keep it to themselves. There is no need to display them in front of an entire army. Or talk about them." The wizard leaned forward to recapture Gunnar's attention. "King Jaggar is our second obstacle when we reach the old wizard's guild. That is where we dangle the carrot. The first obstacle is whoever is leading the trolls on the front lines."

"That's One Eye. He's a particularly nasty brute, huge and hairy. Scars everywhere. He will accept the challenge himself or assign his best soldier. Either way, it won't be easy. You must understand if you lose, they will attack. Even your combined magic would be overwhelmed by a thousand trolls."

"Then we will not lose," the weapons master said.

"Which of your Protectors is up for the challenge?" the general asked. "You will need your very best." All the Protectors raised their hands, including Chase.

"I will do it," Garth said.

Chase looked over. "It's alright. With my red chips, I should be fine. I will do it."

The weapons master turned to the tall boy. "No, I suspect there will be a second challenge when we meet Jaggar. He will bring out the greatest soldier in the troll nation. You can do that one. It will be a good test." He looked away with a bland expression as if discussing the weather.

Chase rolled his eyes, looking around for support. The twins slapped him on the back.

"Don't worry, you got this," Kristan chirped.

"Ya, how hard can it be to face the best troll fighter in the world?" Thomas tried to smile. Ethrang giggled.

"It might not come to that," Chip intervened. "Not if we dangle a big enough carrot before Jaggar."

"What do you have in mind?" Xander asked.

"Northbane, for starters. And then the Orb of Power when we are done with it."

Everyone looked at him.

"That's too much." Eleanor shook her head.

"The Power the Troll King would hold..." Xander muttered.

"The orb should be put into safekeeping—" Eleanor started.

"As long as he aids us in the Last Battle," Chip finished. "I don't think he will survive it anyway."

The others stopped talking, pondering the idea.

"I recommend starting smaller and keeping that in our back pocket," Mary advised. "Let's see what he thinks of getting Northbane first."

General Gunner threw up his hands. "I'm so happy you came by, Garth. You want me to forfeit the city I'm sworn to defend, then give a maniacal Troll King a magic talisman to make him more powerful, all so you can use his library?"

"And garner his assistance in the Last Battle. It's for the common good," Garth added.

"I need a drink," Gunnar lamented. "Ale, anyone?"

As if on cue, the soldiers returned carrying trays of food.

Roasted meats and various birds were placed on the table with steaming vegetables and cups of ale. The talk turned to old Guild stories and lighter subjects. Even the Protectors joined the conversation. Gunnar asked after Maxim, saying he didn't like the man but conceded he was a skilled Protector.

Garth grunted, giving a truncated answer indicating the topic didn't interest him. The general took the cue and switched subjects.

When the meal was over, Bulch walked over to the twins and asked if they could magically insert the unicorn horn into the hilt of his dagger.

"Grand Wizard Xander," Thomas called, "may we try to create a dagger with a bit of magic?"

The wizard looked around, making sure no one was watching. "We are far enough from the front lines that no magic will be sensed, but be discreet."

Both twins nodded as Bulch produced a normal dagger and gave them the horn. Chip came over to watch. The twins concentrated on the old dagger, their eyes flaring a bright blue.

"I got this," Kristan said, "give me the link."

"Fine," Thomas responded. "Don't screw it up."

The more powerful twin sent blue threads of magic into the old dagger, which raised a foot off the table, heating it. The blade began to melt and fall into the hilt. Thomas took the unicorn horn and slowly inserted the fat end into the bubbling metal. Kristan then reformed the hilt, which was now big enough to wrap around the horn since the blade had melted into it. He pressed the metal tight against the horn and elongated the handle until it was symmetrical. Then he pulled out the heat in the blade until, finally, a polished hilt surrounded the unicorn horn. Kristan reached out and grasped the handle then offered it to Bulch.

"Try it," the blond twin said. "I think I did it right."

The giant Protector took the reformed dagger and stabbed it into the top of the wood table. The horn stuck in standing upright. Thomas patted his brother on the back, acknowledging his craftsmanship. Bulch smiled in appreciation and tried to pull the horn out. The hilt came clean off in his hand. He looked at Kristan, bewildered.

"Awkward," the twin said sheepishly. "I don't think it will bind to iron or steel. To be honest, it's not sharp enough to do much good anyway."

The big man grunted and went back to his seat.

Something about the horn sticking out of the table intrigued Chip. He stepped over and grasped the round end. Immediately, he felt a jolt of energy. There was something in it. He broke through his Wall, red eyes blazing, and inserted his presence into and around the object. Everyone stopped to watch.

"It has magic," he breathed. Without thinking, he pushed down. The unicorn horn sunk into the table all the way up to his hand, as if slicing through butter. When he let go, only a few inches of horn appeared out of the wood.

Xander, watching intently, let out a low whistle. "My, my. Wonders never cease."

"How is that possible?" Kristan looked perplexed.

"Cool," Ethrang breathed. The skinny blond boy put his palm on the top of the horn and tried to push it deeper into the hard oak table. It wouldn't budge.

"Maybe you need to use magic?" Thomas offered.

The skinny boy's eyes flared an intense green, and he tried to push it in again. It wouldn't move. "I don't sense anything in it. To me, it's a piece of wood." The orphan shrugged and released his Power.

Chip reached out and felt another jolt as soon as he touched the horn. He pushed down on it with two fingers, and it slid deeper into the wood. Everyone's eyes widened. Now, only the base of the horn appeared above the table.

"Let's see who can pull it out," laughed Ethrang, trying his hardest. The horn looked like it was now part of the table.

The twins tried, then the Protectors. Even Bulch could not take it out. Mary and Eleanor looked at each other, rolling their eyes at the same time.

"It's amazing what entertains men," the Blue Wing Leader muttered.

"They could do this for hours," Eleanor agreed. Both women could not help but smile.

The twins were fighting with each other to go next. Chase was trying to get there first.

"Don't cheat and use magic."

"Let me go!"

"I want to try again."

The Guardian pushed between them and, with two fingers around the base of the horn, effortlessly pulled it out.

"That's not fair!" Thomas pouted.

"He's a Red Level. That's why," Kristan noted.

"He did not use his magic," Xander pointed out. "No, I think it has something to do with the unicorns and the bond. There is latent magic in that horn, and it appears to only respond to the Guardian.

Chip thought about it. "I have an idea." He pulled out the jewelled dagger that the High Wizard had given him.

Xander whistled. "That was King Luminor's. It is an eleven dagger of the finest craftsmanship. If you do what I think you are about to do, you better be right. That dagger is worth a small fortune."

The boy nodded. He held the horn in one hand and the dagger in the other. Embracing his magic, he felt an instant connection between the elven steel and the horn. He could not explain why, but they felt right together.

Chip took a deep breath and infused the dagger with threads of red magic. He released his hand to let it float in the air and copied Kristan's technique, melting the metal and reforming the hilt. He pushed the jewel shards to the outside. Letting go of the horn, he slowly used his magic to insert the round end into the molten hilt. When they touched, he felt a connection. He wondered if the unicorns were connected to the elves in the same way the dragons were. A memory of the dragon egg humming when the boy first met Redmane resurfaced.

Putting his speculation aside, Chip pushed the base of the horn deeper into the molten metal. He envisioned the perfect hilt, reshaping and compressing it as he pulled the jewels to the outside, spacing them equally apart. His magic copied the image in his mind, binding the two objects together. He was about to withdraw his Power but decided to wrap the hilt with red bands of magic, forming concentric rings, and squeezing them tighter until the horn fused with the metal, becoming one.

The unicorn horn gleamed in the air as it rotated, the hilt shimmering with multi-coloured gemstones.

"It's beautiful," breathed Eleanor.

"Well done, lad," Xander nodded in appreciation.

"Cool," Ethrang murmured.

Chip levitated the blade to Bulch. "Try it."

The big man grabbed it by the hilt and then impaled it into the table. Only the tip went in. "Same as before," he rumbled.

The Guardian looked on in puzzlement then pulled the dagger out with his Power until it reached his hand. He then drove it straight into the table up to the hilt. There was no resistance until it hit the metal. Standing up, Chip pulled it out and looked at the stone wall. "May I?" he asked the general.

Gunnar sat back, throwing up his hands again. "Why not? We are trying to give the place away anyway. Have at it."

The boy released his Power, seeing if it would work without it. He still felt a strange hum in his hand. The hilt felt perfect in his grip. He walked over and drove the dagger deep into the solid stone wall then stepped back in shock.

The weapons master whistled. "There is no armour in the world that can stop that. Will be useful in a fight."

"Amazing," the twins breathed as one. Chip left it in the wall. The men ran over to try and pull it out one by one. The women rolled their eyes again. Bulch went last, his immense forearms bulging, but it wouldn't budge. The boy walked over and withdrew it without effort.

"It made for you. You keep." Bulch chortled, slapping him on the back.

Chip grimaced. "Thanks."

The companions talked for a good while longer, swapping stories and forming a stronger bond. The ale helped loosen tongues no doubt, and even Mary and Eleanor began to converse. At first, it was only sarcastic comments about the men, who had moved off to play silly games or spar lightly, but then they began to discuss matters of court and nobility that Chip knew nothing about. He always listened when he could, for the weapons master made it clear that people should always be trying to learn. What better source of information for knowledge than another's experience?

He chuckled inwardly at an example Garth used of ten blind people touching one part of an animal, such as a fanged black bear. Each would have a different view of the animal depending on which part they touched, but in the end their views together would complete the picture.

He knew it was the same with human experience. The different views expressed by everyone, especially different cultures, whether agreeable or not, would complete the whole picture. Listening to someone else's experience was beneficial to refining a person's worldview. Everyone had something to teach. Or at least make you realize what not to do.

Chip grinned as he watched Ethrang try to score points on the Protectors as they sparred lightly with their hands. The skinny blond boy was quick, and though they dodged most of his punches, he managed to connect a few times, surprising even them. He hit Sheldor, who was built like a tree, in the stomach, causing him to double over and smacked Hunter in the side of the head. Growing up in Banfar as a street kid had forced him to be a decent fighter. His shapeshifting ability and fearless attitude made the green-robed boy a powerful ally. Even more surprising, Carvor and Chase, the two finalists in the Silver Sword tournament, were jesting with each other. His best friend even showed Maxim's star student a few sword techniques to shore up his weaknesses.

At the end of the evening, General Gunnar stood up and raised a toast. "Good luck on the morrow, my friends. I have already sent out word to have the entire city ready to come to your aid if necessary. We must keep our distance, or the enemy will think we are mounting a major assault, causing the consequence we hope to avoid. The trolls look brutish, but they are cunning. They have been raised only to know war. You will need all your talents to achieve your goal. Luckily, as much as it pains me to admit it, you are led by one of the greatest Protectors who ever lived. Heed his orders and advice. There is no better. High King Dominor may have my head if I lose the city, but I can always say the Guild strong-armed me."

He winked at Xander then turned to Chip. "I will have a scabbard made by morning for your horn dagger. Pick it up at the leather smith next to the forge on your way out. Something that beautiful needs a sheath." His face lost its smile. "There's a thousand trolls on the front lines and more in the old wizard's fortress. Once you cross the trenches, you are on your own. We will be watching to lend aid if necessary, but we may come too late if they descend on you all at once. It is the risk you must take.

"The only reason we hold them back is our archers. For some reason, trolls do not use bows and arrows. I think it's because their fingers are too big. I've also heard them shout that it's dishonourable. They like looking a man in the eye as he dies. One-on-one, a good soldier will usually lose to a troll. We hold them back only through superior weaponry and tactics. You are a powerful group but cannot withstand an entire army. They also have mages in the old Guild. Remember, King Jaggar is ruthless, but he may listen if he sees an opportunity.

"My men will take you to guest rooms in the keep. They are sparse but serve their purpose. Going forward, you will encounter a world of stone. From Northbane on, everything is made of stone: the old Guild, the troll capital Rathgar, and the mountains themselves. Before King Jaggar united them, the trolls liked to set fires to warring tribal villages. They quickly learned to make everything out of stone. The Troll Kingdom is often called the Stone Kingdom. It's hard and bleak out there. Dress warm, for once you get into the mountains, it gets cold, even in autumn. May the Creator's light shine fortune on you."

Everyone raised a glass, and the general departed. Shortly thereafter, the guards escorted them to their rooms, which contained two functional beds against opposite stone walls with a small desk in the middle. One thin, slitted window provided weak moonlight. Chip and Chase shared a room, and surprisingly so did Eleanor and Mary.

Chase collapsed on the hard but serviceable bed. "I guess Carvor isn't that bad after all. It's funny how if you give people a chance, they aren't so bad."

Chip thought about it. "The weapons master said you can quickly turn enemies into friends with a common goal. Or do something exciting or thrilling with someone, and bonds can form instantly. He said if friendship ever wavers, start doing the type of things that made you friends in the first place. Better yet, try exciting new things."

"Makes sense. There is nothing like camaraderie." He sat straight up. "Wait. Does that apply to bonding with women too?"

Chip laughed. "Yes, of course. Bonds form as long as you pick fun, exciting things to do. It can also rekindle a stale relationship. So who's the lucky girl?"

His best friend put a finger to his lips and closed his eyes with a smile. "That's for me to know."

"Well, whoever it is will have to wait. First, you must defeat the greatest troll warrior in the Stone Kingdom."

Chase made a face. "Don't remind me."

The boys didn't talk much after that as the gravity of the situation began to press on them. Chip remembered going to the baths in Vanalon long ago as a small child, daydreaming he was a captain issuing orders on the walls of Toron while a troll army attacked the capital. Tomorrow, he would not have to imagine anymore. He would finally meet the trolls.

The thought did not help him sleep.

5

The day dawned cold and grey in their stone rooms. The companions put on extra layers of clothing and gathered in the main hall. They ate a light breakfast consisting of smoked bacon and eggs, washed down with cool river water. The general was absent, likely preparing the men.

When finished, a soldier led them out of the squat fortress towards the front gates. A thick bank of clouds had rolled in overnight but did not retain the land's heat, as a cold wind was blowing in from the north. To the southwest, darker clouds gathered on the Great Plains. The Toron soldiers were bustling about, making breakfast, sharpening swords, and donning armour. The group stopped at the leather smith's shop and a large man with a pot belly greeted them. Tools jutted out of his apron.

"Ah, there you are, laddy," the man said, singling Chip out. "I was told to make a sheath to hold a special dagger for a young man in red robes. You fit the bill. Give me a moment."

He went inside and returned with a short round sheath ending in a point. "The general gave me rough dimensions, but let's see how she fits." Chip pulled the horn from his rope belt, holding it in the wan light. Even so, the gems sparkled, and the smooth brown unicorn's horn gleamed. "She's a beauty, isn't she," the man's eyes widened. "Normally, a scabbard is made of wood wrapped in leather, but this is a flexible sheath with stitched leather and a ring around the top. When empty, you won't even know it's there. Let's give it a try." Chip slid the horn point first into the sheath until only the jewelled hilt showed. "Ah, snug as a bug." The man beamed.

"Thank you," Chip said. "It's perfect." He then removed his rope belt to slide it through the loophole.

"No, no, that will never do. A lad of your station needs a proper leather belt." He went back inside and returned soon after with a belt and buckle. The boy slid his sheath and sword scabbard through, then buckled them tight.

When he finished, Chip asked, "Can I give you money for your efforts?" The boy then realized he had none.

"Ya, but I wouldn't take it. A favour for the general. Besides, Toron pays for everything," he said, waving his hand. The man stepped back to his shop door. "If that is all, I have another ten orders to fill. Take care, laddy."

"Thanks again," Chip called after him, but he had already disappeared inside.

They headed north down the main street towards the gates. More men paused to give them distrustful looks. Their scarred faces and bleak demeanours spoke of the hardships of battle. Chip hoped he could end this war but knew that it would not be easy after a thousand years of fighting.

General Gunnar met them at the front gates. He was calling out orders to soldiers who ran off to fulfill missions. A squadron of ten men in impeccable uniforms sat on horses in perfect formation, awaiting orders.

"There you are. I thought for a moment you had changed your mind." The man grinned and clasped Garth's hand. He then lowered his voice. "The men aren't happy a group of wizards are crossing the front lines, but we are here for you. Regiments have been instructed to follow but remain out of sight. We can relay messages back quickly for reinforcements. The men withstood a skirmish two days ago so the trolls will be in a foul mood. Do you still have your mounts?" The general glanced at Chip.

"I will call them," the boy said. Gunnar gave him a puzzled look but didn't say anything. He sent his presence out and almost immediately connected with Redmane who was about a league away. The unicorn responded and began moving towards the city. "They will be here shortly."

The general looked at him funny. "You do know that trolls eat horses, right?" Chip's eyes widened.

Chase looked confused. "Do trolls not ride horses?"

"Ha," Gunnar laughed. "Of course not. Horses are terrified of them. I think it's the smell."

"So what do they ride?"

"Ride? They run. And fast. If the trolls need to send a message faster, they use trained mountain hawks. Half the time, our pigeons don't make it back to Toron. The hawks have been ordered to intercept them. Keep an eye on those unicorns. Horse meat is a delicacy in the Stone Kingdom."

The boys looked at each other.

"Now, now," Xander interjected. "It shouldn't come to that." He gave them a weak smile.

The sound of horse hooves interrupted their conversation, and a blur of white led by a spot of red materialized into a herd of unicorns as they slowed on the road leading up to the open gates. The unicorns stopped a safe distance from the city and waited, horns gleaming.

"Looks like our ride is here." Ethrang grinned.

"So it is," Gunnar said. "I will be behind you with my men. See you on the front lines." They all nodded and walked up to the waiting horses. Redmane danced excitedly before Chip, then stopped and lowered his head until the shiny white horn touched the boy's side where the unicorn dagger rested in its sheath. He felt a hum in his side for a moment, and then the horse neighed in approval and bent a knee. Chip breathed a sigh of relief and leapt on. The others tied their packs to the saddles and did the same. In a few moments the herd was ready, forming a triangle.

Redmane let out a musical whinny and responded to the boy's nudge. Chip kept the pace brisk but restrained the great animal from galloping too fast to allow the general and his men to keep up. Looking back, he saw several regiments had formed inside the city. According to the general, they would be spaced from Northbane to the front lines to assist as required.

The small party travelled for several leagues before the surrounding low hills began to recede. The trees also thinned as if life was pulling back, aware that a war had been raging for a thousand years, leaving even the land cold and dead. The wind grew stronger, bringing a deeper chill from high up in the mountains. They crested a last rise between two hills and found themselves on the front lines. Chip caught his breath at the vista before him. The land fell into a brown, arid plain stretching almost as far as the eye could see. In the distance, towering mountains rose on the horizon, glowering at them like ominous sentinels. There was a massive trench before them with a thousand men scurrying inside and behind it like ants.

In the middle of the plain, a large mass of moving bodies appeared and disappeared in their own trench. He could not see their features from this distance, but they looked big. Between the two trenches were multiple red spots and broken armour. Smaller white and brown things littered the land, and with a shudder, Chip realized they were pieces of trolls and humans. The red splotches gave a garish splash of colour to the desolate landscape as if an evil painter had embellished a plain portrait with the blood of his victims.

The general rode up and reigned in as they stopped to look at the stark landscape.

"Welcome to the front lines, gentlemen. This plain is soaked with the blood of generations of men and trolls. Quite depressing, isn't it. You can't make it out from here, but the old Wizard's Guild overlooks this plain. It is nearly impregnable. The only way in is through invitation. Use the small wooden makeshift bridge to cross our trench. You are at the enemy's mercy once you set foot on the other side. Everyone is fair game on the plain. What signal should I look out for if you need aid?"

Xander pushed forward. "Look for an inferno of bright blue, green, and red fire. Then listen for loud screaming. Don't worry, you won't miss it."

"Ha. I will keep my eyes open."

Gunnar led them down the hill as the men on the front lines began pointing and muttering. They had dark looks on their faces as they buckled on swords and filled quivers. At the bridge, the general spoke with what looked like a captain and waved them across.

Chase looked around at the Torons' angry faces. "I guess no lunch before we head out?" he asked hopefully.

Eleanor rolled her eyes. "I would not recommend it. These men might turn on you since you are protecting wizards who look to be breaching a treaty that has stood for a thousand years." Mary smiled at the boy's chagrin.

"Right, let's get this over with," Chase muttered.

Several men in the trenches spat to the side as they crossed. Within moments, they were on the bloody plain. Redmane became jittery as they walked across the hard, unforgiving ground, stepping around pieces of broken armour and body parts. There was a large brown thing to Chip's left, which he realized must be a troll head. Stringy, bloody hair was matted on the back of the dented skull. The size of its head alarmed him.

Guttural shouts rang out ahead, and the milling mass of bodies began to grow and spread out. The boy realized he was approaching a troll army trained to rend humans limb from limb. Xander reached into his robes and produced a white flag, raising it high. He held it aloft as they continued forward. A foul stench suddenly filled Chip's nose, which wrinkled involuntarily. It spoke of unwashed bodies, stale sweat, and wild animals. The wizard took the lead as the distance diminished. They could now make out the trolls.

"Good grief," Thomas whispered, covering his nose.

"They look worse than the stories," Kristan added, face grim.

"They have fangs!" Chase exclaimed. "Great."

Chip's eyes widened at the sight. The trolls were massive, upright creatures covered head to toe with thick, ridged skin resembling tree bark. Their bodies ranged from six and a half to seven feet tall, with heavily muscled limbs. The faces were blunt, holding deep-set eyes and large mouths sporting two fangs long enough to extend below their lower lips. Various bits of leather and metal armour covered them in mismatched fashion. Some of it was human-made, meaning they picked it up off the battlefield. Their mannerisms were restless, appearing disorganized, but they held the line.

With a start, the boy realized the ones with long hair must be women. They were slightly slimmer than the men but appeared even more agitated. It was the look in their eyes that got him the most. They seemed to be in a constant state of frenzy, only happy if they could run rampant at the enemy to tear them apart.

The trolls carried all manner of weapons. Most seemed to favour a cudgel to bash their opponents to death, while others held short, blunted swords. Maces and axes were also prevalent. The few long swords were manmade. These creatures used anything at their disposal against the enemy.

More piled out of their trench to spill onto the plain. A massive, hairy troll stood before them, covered in patchy leather armour, muscles bulging. He had a scar running through one eye diagonally down his face. That eye shone milky white. He carried an immense club. When they were close enough to speak, Xander reigned in his unicorn. The one-eyed troll raised his arm and made a circular motion.

Chip feared he was going to attack without trying to parlay, but the trolls spread around them in a large circle, keeping their distance. With teeth gnashing, they began grunting and snarling, shifting their weapons from one hand to another. Many looked hungrily at the unicorns, licking their lips. Some of their mounts neighed shrilly, eyes darting to and fro. Chip realized that even with his magic, if a thousand trolls attacked at once, he would be hard-pressed to make it out alive.

The troll in front lumbered forward, raising his arms. The noise died down, but they could still hear heavy breathing. He stopped a short distance from Xander, scanning them with one good eye, giving them an evil grin.

"Wizards, eh?" His deep voice rumbled. "You violate the treaty, humans. Even your magic won't stand against us all." He licked his lips and started to raise an arm.

"You will break the treaty, not us, Captain. The point is there is room to parlay in the treaty. We come to do just that. We do not intend to use our magic against you," Xander reassured.

The troll gave him a cunning look. "If we attack you, will you use your magic?"

"Why, of course, we must defend ourselves, but it won't come to that..."

"We will attack, and when you use your magic and break the treaty, we will eat you." He began to raise his arm again.

"Oh, King Jaggar will not like that," Xander shook his head. "Not at all."

The troll captain lowered his arm. "Why not?" he growled.

"We have an important message for him, one he's been waiting to hear for a long time. You see, I know your king. I wrote the treaty with him a thousand years ago." The wizard sat tall. His blue eyes sparkled with menace. "If your king finds out you tried to kill a messenger with important news, he will put your head on a spike for all to see."

The troll grunted. "Why should I believe you, wizard?"

"My goodness, you don't have to believe me. However, if I'm telling the truth, you will suffer more than any troll who has ever lived. King Jaggar will skin you alive, for starters. I've seen him do it. Why not escort us there, and then, if we are lying, Jaggar will gladly let you eat us. Now, if that is all, let's be on our way. The king does not like to wait."

The troll's face contorted as he weighed his options. Finally, he nodded in resignation and lowered his weapon. "Very well, human. I am Captain One Eye. We will escort you." Xander bowed his head in appreciation. "After you hand over your horses. My army is hungry." Chip's fists tightened, and the Wall appeared in his mind.

"We ride the horses. They are ours." The wizard's eyes narrowed in menace.

"Give us the horses, or we will kill all of you." One Eye looked specifically at Redmane and licked his lips. "Your message can be delivered without them. That is the price for you to pass." Saliva began to drip off his fangs.

Garth Stone moved his horse forward between Redmane and the captain. "They are my horses, troll scum. Let us pass unhindered, or you will force me to challenge you to a duel."

The captain's head snapped up. The other trolls began gnashing their teeth. "You dare talk to me like that, puny human."

"I would stop talking if I were you, ugly beast. If you continue, I will challenge you. I heard trolls have honour, but I only see scared animals."

"I hope he knows what he's doing," Chase whispered. The twins nodded, wide-eyed.

Xander snorted, looking at the weapons master. "You called them names, and they still haven't challenged you. How could they have honour?" he said in a loud voice.

Grunts and bellows started erupting from the trolls in the circle. The captain looked at his army, which now required blood. "How dare you. Trolls know honour. You have insulted my people. I challenge you to a duel!" He pointed at Garth.

The weapons master's face hardened. "If I win, we keep the horses, and you escort us to King Jaggar."

The troll nodded. "And if I win, we eat the horses...and you."

"That's agreeable." Garth jumped down from his unicorn.

"But you fight my proxy." One Eye grinned, fangs gleaming.

"Your choice," Garth said. "It matters not who I beat when honour is at stake."

One Eye stepped back with a ferocious grin. He turned to the circle. "Smasher," he called. "Defend our honour."

There was a flurry of activity in one part of the circle, and then a monstrous misshapen troll broke through, emerging into the dull light. He was hideous. His arms were extra long, and he dragged a large cudgel across the ground behind him. Bulging muscles rippled as he stepped forward with fangs bared. Despite his size, he moved with a fluidity learned through years of training. Various weapons surrounded his mismatched armour.

Garth Stone looked at One Eye. "To the death, I assume."

The captain grinned. "Death or submission and trolls do not submit."

Everyone stepped back, giving the combatants a wide berth.

The weapons master pulled out his sword, face turning to granite. He circled the giant carefully. The Protector seemed tiny compared to the massive troll, but Chip knew his body was a living piece of iron.

The attack came suddenly. One moment Smasher was twirling his cudgel and then he leapt in with stunning speed and agility. Garth was faster. As the cudgel came straight down towards the weapons master's head, he darted in and to the side, slicing down with his sword clean through the wrist of the beast. The cudgel fell to the ground with the severed hand still clutching it. The weapons master danced back, avoiding the dagger that had appeared in the troll's left hand. Smasher bellowed once in pain then began circling again. Off to the side, One Eye growled with displeasure.

Garth Stone stayed on the side of the troll's severed arm and began leaping in, jabbing the monster's shoulder until his whole arm was a bloody mess. The creature threw his dagger straight at Garth's chest, but the Protector turned at the last instant, and the blade sailed through the air to impale itself in the thigh of a troll standing in the circle. Raucous laughter erupted from the other trolls nearby as their comrade howled in pain. Smasher pulled a large two-sided axe from his belt and circled again.

The troll must have sensed that time was running out, for he ran into Garth's sword on purpose and twisted his body to wrench it out of the Protector's hands. Quick as thought, the weapons master drew two daggers to block what would have been a fatal axe blow to his neck. In quick succession, he drove both daggers to the hilt in the troll's midsection and stepped back with a mace in his right hand. Smasher fell to his knees, holding his stomach. Garth went in for the kill, swinging his mace in a deadly arc.

He never completed the swing.

Smasher's left hand shot out, releasing a grey powder straight into Garth's eyes. The weapons master grunted and stepped back. He blinked and tried to rub his eyes, unable to see.

"That's cheating," yelled Ethrang.

One Eye looked over and grinned. "I didn't see anything."

A strong front kick struck the weapons master in the chest, sending him sprawling on his back. He regained his feet and crouched low, listening with eyes closed. The troll closed the distance in a single bound, and the axe rose high for the deathblow.

"Overhand!" warned Ethrang.

Right before it struck, Garth spun and executed a full force back-kick to the troll's midsection, causing the beast to land hard on his behind, wheezing for air. The axe flew out of his hand.

Chip had never seen the weapons master look mad before. His normally calm, granite face became downright angry. Garth ran in with eyes closed, swinging the mace with deadly intent. The troll tried to scramble backwards, finally showing fear, causing the mace to miss Smasher's head, but it impaled itself in the troll's groin.

This time, there was no bellow. A high-pitched scream erupted from the monster, cut short as various weapons appeared in Garth's hands, impaling themselves in different parts of the troll's body. The weapons master, enraged, drove every tool he had into Smasher, all with eyes closed. When it was clear the troll was dead, Xander politely coughed, causing his Protector to stop. Garth Stone stood up, regaining his calm, granite demeanour and stepped back.

Smasher looked like a pincushion. A large pool of blood surrounded him. Nobody made a sound. Even One Eye gaped in shock.

"Take us to see King Jaggar," the weapons master said.

The captain could only nod. The rest of the trolls grunted then beat their chests with both hands, nodding in appreciation at the spectacle. Xander moved his unicorn up to Garth and touched his face. The wizard's eyes blazed blue, cleaning out the debris in his Protector's eyes, and Garth looked around with sight restored.

"You're next," the weapons master said to Chase as he mounted his unicorn. "Good luck."

Chase rolled his eyes. "Why me?"

The trolls returned Garth's weapons to him but split the rest of Smasher's armour amongst those fast enough to scavenge it. Several fights ensued about who would get which piece.

The captain signalled a troll to step forward. The soldier held his arm out to the side and whistled. A large mountain hawk plummeted from the sky to land on his gauntlet.

"Send word to the king that we are escorting a group of seven wizards and eleven Protectors to the old Guild to speak with him," One Eye instructed. The troll nodded. The captain then turned to a thinner, nasty-looking troll with long hair covered in scars. Chip realized with a start that she was a female. "Widow, you're up. If you see any funny business from the Torons, mount an attack."

"I recommend you don't engage until we return," Xander suggested.

One Eye looked at him. "Why's that?"

"If things go right, we could end this war."

The captain stared at him for a moment, his deep-set eyes widening. Then he reared his head back and let out a deep rumble that seemed to be a laugh. The other trolls started chortling. Several were holding their bellies, letting out loud guffaws, enticing others to join in. Soon, the whole circle bent over, emitting toad-like bellows of laughter, strangely causing many of them to loudly pass wind. The stench went up a notch, making the twins go green. Mary covered her mouth, trying not to vomit. Ethrang found it hilarious.

Finally, the captain wiped a tear from his one eye. "You humans can be funny at times. If we ended this war, what on Earth would we do?" He opened his hands. The other trolls looked at each other blankly. None could come up with an answer.

"Never mind." The wizard turned his unicorn northwards. "Shall we?"

The captain nodded and commanded the circle to open, allowing the party to ride across a makeshift bridge over the enemy's trench. A large contingent of trolls on foot, led by One Eye, surrounded them as they headed north towards the distant mountains and the old Wizard's Guild.

Chip ensured Redmane moved at a canter so the trolls could keep up. The beasts jogged around them, forming a large circle. He slowed to ride alongside the weapons master. "I was about to break through my Wall to protect you at the end, but Ethrang's warning was enough."

"No need," Garth replied. "I could hear Smasher coming. While I was crouched low, the only attack available to him was an overhand swing. I knew with his hands raised that his stomach would be vulnerable. Understand that in each fight or challenge in our lives, we learn something. I did not expect him to cheat in a fight of honour, which cost me. I won't make that mistake again."

"I've never seen you mad before," the boy commented, glancing sideways.

The weapons master grunted. "It has been a while. Calmness is mastery, and I let myself slip today. I do get angry when someone is dishonourable. Rage can lead to costly mistakes in any contest. You need anger to use your Power, which is why it's dangerous. Sadly, it's a necessary evil. Perhaps the Balance does have a twisted sense of humour. Always seek to calm your rage or at least understand it so you can make rational decisions. It's a fine balancing act. Giving in to anger can become habitual. Understand that there is always a thought that precedes anger. It's normal to experience wrath and other negative emotions. It is a part of life. The danger lies in acting out on those emotions by doing something you will regret. In other words, those negative emotions can lead to negative behaviour that hurts yourself or others."

Chip thought about it. "So how do you stop negative emotions like anger, jealousy, fear, depression, and hate?"

"Find the thought or belief behind them. Even when they seem automatic, a flawed thought triggers them. Once you identify the thought, change it."

"That sounds pretty simple," the boy said.

"Talk to yourself, don't listen."

"Huh?"

"Tell yourself the new thought out loud. Talk to yourself. Don't listen to the old thought. It will still be there for a while until the new thought replaces it."

"I think I understand. Changing my thoughts stops me from feeling negative emotions, which stops me from doing something I will regret."

"Exactly."

"Care to give an example?" Chip asked.

"Sure, here's a few. Nobody likes me. It's not fair. I am worthless. It's alright to hurt people to get what I want. I deserve it."

"Yup, those sound pretty negative," the boy agreed.

"The key is to change each one, but don't simply say the opposite because your mind might not believe it. For the first one, it's alright if some people don't like you. They are probably not worth your time anyway. There are always family or friends you can be grateful for. Plus, don't forget that you are enough."

"I am enough." Chip remembered that bit of wisdom when he realized the preciousness of life in Death's realm.

"Once you have the new thought, keep saying it to yourself and stop listening to the old thought. In time, it will replace it and stop the negative emotion. There are other techniques too. The problem is people can't think straight when they are under the influence of a negative emotion. That's why calmness is mastery. For anger, learn techniques to maintain calm. Deep breathing does wonders, and almost always, taking a walk will do the trick. Remove yourself from the negative situation. Remember the twenty-minute rule. That's how long it takes for us to fully calm down."

Chip grinned. "Are you calm yet?"

Garth arched an eyebrow. "It hasn't been twenty minutes yet."

The boy laughed and resumed the lead.

The trolls turned out to be excellent runners. None of them showed signs of fatigue. One Eye had chosen over one hundred to escort them, but Chip knew they would attack at a moment's notice if they tried to break through the circle. Ahead of them, the mountains grew in size, their snowcapped tips nearly touching the dark clouds. The wind increased, causing him to shiver. The boy was amazed at how the flat plain up ahead ended and the mountains began. He felt like he was running into a giant wall.

He could now make out the old Wizard's Guild. It stood on a massive cliff at the edge of the plain, blending into the gray rock of the mountain behind it. Stone spires rose around a rectangular structure with narrow windows. On top of the crenellated walls, he could make out tiny figures. Flashes of blue, green, and yellow indicated they wore mage robes. The boy realized that once inside, they would be surrounded by troll mages and soldiers. A moment of anxiety rippled through him at the thought of all those stones surrounding him like a tomb, full of the enemy. Flashes of the Dim chasing them through the Demon King's caves surfaced, making him shudder. They were going into the lair of the beast.

It took the better part of the afternoon to reach the cliff wall. Chip craned his neck to see the old Guild towering a thousand feet above

"This way," One Eye grunted, leading them around the cliff through a pass between two mountains. The trolls had a light sheen of sweat on them, magnifying their rank odour. He noticed Mary wrinkling her nose in disgust. The boy looked at Eleanor, who gave him a smile of encouragement. He always marvelled at her calm and poise, regardless of the situation. The twins winked at him, but their faces showed a slight strain. Even Ethrang looked a little nervous as he gazed up at the fortress.

They followed the trolls through a dark, winding pass, circling the Guild. The captain stationed half the trolls at the entrance to the pass, causing everyone to share dark looks. The only way was forward. The pass opened into a dark meadow with stunted grass.

"Leave the horses here. You must walk the rest." He pointed to the side of the field where stone stairs wound up the mountain to reach the Guild. One Eye noticed the boy's trepidation and emitted a deep laugh. "Don't worry, we won't eat them…yet."

"You will never eat them," Garth said, dismounting. The captain smiled, fangs gleaming, but said nothing. Redmane looked nervous, so Chip held his head and showed him calming images. He explained in pictures that they would be up the mountain for a while but would return. The boy understood if the unicorns wished to leave. Otherwise, they could graze in the meadow and roam around the mountains until the party returned. He warned him not to go near the trolls, which the horse understood readily. Everyone took some items out of their packs to carry up the stairs. The boy hugged the magnificent beast's neck and patted him on the side. The unicorns sprang forward as one, running to the edge of the meadow, far from the trolls.

They looked at Red Eye for instructions. The troll grinned wickedly. "After you." He pointed up the dark stone stairs.

Everyone looked up at the ominous fortress high in the sky. Dark windows in the stone walls seemed to stare at them with spectral eyes. A breeze suddenly blew through the pass, whipping their cloaks sideways, emitting a mournful howl. A sense of foreboding filled the air. Huddled together, the small party began climbing the stone stairs to the old Wizard's Guild.

6

The Demon King stood on the slopes of Cave Mountain, staring at his ancestral lair. One hundred thousand demons fanned out behind him, covering the land down to Fang Forest. He looked at the misshapen peak in disbelief. Murk had sent a tracker to inform him of what transpired here, but he had scarcely believed it. The Lord of the Dark Elves sent his presence out, assessing the damage. Half the peak had fallen in on itself, looking like a bent old man. The lake with the small island in the middle was completely buried. He probed the bowels of the mountain, searching for the black egg. A presence suddenly connected with his. The dragon egg was still in its diamond womb. It sent him a flurry of images, showing the boy with red eyes picking up the white egg and then fleeing with his companions from the Dim.

A rage like no other began to build in him. The boy had first killed his black dragon, Fang, and then stolen one of his eggs. The presence in the black egg expressed its discontent, thirsting for revenge. *Soon,* he projected, soothing the powerful creature.

Killian continued searching the cave system with his mind, noting the destruction. His throne room had spiderweb cracks but remained intact. The damage to the demon chambers, however, was significant.

For a moment, he felt overwhelmed with rage and spasmed. The coils of red Power that slithered across his body like crimson serpents flared outward. The Inner Circle and Dark Elves scampered away, but two of his demon guards instantly combusted.

The thought of the Dim tamed his anger enough for him to think again, and he moved his presence to the other side of the mountain, searching. The cavern below the eastern slope had completely collapsed and filled with crushed stone. He found the empty spot almost immediately and realized it was moving. The Dim was scraping at its stone tomb with one hand, trying to claw its way out.

With enough time, it would.

The Demon King rarely felt apprehension, but knowing its touch would kill even him was disturbing. Life forms were easy to recognize, but this creature was made of...nothing. And now, for some reason, it had stopped obeying commands. A ripple of disquiet passed over him. He would leave it snug in the buried rock until he unearthed the black dragon. Then, he would surround the Dim in a diamond prison.

The thought of unleashing it in the Last Battle sent a shiver of ecstasy through him, but the rage returned. The fact that someone had damaged his home was unforgivable. For a moment, he realized that an eternity of torture for those responsible would not be enough. He clenched his gloved hands in fury.

The Demon King's black cape billowed in the wind as the sun began to set.

Killian turned to his nearest advisor. He was a Dark Elf named Wormwood whose sibilant voice usually soothed him. "Ready the hordes," he ordered through gritted teeth. "We march on Toron now. I seek revenge."

"Master, please reconsider," Wormwood hissed, "winter comes early on the Great Plains. The demons will freeze to death."

The Lord of the Dark Elves was as close to shock as he had been in a long time. His advisor had questioned his command. He prided himself on patience, but this was too much. Killian's gloved hand shot out and seized Wormwood's neck. With one squeeze, he broke the

Dark Elf's spine then flung him against the side of the mountain, breaking most of the bones in his body. He sent a stream of red Power into the corpse, incinerating the remains until it was ash that the wind picked up and swept away.

Wormwood's death gave him enough joy that it subdued his rage so he could think. A pang of disappointment at losing an advisor who had been with him for a thousand years briefly entered his thoughts, but then he realized his anger was justified. How dare he question his Master in front of the army? He looked down at his pets, who were wailing in agony at his displeasure. Some of the weaker ones were clawing their eyes out. More food for the stronger ones.

Something pricked his thoughts. What had the advisor said? Something about the demons freezing on the plains in winter. He was about to dismiss the thought but reconsidered. The advisor had a point. If an early winter storm struck, the demons would freeze. It wouldn't affect him or the Dark Elves, but his main army would suffer catastrophic losses. And he would not be able to fly over the burning remains of Toron on his black dragon if he didn't wait.

Killian had waited three thousand years for his revenge. A few extra months would not hurt. He could unbury the black dragon and birth him. With his magic, he could grow the beast to full adulthood by winter's end then ride the glorious creature in the Last Battle. In the meantime, he would rebuild Cave Mountain and put the Dim in a diamond prison. Yes, it all made sense. The advisor had been right.

He almost felt a stab of pity for Wormwood but threw aside the feeling. Pity and sympathy were for the weak. He had been taught that over and over. It was his advisor's fault for not getting his point across. The Demon King's reaction was appropriate. He had learned long ago that anger and rage solved most problems. He conceded that thinking things through occasionally had merits, but he felt so much better when angry. The gratification was instantaneous, even if the problem remained unsolved. He permitted himself a small smile and even reached out to pet the head of one of the larger demons, who was prostrate on the ground, grovelling at his leisure. The rest of its brethren, seeing their Master display affection for them, started shrieking with joy, basking in his temperance. He was a merciful king. They were lucky to have him.

At that moment, a black speck appeared in the sky, growing larger. It was a wasp demon. The Lord of the Dark Elves smiled under his horned helmet, awaiting the good news. He did not show his face to his pets. They did not deserve to look upon his handsome countenance until his enemies were vanquished. Then he would grace them.

The creature swooped in under the dark clouds, landing at his master's feet. It immediately grovelled, folding its great wings.

"Master," it croaked. The creature's jaws were not built for speech, but the words were decipherable.

Killian nodded. "Is the boy dead?"

The wasp demon looked up, black eyes betraying its fear. "They killed us all."

The Demon King began to shake. "How?" he managed.

"They ride...unicorns. The red one saw us coming. We fell to their magic."

A sudden image of a white unicorn appeared in Killian's mind. He had ridden one as a boy. For a moment, he was back in the elven forests, riding on the magnificent animal, wind whipping through his hair, wild and free. The sounds and smells of nature invigorating him as he frolicked with the horse on long, sunny days.

Then his rage returned.

He lifted the wasp demon in the air, sending tendrils of red magic into its body. It started coughing out smoke, and its wings burned away. The creature's armour became red hot as he slowly cooked it. Killian was showing tremendous restraint by not killing it instantly. The suffering was necessary to show the other demons that failure was not an option. A thin, high scream escaped the creature's burning lungs as it writhed in agony.

After a while, even the Demon King's commendable patience ended, and he smote the wasp in the chest with a red fireball. Its burnt body blew apart in a shower of cooked flesh and bone fragments. The other demons mewled and howled in commiseration with their Master's discontent.

Satiated by his display of Power, Killian reflected on the wasp's words. A red unicorn had appeared. From his childhood connection with the white unicorn, he knew a red one was extremely rare. It allowed them to form a bond in times of need. It seemed the Balance was always at work. He shook his head at the unfairness of it all.

Brushing his memories aside, he vowed to kill all unicorns. His source in the new Wizard's Guild had not mentioned them. The boy with red eyes and his companions might have acquired them after departing on their mission to find the Light Elves. He shrugged. It was a slight wrinkle. He knew what to do.

The Demon King turned to his Inner Circle. "Hagatha, come."

A thin, skeletal Dark Elf with long white hair emerged to stand before him. She bowed low but did not prostrate herself. "I serve at your leisure." He allowed such a breach of protocol only because of her rank. She was the mother of his childhood friend Bashan. For a moment, a wave of rage washed over him, thinking of his treacherous friend. Bashan had fled to Banfar to indulge in his creative pleasures. A report by one of the Dark Elves who escaped the city said he died at the hands of the red-eyed boy. Killian should have seen his betrayal coming. After Bashan criticized him for not releasing the Dim in the Great Battle, he had enjoyed torturing his friend for centuries.

With the orb, there had been no reason to release the creature. Then, that thieving wizard boy stole the talisman, and he was forced to retreat from the Great Plains. Afterwards, Killian did try to release the Dim, but Arkan was clever and cut him off. In the end, he fled to Demon Island.

He studied the old female elf before him. As a child, she was like a second mother to him, nurturing Killian to become the Lord of the Dark Elves. She and Morgo showed him the folly of sympathy and the benefits of narcissism. Unlike her traitorous son, she valued loyalty, and hers was unwavering. Hagatha would have killed Bashan herself for his treachery.

She had done well so far, unlike the others. Vanalon had fallen easily under her command. All Killian had to do when he entered the city was walk across the human bones, picked clean by the demon hordes. He had stopped on purpose in the courtyard next to the tallest tower in the palace, recognizing the garments of the Queen of Vanalon, who had fallen to her death. He ground her skull to dust with his boot then gave the Dark Elf a rare compliment. Hagatha was a severe woman almost devoid of emotion, but the gesture caused an almost imperceptible smile as she fawned before him. Yes, she had done well, but now he had a task of higher importance.

After the loss of General Morgo and three of his Inner Circle, he needed to send someone more cunning. Elohan, Marta, and Murk had their talents but were fools. Hagatha was worth all three. Besides, her Blue Level of Power was nearly unmatched. The Orb Stealer, that pathetic son of Arkan, would not stand a chance against her.

Yet even so, he needed something more.

"Get me, Blade," he commanded in a loud, deep voice.

A moment passed as the demons milled about, frantic to fulfill his command, and then a figure smoothly detached itself from the throng. The Dark Elf moved to stand before him with unmatched grace. A smidge of grey hair coloured his temples.

He was the greatest weapons expert who ever lived.

Granted, his pupil, Victor, had recently surpassed him, but not by much. Blade's disciple still lacked his teacher's wisdom.

The Lord of the Dark Elves looked at his finest specimen. Commander Blade was taller than most elves but not anywhere near the size of Victor, who was a new breed of deadly. However, beneath Blade's green tunic was a body hard as iron, strengthened by Killian himself through magic. Blade had shown promise as a young commander on the battlefield millennia ago, many times being the only survivor during the Elf Wars. His prowess and military tactics in the Great Battle saved them from defeat. He was only a Yellow Level magic user, but that was his greatest strength. He could heal himself almost instantly.

Killian had nurtured Blade on Demon Island, feeding him Power from the white-eyed demons, strengthening his skin, and amplifying his ability to heal. A sword could barely cut him, and even then he would use magic to heal himself. Blade had trained for three thousand years with all manner of weapons, perfecting the art of fighting. Only his pupil Victor, who was also cultivated in a similar fashion, had bested him. No human would stand a chance, even the so-called Protectors from the Guild. Blade could carve through a dozen elves without a scratch on him. Even Killian marvelled at what he created.

The Demon King paused. His source in the Guild had talked of a young Protector with red chips in his eyes. The red-eyed boy had transferred some of his Power—how he did not know—into the Protector, giving him superior traits. An exceptionally gifted teacher also trained him, a weapons master. The Demon King chuckled. It did not matter. Blade was without equal. He turned to his two underlings.

"I have a task for you."

They bowed without speaking, knowing their place. "The red-eyed boy, accompanied by a group of wizards and Protectors, seeks the missing Light Elves. They travel north to the old Wizard's Guild. King Jaggar holds sway there. I do not know his allegiance. He betrayed me by joining forces with the humans in the Great Battle, but he is an opportunist, always amenable to options. Do not reveal yourself until you know the location of the Light Elves." He paused to contain his hatred, especially for his uncle, King Luminor. He wanted to turn the old man into dust. "Send a message to me when you find out their location. After that...kill them all."

The Lord of the Dark Elves could not afford another failure. As much as he desired to torture his enemies, he needed to exterminate the threat. Only one red-eye could know the knowledge of the Great Forget. He would, for once, put his desire for satisfaction aside. The thought rankled him, but it was a noble sacrifice on his part, done for the common good.

He looked at both of them. "Make sure you only attack if victory is assured. Do not make the same mistake as the others. Ride two of the four-legged speed demons. They can cross the Great Plains in a third of the time. Bring another mount to send back with a message. If they freeze to death, continue on foot."

Blade prostrated himself. "As you wish, may we grovel at your leisure."

Hagatha bowed low. "Master, may I inform you of something else?"

Killian was about to wave them off then dropped his hand, trying to maintain patience. "Yes."

She came straight to the point. "A white-eyed demon used magic today."

Being shocked was a rare occurrence for the Demon King. It led to hesitation, which could prove costly. He regained his composure, subduing a vein of excitement. "Show me."

Hagatha signalled to several guards. "Bring forth the white-eyed one."

There was a flurry of activity, and a small demon emerged from the mass of bodies. It was still a youth, likely born a few months ago. Its eyes should have turned black by now. The thing's claws and fangs were growing admirably. It had the characteristic blunt demon face with gray-black skin, but glowing white eyes set it apart.

"Master," it said in a high voice, nodding.

If any other demon had acknowledged him without prostration in that manner, its death would be sealed. Yet Killian barely noticed the infringement, such was his excitement. "Show me your Power," he commanded.

Nothing happened. The Demon King gave Hagatha a cold look.

She turned to the demon child. "Use your rage to break through the Wall in your mind and then show us. Think of the one who tried to hurt you today." The small creature cocked its head, then its white eyes blazed a powerful green. The Dark Elves nearby gasped.

Killian stood in awe, experiencing a rush of elation. He pulled off his right glove and put his hand on the small demon's head. The hordes started mewling and purring with ecstasy at their Master's benevolence. The Lord of the Dark Elves had touched one of them with his bare hand! Even the Inner Circle looked on, mouths agape.

Killian's eyes flared a bright red as he probed the white-eyed demon's mind. He assessed its Green Level of Power. It was very strong. The enormity of the implications staggered him. Finally, the Balance had seen his just cause and supported the evolution of his offspring. He decided to examine the memories of the small being and watched in its mind as a larger demon tried to eat it. The white-eyed demon had felt a deep rage and broke through its Wall, shooting green fire from its clawed hands into the attacker, melting the larger demon's skin until it was a steaming husk. Killian also realized it was more intelligent than the others.

The Demon King patted the top of its wrinkled head. "I name you Miracle," he breathed. The creature cooed softly in response, its eyes returning to a shiny white. He turned to his giant army. Some of the demons wept openly at the display of affection. "Step forward, my white-eyed brethren!" His voice carried down the slope of Cave Mountain, amplified by his Power.

A minute fraction of his demons were born with white eyes. They could never access their Power, and within a few months, their eyes turned midnight black, unrecognizable from other demons. In Morgo's time, he would eat them in an enjoyable ritual, absorbing their Power. They were exceedingly rare, but over three millennia, he had grown strong. He occasionally served the delicacy to his Inner Circle and, of course, Blade and Victor. Now, without the general's dark arts, the practice regrettably stopped.

He waited as more white-eyed demons moved forward. All were small and born within the last few months. In total, two dozen amassed before him. He sent his mind into theirs, searching with bated breath. It took him only a few moments to realize they all had Walls. Most had not smashed through, likely unaware of how special they were. A couple of others had used magic alone, not knowing what it was. One, a spider demon, was a Blue Level. He examined its memories. The demon had killed another of its kind using its Power, but no one witnessed it. The carcass would have been eaten by other demons as soon as they found the body.

He approached the baby spider, patting its bulbous head. It

emitted a happy squeak and trembled with joy. He was about to remove all their Walls, but something stopped him. If he did, their eyes would go black from continued use of the Power, and they would be indistinguishable from their kin. Not knowing which had magic could be a threat to him. He reminded himself that the Balance had a sick sense of humour. His Power protected him, but it was better to leave them with white eyes for now. They would be trained immediately in magic use and language. He would set a group of Dark Elves to the task. He looked upon the white-eyed demons arrayed before him.

Killian felt invincible.

The uses for these demons were profound. With their magic, they could provide themselves with heat, never freezing. Trained as assassins, they would be almost unstoppable. Only magic wielders would stand a chance. Their different Levels of Power delighted him. The Demon King projected his voice to his minions. "Any who threatens a white-eyed one will be tortured and fed to them."

"Master," Hagatha said when he finished, "these are only a few weeks old, not a few months. They are growing faster than the others. Their birthrates are increasing."

He turned to her, red eyes blazing. "Once they reach adulthood, we can breed them. Soon, I will have an army of white-eyed demons." He let out a rich laugh. The hordes began shrieking with joy. The Balance had rewarded him for his persistence, all but assuring victory. Nothing would stop him now, not even the Orb of Power. He looked at the skeletal Dark Elf. "Go now. Do not fail me."

Both Hagatha and Blade bowed and turned, summoning the speed demons. The creatures were a special breed, taking centuries to perfect. They looked like a cross between a large horse and a mountain wolf but with extra-long, muscular legs built for running. Their fanged teeth could tear a charging buffalo apart. The beasts covered the ground at an insane speed, running all day. The speed demons came forward, and the pair leapt on their backs, with a third ready to follow. They bowed again and departed.

The Lord of the Dark Elves gazed at the hordes gathered on Cave

Mountain. "We winter here and rebuild our home," he boomed, "then we go to war!" He raised both hands to the sky as the demons shrieked with joy.

The Demon King turned with his black cape billowing and strode into the center cave, not stopping until he reached the throne room. He floated red balls of light into the air, illuminating the huge cavern. Killian walked past the immense, dusty table and climbed the steps to sit on his glittering diamond throne.

After three thousand years, he was finally home.

7

The small party ascended the stone steps to the old Wizard's Guild. The walls pressed in against them as they climbed, muting the wailing wind until it was a faint whine. The air was cold but heavy. The stones themselves seemed to emanate a sense of dread. They were walking into the enemy's lair. For a thousand years, trolls had fought humans, breeding enmity and lust for vengeance. They would be surrounded by mages and soldiers, all led by King Jaggar, a warlord with vendettas against King Luminor, who slew his father, and Balor, who seized the position of High Wizard without a vote.

Chip prepared for all eventualities as he climbed, running different scenarios through his mind. Nothing was more important than finding the Light Elves. They held the Orb of Power, a light against the darkness. That was the goal. The weapons master had always stressed the importance of goals. "Set goals but surrender the outcome," he had said. "Sometimes, our journeys will send us on a different course, forcing us to revise our goals and the steps needed to achieve them. Use your mental fortitude to react as necessary. It's the one thing you have control of. Life is about challenge. There will always be things beyond your control. Surrender the outcome." Chip strengthened his resolve, willing to accept and adjust as necessary.

Xander led the way with the other wizards in the middle and the Protectors grouped at the back. They were the buffer between them and the trolls, commanded by Captain One Eye, who followed close behind. Chip looked back at Eleanor as she whispered something to Mary. He was happy they were getting along despite the look of revulsion on the Blue Wing Leader's face at the stench of the trolls wafting up the stairwell. The boy had spent much time with the queen and knew that healthy relationships required friendship and time apart. Auntie Clare once told him that there were many forms of love. There was love of your partner, your parents, your friends, the Creator, and yourself, among others. She said if you only focused on one, you would eventually be unhappy. All of them were important. People needed time apart to enjoy the other loves and feel fulfilled. He was happy she had made a new friend. Chip looked at the skinny blond orphan behind him.

Ethrang flashed him a grin. "Hurry up, old-timer. We don't have all day."

"We are the same age," Chip replied. "It's not my fault you found your Power two years earlier. That's the only reason you look younger."

The green-robed boy laughed and whispered. "You realize I could fly to the top."

"Yes, but there's a thing called the element of surprise," he reminded him.

"That's why I'm still here. Don't worry, Guardian. I've got your back."

Chip smiled and continued climbing. He was pleased they had formed a strong connection. Growing up as a street kid in Banfar must have been hard. Ethrang's happy-go-lucky attitude and positive outlook had served him well, but he was quick to anger and had admittedly done bad things. The Guardian believed in redemption, plus he genuinely liked the orphan. Even though they were the same age, his younger appearance made the Guardian feel like an older brother. In a way, the two orphans shared the same story.

"If you can't keep up, I will levitate you to the top," Chip called behind him.

"Ha, what about the element of surprise?"

"Good point," he admitted. "I guess we will have to use our legs."

They continued climbing the endless stairs. All jesting aside, the boy was beginning to wish Ethrang would fly him to the top. Chip was in good shape, but his thighs burned, and the oppressive feeling of the dark walls began weighing on him. Images of the stone slab pressing on his back at Cave Mountain with the Dim reaching for his ankle caused his heart to flutter. He took several deep breaths and focused on each step. Making matters worse, the sun was setting, causing the light to fail.

"Not much farther," Xander called back.

"I think my legs are going to fall off," Thomas answered from the middle. "No big deal."

"I'm sure the old Guild has the same amenities as the new one," Kristan assured. "We can relax in a nice hot bath provided by our gracious host."

Xander snorted from the front. "I hope you like stone, and 'gracious' is the last word I would use."

A short while later, they emerged on top of the cliff. The sun had almost set, but the view of the Troll Mountains to the north was breathtaking. To their right, the fortress loomed dark and cold. Twelve robed figures stood in a semi-circle on a giant stone verandah extending out the back of the Guild. Each wore a hooded cloak pulled tight.

All their eyes blazed blue.

"Xander," Kristan warned, clearly about to seize his magic.

The wizard held up his hand. "Don't." He walked to the stone steps leading up to the verandah. "Greetings," he called amicably. "I invoke the right to parlay, set down four millennia ago by the council."

"If it were up to me, I'd blast you off this mountain right now, wizard." The figure in the center removed his hood, revealing an angry troll face framed by white hair. His eyes shone a menacing blue."

"I'm happy it is not up to you, Grand Mage Rafael." Xander's face hardened. "We seek council with King Jaggar under the Parlay Treaty, not to mention winning a duel by combat. I assume the trolls still follow the code of honour."

Rafael snorted and released his magic. The others followed suit. "You humans should not talk of honour. Very well, you have earned the right to speak to His Eminence. Then we will blast you off the mountain."

"Very kind, thank you." The wizard feigned a broad smile.

"Follow me." Rafael turned and walked through two massive open doors into the fortress. By now, One Eye and his trolls had spread out behind them. The other robed figures moved to the sides to allow them to pass.

Chip marvelled at the size of the place. It reached into the sky like a giant stone hand, each finger a spire. Dark clouds roiled above them, and then a crack of thunder reverberated against the stone. The wind began to howl again as if warning them not to enter. The new Guild was the largest building in Amrika, but this was impressive.

They entered the fortress as torrents of rain began pelting the ground behind them.

"Welcome to my childhood home," Xander whispered. "Nice, isn't it?" They entered a huge circular hall with a high vaulted ceiling. To the sides were stairs leading up to the second level. The hall was ringed by a stone balcony so people could spectate. On the opposite end, massive windows with doors opened out onto a large stone patio looking south over the plain. The view, even from here, was breathtaking. The low hills ending at the plain from the Northbane side looked like a smudge on the horizon.

"In the old days, the students gathered in this main hall to practice magic while the rooms on the sides were used for academia. The council room resides on the second level."

Grand Mage Rafael led them up the stairs, which went right and turned left onto the balcony. They followed the circle around until they arrived at two smooth wooden doors. Chip realized no gold, silver, or intricate details adorned anything. High Wizard Balor, on the other hand, went the opposite way, spending a century making the new Guild as lavish as possible, sparing no expense.

The mage turned back to One Eye, who stood in the hall with his regiment of soldiers. "Stay there," he ordered.

The captain bowed low. "As you wish, Grand Mage."

Rafael turned back and knocked three times. Far away, a deep voice rumbled.

"Enter."

The troll mage opened both doors to reveal a large oval room overlooking the plain. In the center was an immense oak table. Chip remembered seeing this room in Xander's memory in the barn of the White Deer Inn beside the One Road. It felt like a lifetime ago.

Sitting at the head of the table was a massive troll wearing a stone crown. King Jaggar sat in the same seat as High Wizard Arkan did all those millennia ago. The troll rose, well over seven feet tall. He wore a soldier's uniform instead of mage robes over his heavily muscled limbs. His short black hair bore streaks of grey, but his face still looked late middle-aged, younger even than Balor. Behind him stood twenty guards in full armour, ten on each side. To his right stood a female troll with long hair. She looked fearful.

"Grand Wizard Xandrostika, it has been a long time. Sit." He gestured to the seats on either side of him. "Your Protectors can wait outside."

"Thank you, King Jaggar, but our Protectors will remain with us."

"You will address me as High Mage, Xandrostika." He paused then shrugged. "Your Protectors may stand behind you." He gestured to the dozen blue-robed mages who entered with Rafael, indicating they should sit at the far end. The table could easily hold everybody.

Jaggar sat back down, then surveyed the others. His gaze lingered on Chip then returned to Xander. "Who are they?"

"Forgive me," the wizard said. "This is Queen Eleanor of Vanalon,

Blue Wing Leader Mary, council members Kristan, Thomas, Ethrang, and the Guardian, Chip Oathbinder."

"Guardian?" he rumbled, his voice sounding like the noise an oak tree would make if it could speak.

"Yes, he is the one true hope."

"Hope?" A deep, booming laugh erupted from the king, echoing off the walls. The twelve blue-robed troll mages joined in, mimicking their leader. Halfway through, he abruptly stopped and leaned forward. The laughter of the other trolls nervously died off. "You're a foolish old man. Our only hope back then was to finish Killian, not imprison him." The wizard raised his eyes at the mention of the Demon King's name but said nothing. Noticing the reaction, Jaggar smiled. "Don't worry, he cannot reach me. Even if a demon army attacked in summer, I could retreat north to Rathgar, where it is always cold."

"Can you withstand the Demon King and a thousand Dark Elves?" Xander asked mildly.

King Jaggar paused. "I have...protections. Or I could hand this boy over to them and form an alliance."

Xander's face went cold. "You would not survive the attempt." The king's face darkened, and several gasps rang out amongst the mages. Before he could react, the wizard continued, "Listen to me. Killian is much stronger now. He doesn't need alliances. He will use you and then kill you. He will rid this world of all life. The prophecies speak of it."

"Prophecies?" Jaggar's voice rose, and he slammed his fist on the table. "I make my own Path!" The hands of his guards went to their sword hilts. The Protectors shifted slightly, widening their stance. The tension in the room was palpable. The king stood up. "You want me to ally myself with your treacherous brother, who robbed me of my right to be High Mage of the Council?" he yelled and began to raise his hand.

The female troll behind him stepped forward and clasped his wrist. "Father, please listen to them," she begged. Jaggar wrenched his hand free and slapped her hard across the face in a blur of motion. She staggered backwards.

"Know your place, Daughter."

Chip stood up, eyes blazing a ferocious red. King Jaggar recoiled then seized his magic, eyes turning an insane blue. Instantly, all the wizards and mages' eyes lit up. The peculiar crackle of magic filled the room.

"Enough!" Eleanor screamed. She was the only one not seizing her magic. "You are all acting like schoolchildren. High Mage Jaggar, we offer to parlay."

The king was so shocked by the interruption that he stared at her. Then he looked at Chip, eyes blazing. The boy held his ground.

Jaggar's face softened. "Such Power...perhaps there is still hope." He sat down slowly, eyes returning to normal. The other mages looked at each other in disbelief, and then, one by one, the magic left their eyes.

The wizards followed suit. Chip glanced at the troll princess, who stared at him with wet eyes. He was still angry, but he released his Power.

"That's better," Eleanor said calmly. "If I may, Grand Wizard Xander?" The old man nodded. "We seek to examine the archives room, likely for at least several days. We need a document. In return, we will surrender Northbane."

"As long as you declare the war ended," Mary interjected smoothly. "And assist us in the Last Battle," she added as if as an afterthought.

Jaggar looked at her in disbelief. "No."

"What do you want in return?" Eleanor asked, deflecting his mounting anger at Mary.

"I want the new Wizard's Guild."

There was complete silence in the room. Xander smoothed out his robes. "I'm afraid that's not on the table."

"Why not?" Jaggar's voice rose. "It's the least your treacherous brother owes me."

Xander's face darkened, and he stared at the king. "If we come to no agreement here and Toron falls, you will be all alone against the Demon King. Together, we stand a chance. Your assistance last time achieved three thousand years of peace. My brother felt he deserved the place of High Wizard because our father, Arkan, made the ultimate sacrifice. I agree he acted in haste. There should have been a vote. The council disintegrated because of it. What's done is done, but in fairness, you did end up with the old Wizard's Guild. If we win this war, a new council can be created where we all sit at the table and vote. If you don't help, it will be the end of all of us." He leaned forward in earnest, and a strange yearning Chip had never seen before filled his eyes. "High Mage Jaggar, we need to finish it this time."

The king sat back, pondering his words. "I always respected you, Xandrostika. You would have made a far better High Wizard than your brother." He sighed. "What document is so important you need to give up a city?"

"It will tell us where to find the missing Light Elves," Xander said simply.

Jaggar's eyes narrowed. "King Luminor betrayed us all." He spat on the floor.

The wizard nodded. "I understand the sentiment. Luminor felt the Orb of Power was proper compensation for their sacrifices during the Elf Wars and the price they paid in the Great Battle. However, I don't disagree with you. The orb should belong to everyone. I'm the one who stole it, after all...with your assistance, of course," he added.

"He killed my father, King Malkor," the troll said quietly. A dangerous glint appeared in his eyes.

"And King Malkor slew Luminor's father before that. It needs to end," Xander urged.

"It will end when Luminor is dead," King Jaggar screamed, slamming his fist on the table again. His daughter, the princess, whimpered, wringing her hands.

Chip saw where this was going. "You are forgetting about the Dim," the boy said loudly.

Jaggar stopped, head whipping sideways. "What do you know of the Dim, bane of the trolls?" he growled.

"I know that if the Demon King wins, the Dim will destroy the world. In fact, it will destroy everything. Soon, nothing will contain it. It eats the Paths."

"You dare speak of this creature as if you know it. The trolls suffered dearly after the Great Forget. The Dim almost wiped out our race." He gave him a scathing look.

"I know. I was in its mind. I saw everything." Chip stared at the Troll King, unflinching. He knew that Jaggar saw the truth in his eyes.

"How?"

"The Demon King imprisoned it in a tree in Fang Forest. An Inner Circle member, Zoran, released it to hunt us. I looked into its mind and saw all its memories. It appeared after the Great Forget. It even witnessed the lights in the sky. Then it investigated our world by touching living things. It started with small bushes and trees. Then a troll mage wandered into the valley, and it hunted him down, attacking your villages until the remaining trolls united and buried it under a mountain. The Demon King used the Orb of Power many centuries later to unearth it, though it had nearly escaped on its own. Morgo was able to control it, but I showed the Dim his death by my hand, and it freed the creature from bondage. I escaped its grasp, but it chased us through Cave Mountain. It killed Zoran, and in the end I dropped the mountain on it." Jaggar's eyes widened. "You must understand. It is not alive. It will never stop, ever. If we don't retrieve the Orb of Power from the Light Elves and kill the Demon King, then the Dim will destroy the world. If Killian wins, you lose." Chip let the words sink in.

Jaggar's anger vanished. "And how will you kill the Dim?"

The boy wrestled with the answer, deciding how much information he should disclose to the king. He sensed it was best to keep the dragon's existence a secret. "I have the means. It is all I can say."

Jaggar's eyes narrowed, but he didn't press it further. "Very well. I will grant you access to the archives. In exchange, I will occupy Northbane and end the war. I will also assist you in the Last Battle."

Everyone breathed a sigh of relief. "In exchange for the Orb of Power, if we win the Last Battle."

Xander's face tightened. Eleanor and Mary glanced at each other, struggling for a solution.

Chip turned to the king. "You can have the Orb of Power if your best fighter can beat my Protector in combat. Our honour will bind us."

Jaggar looked at him in surprise then began to laugh. The other mages took the cue and joined in. Even the guards in the back started chuckling. The king finally wiped his eyes. "With all due respect, your Protectors are good fighters, but against my best warrior...not to mention the size difference. I myself could beat them in physical combat, but my best fighter... It will not even be fair." Chip waited, not breaking his gaze. The Troll King shook his head in disbelief. "Deal. I need some entertainment anyway."

"I do ask that it not be to the death. Submission is fair, yes?" Chip asked.

His question elicited another outburst of laughter. The whole room reverberated with guffaws and bellows. "Trolls do not submit, but humans certainly do. Agreed. I warn you that by the end of this, your Protector will not be healable."

"I will take that chance," Chip said, glancing at Chase, who rolled his eyes, muttering.

The Troll King looked at one of his guards. "Fetch me Furiosa."

8

Everyone left the council room to stand along the balconies overlooking the main hall. One Eye and his trolls joined them to watch. The captain looked upset that Jaggar had let them live, but his disappointment turned to excitement to watch the combat.

King Jaggar stood with Xander on one side and Chip on the other. The boy looked over to see Eleanor and Mary talking with the troll princess, who seemed grateful for their company. All eyes were on Chase, standing alone in the middle of the hall.

"Good luck," Ethrang called out.

"Go get him!" Kristan yelled.

"Tear him apart!" shouted Thomas.

The trolls jeered at the remarks, laughing and bellowing insults.

Suddenly, the front doors opened, and a guard let in a cloaked troll that made Jaggar look small.

"She was out in the yard lifting stones for fun," the guard called up.

"She?" Chase exclaimed. Chip watched as the massive figure removed her wet cloak and threw it away. It landed on the balcony.

Standing before his best friend was an eight-foot troll with long, stringy hair. There were so many scars on her face that she was nearly unrecognizable. Without the telltale bark-like skin, people would be forgiven for thinking she was a monster.

Chase turned to give Chip a pleading look. Not knowing how to respond, the boy gave him a thumbs up. His best friend groaned.

"Welcome, Furiosa," Jaggar boomed. "I would like you to represent me in a combat of honour. You may use weapons but no death blows. The goal is submission."

Furiosa gave him a funny look and then shrugged. She stared at Chase. "First, I break you. Then you submit." Her voice was disturbingly deep.

"Begin," Jaggar shouted. The trolls went wild.

Furiosa pulled out a cudgel from her belt. It looked like a small toy in her massive hand. With the other, she drew a wicked curved dagger.

Chase sighed and pulled out his sword, standing at the ready.

Her charge was insane. She screamed a deep war cry, eyes full of fury and ran at the boy, who looked outrageously small. Her club came down with blistering speed. Chase turned at the last instant, the weapon whistling past his nose, then struck her in the face with the pommel of his sword. There was a loud snap as her nose broke, but not before she sliced him across the thigh with her dagger. He leapt back in surprise at her speed. She was already circling, smiling as blood poured from her face. The trolls shouted with glee.

She then attacked him with reckless abandon. Club and dagger came at him from all sides. Chase parried the blows but her onslaught forced him to retreat. He ended up against the wall, which seemed to be her objective. Chip knew he was hesitant to go full force against a female, which cost him dearly. Furiosa used the club and dagger at the same time, pinning his sword against his body and then twisting both to wrench it out of his hand. The weapon clattered across the floor. He instinctively tried to pull his daggers, but she delivered two bone-crushing elbows to his jaw and bit his shoulder.

"Ow!" he cried. She spit out a chunk of his flesh, then dropped her weapons to pick him up by the neck and groin. Lifting him high over her head, she turned and threw the boy across the hall to land with a splat against the far wall. Chip grimaced. There was a moment of silence, and then the trolls went wild, slapping each other on the back.

They started chanting, "Furiosa! Furiosa! Furiosa!"

Jaggar turned to the Guardian with a smile. "Sorry it took so long. I expect you to uphold your honour."

"It's not over," the boy answered.

The king laughed and turned back. "Your Protector is dead. Look at him…"

Chase stood up, rubbing his shoulder. He then stretched out the kinks. The chips in his eyes glinted as an angry expression surfaced.

"How is this possible?" Jaggar said in disbelief.

"He is special," the boy replied.

Furiosa watched him stand up and then cocked her head, trying to understand how he was alive. She then shrugged and charged at him, pulling out her mace. Chase already had a dagger in each hand and ran to meet her. Expecting an overhand attack, she swung the weapon sideways at his chest. He adjusted instantly, sliding underneath the blow to bury both daggers in her thighs.

She caught him with her backhand, sending the tall boy somersaulting across the floor. The troll grabbed the hilt of each dagger and with a smile wrenched them out of her legs. Fast as thought, she flipped each one so her fingers held the blade and whipped each with expert precision. The boy was still getting up but heard the dagger whistle through the air and turned in time to avoid the first one. The second went through his hand up to the hilt.

"Ow!" he cried. The trolls erupted again, beating their chests. Furiosa charged, giving him no reprieve. He yanked the dagger out with a grimace, eyes flashing with menace and threw it back at the monster. It buried deep in her shoulder, but she ignored it, slamming him into the opposite wall. She began uppercutting him with a flurry of rib-breaking strikes. Audible cracks sounded. Grunting, he latched onto her massive neck and swung himself over her body to land on all fours behind her. Leaping into the air, he struck the troll with both feet in the center of her back. Furiosa's face made a squelching sound as she struck the wall. Several teeth fell to the floor.

Chase staggered backwards, holding his stomach and then slowly straightened. He was healed, eyes glinting as his anger flared.

The king gave Chip an accusing look. "He has magic?"

"Nope, mine rubbed off a little when I healed him. I told you he's special." Jaggar grunted. The other trolls were pointing at Chase in surprise. Some even began to nod at his prowess.

Furiosa turned around. Her face was unrecognizable, and blood leaked from her thighs and shoulder. Incredibly, she grinned, revealing one tooth still intact. Again, she charged, pulling out a small axe from the back of her belt. Chase ducked at the last instant, swinging his right leg in a full circle, foot sweeping her. She landed hard on her back. He wrenched the axe from her hand, eyes glinting with rage. The boy screamed and swung it full force to decapitate her. At the last instant, he realized he was about to kill her and stopped the axe's flight, barely piercing her skin. The pause allowed her to reach up and seize his neck with one massive hand. She stood up, holding him tight.

His feet dangled from the floor. He grabbed her wrist with both hands to break the grip, but she bent down, picked up his foot with her other hand, and swung him around in a circle. With a scream, Furiosa threw him at the end of a full rotation.

Chase flew through the air like a living projectile, crashing through the stone balcony into a pack of One Eye's soldiers. Several trolls slammed into the wall and didn't get up. Chase collapsed in a twisted heap. Jaggar smiled, clearly thinking it was finally over.

The tall boy groaned and stood up. Chip watched in fascination as his broken body realigned. Trolls nearby stepped back in shock, giving him space. Jaggar's smile vanished.

Chase Longfellow was mad.

He leapt off the balcony and landed cat-like in front of Furiosa. She tried to attack him with her massive fists, but suddenly he was beside her, side-kicking her right knee with terrifying force. Her leg snapped in half. She grunted, trying to stay upright.

In a blur of motion, he was on her other side, breaking her left leg in the same manner. She fell on her back with a loud thud, bellowing. He picked up her right wrist and slammed his knee into her elbow, bending it the wrong way. Another audible crack sounded. In a flash, he grabbed her left arm and broke it the same way. Furiosa began writhing on the ground, limbs flailing at unnatural angles. Chase seized her neck and twisted.

"Submit," he snarled, eyes shining.

She groaned in pain. There was a slight crack in her neck as one of the bones broke. He twisted harder.

Furiosa wailed. "I…submit."

There was dead silence in the room.

Chase stood up, red chips gleaming. He looked at Jaggar. "Uphold your honour."

The king looked around, speechless. The other trolls began slapping their fists to their chests, the sound growing in volume. Jaggar finally sighed and nodded.

"Let me heal her," Chip said.

"No." The king's eyes blazed a stunning blue, and a coil of blue fire shot out of his hand, turning Furiosa into a blazing inferno. Then he released his Power.

The Guardian turned in shock to the Troll King, rage igniting. "Why?" he said through gritted teeth.

Jaggar looked at the boy with an evil smile. "Trolls do not submit. If your Protector had submitted, I would have done the same to him. Combat is always to the death." He spun and began descending the stairs. "Come. It's time to eat."

It took significant control for the boy not to seize his Power. Eleanor came over to rest a hand on his arm. "Don't, there's too much at stake." He nodded grudgingly.

Chase came over, looking equally perturbed. "He didn't have to do that. She submitted."

"I know," Chip sighed. "It is the troll way. I don't like it, but Eleanor is right. There's too much at stake."

Xander and the weapons master came over to congratulate Chase.

"Well done, lad. You had me worried for a moment." The wizard patted his shoulder.

"There is room for improvement, but you did well," Garth stated. Noticing the boy's sour demeanour, he lowered his voice. "You had no idea Jaggar would kill her. I can assure you that if Furiosa had survived, she would have thrown herself off the cliff in shame. It is the troll way. Do not fret over what we can't control. Surrender the outcome. We must stay on the king's good side until we find what we seek. He is unpredictable. Let's eat."

The others had come over to listen in and nodded.

"I knew you had it in you," Kristan said, slapping Chase on the back. The tall boy's eyes muted to normal as his anger receded.

"Yep, never doubted you." Thomas gave him a weak smile.

"Ha, I thought she had you, but good show. I wouldn't want to fight her." Ethrang grinned. A thought seemed to cross the blond boy's mind, and he dashed down the stairs to touch her burnt remains. He then seemed to change his mind and reached down again to touch the sole of her right foot, which was the only part of her untouched by the fire. Incredibly, it was still twitching. Then it went still.

One Eye turned to stare and narrowed his eyes. "What are you up to, boy?"

Ethrang, noticing he was being watched, said in a loud voice. "Yup, she's dead, alright."

The captain shook his head. "Humans. Come to dinner now, the lot of you. You get to eat real food for once, not that human slop."

They all followed him through a set of doors into the dining room. It was almost as big as the first hall, with long rows of tables. About one hundred troll students were eating at the far end, wearing different-coloured robes. Jaggar sat at the head of the largest table, with his daughter beside him, and he gestured for them to take seats nearby.

Chip began to understand what One Eye meant by "real food." Troll servers in dirty white aprons brought in heaping trays of unrecognizable meats and vegetables—at least, that was what he thought they were.

Jaggar was tearing at a morsel of flesh and bone. "This is mountain bear. Delicious." Liquid fat ran down his chin. "Over here is snow ape. It's a rare delicacy. Few can catch it because it tends to kill the hunter first. They blend in with the snow. This tray over here is wild cow testicles, a common staple amongst the trolls."

Mary and Eleanor looked at each other, trying not to make a face.

The king continued, "There are many denizens in these mountains you won't find anywhere else. Even the hardiest trolls avoid certain areas. Some creature with yellow eyes comes out at night, slashing throats and drinking blood. In the morning, the bodies are dried husks. We think it's a cat, but no one is sure. It would be interesting to try its flesh. Usually, the most dangerous are the most delectable ones. Slow-cooked, of course."

Chip could tell most of the wizards were losing their appetite. The Protectors grunted, eating happily. Chase was helping himself to seconds.

Jaggar glanced at the Guardian. "Tell me the story of how your Protector got his...abilities."

The boy recounted the events in the cornfield, excluding Eleanor's part. The king listened attentively.

"Can it work on anyone?" Jaggar asked.

"No, High Wizard Balor tried to use my blood, but it failed. He believes there has to be a bond involved that can't be forced."

The king's face dropped. "Creating an army like that would be nearly unstoppable."

Xander put down his fork. "It seems the Balance has allowed the creation of only one." The wizard glanced briefly at Eleanor. He also did not want to disclose her red chips to the king. She nodded subtly. Chip thought for a moment that Jaggar noticed the nod, but when he looked fully at the troll, his eyes were down.

"May I ask your daughter's name?" Chip inquired.

Jaggar didn't bother looking at her. "This is Miriam, born during the war. Her mother died in battle." He gripped a goblet of ale and noisily washed down his food.

She nodded to them. "Nice to meet you."

The king paused as if deciding whether she had the right to speak. "Miriam means well, but she doesn't understand politics. I always keep her close by, as she is my only heir. She has much to learn. I know I coddle her too much, but she understands." The princess looked down, but not before her eyes betrayed disagreement.

"Perhaps she could help us look through the archives," Mary offered. "You need someone to keep an eye on us." She smiled warmly without a hint of deceit.

The king studied her for a moment. "Very well, but understand if anything happens to her, nothing will stop my vengeance." He roughly squeezed the princess's hand, causing her to pull back and look down.

Eleanor chimed in. "I assure you our intentions are pure. We wish no one in the Troll Kingdom harm. We seek allies for what is to come. Together, we are strong."

"I've heard that before," he said with narrowed eyes. The king grabbed a napkin and wiped his chin. "The guards will take you to your guest rooms. Do not wander about my home. A guard will escort you to the archives. He will wait in the hall until you are finished and take you back. Use the same route each time. We will gather here for dinner every day. You may go through the main hall to get some air. Do not attempt to go down the mountain. That is all."

The Troll King stood up and left the dining hall with two soldiers flanking him. Grand Wizard Rafael stared at them with a sour expression then got up and followed him out. The others looked at each other, saying nothing, as troll guards were within earshot. Mary and Eleanor asked Princess Miriam to sit closer to them, and they all began whispering.

When everyone finished eating, they were escorted to their guest rooms, which reminded Chip of Northbane. They contained bare stone walls with a bed and washbasin. Xander gathered the wizards in his room, along with Chase and the weapons master. Two guards were stationed outside in the hall. He kept his voice low.

"We've had a busy day, for some more so than others." He glanced at Garth and Chase. "That was a close call today, but so far we managed to garner the support of the trolls in the war to come and gained access to the archives. Mary and Eleanor, your intercession at the council was much appreciated. We were moments away from turning that room into a blazing inferno of magic."

"You boys can be hot-headed at times," Mary stated.

The wizard nodded. "Now, unless you are too tired, it's still early evening, and I see no reason we can't begin our investigation of the archives. Currently, we are in a wing of the student dorms. I know this fortress like the back of my hand. There are more opulent rooms for guests of import near the council chambers, but Jaggar has chosen to treat us like underlings. He is trying to make a point. Tread softly around him. His mood changes without warning. The king still holds great enmity for humans and Light Elves. Chase and Garth, I would like you to help us search. We must be on alert at all times." Everyone nodded.

They conferred briefly with the other Protectors and then approached one of the guards. He was a large troll with an impassive face, bristling with weapons.

"May we see the archives room, please?" the wizard asked politely.

The troll grunted. "Follow me." He turned and led them down the hall, his leather armour creaking. They could hear muffled chatter in a different wing.

"How many students reside here?" Eleanor asked.

"Don't ask questions," the guard snapped. The queen looked at the others and shrugged. Ethrang released a faint giggle, causing the twins to grin. Mary rolled her eyes.

They followed the soldier through an iron door down dusty stairs. This part of the Guild seemed less used. King Jaggar was keeping them separate from everyone else. Chip knew the king still distrusted them, and he began to wonder about the troll's true intentions.

They travelled down three flights of stairs and exited into a hall dimly lit by oil lamps. The guard turned left, leading them to a much bigger iron door. He selected a large key from a ring attached to his belt and opened it. Immediately, a musty, stale smell assaulted them mixed with an odour of sweat and urine.

"The archives room is above the dungeons," Xander explained.

They travelled down three more levels of stairs before they heard muffled shrieks and screams from below. The guard noticed their reactions and grinned but said nothing. He produced a different key, and they followed him through another door into a smaller hall. Someone had already lit an oil lamp to provide illumination. They reached a locked wooden door at the end of the hall. The troll opened it and waved them in.

"I wait here. When you are finished, I take you back."

"Thank you kindly," Xander answered. He sent a faint blue ball of light into the dark room and lit several lamps.

Chip's eyes widened. The room was larger than he imagined. Books and scrolls lined the walls from floor to ceiling. Several small tables were arranged in the room for reading. Each table was covered with paper, books, opened scrolls, and a thick layer of dust. The trolls evidently did not care about old writings. A smell of old leather books and dust greeted them.

Ethrang groaned. "This is going to take forever."

"Oh my," Kristan breathed. "We have our work cut out for us."

Xander studied the tomes with a form of reverence. "These works predate the Breaking between the Light and Dark Elves. It is a collection of writings from the Great Forget to the rise of the dragons and subsequent Elf Wars. One thousand years of history gathered from the learnings of the early elves, trolls, dwarves, and humans. After the Great Forget, many events unfolded. The elves were a group of wandering tribes who united to fight the trolls and establish boundaries. After five centuries of war, they agreed to a truce. The trolls held the north and built Rathgar, while the elves constructed the beautiful city of Tarana where Toron now sits in the south."

"I know little of this stuff," Ethrang commented. "The streets of

Banfar are not ideal for getting an education. I only know how to read because the cult insisted on it so I could memorize their scriptures. I do find this stuff kind of cool." The blond boy grinned, waiting for the wizard to continue.

The old man produced his pipe and pulled a pinch of tobacco from his pouch. Everyone glanced at each other but didn't roll their eyes. They were interested in refreshing their historical knowledge to contextualize their search. Chip also found the stories fascinating. The wizard lit his pipe and took a long pull before releasing a perfect smoke ring. It wafted to the high ceiling. The smell reminded the boy of old times.

The wizard sat in a dusty chair, which creaked. "Two dragons appeared after the Great Forget, birthing the twelve Originals. Five hundred years later, the trolls found the eggs in these very mountains and kept them hidden in Rathgar. The elves felt the pull and only determined the source when Malkor, the Troll King, smashed six of them a couple of centuries later. King Luminor, ruling in Tarana, brought his army of elves to investigate. When Malkor offered him the six remaining eggs and then tried to rescind the deal, a fight ensued. King Luminor slew the Troll King and managed to retrieve three of the eggs but was forced to retreat. Jaggar pulled the crown off his dead father's head and vowed vengeance. No one knew what happened to the other three eggs, but they ended up in the Demon King's hands. You hold one of them, Chip." The boy nodded.

Xander took another pull on his pipe. "King Jaggar vowed vengeance and started the Retribution Wars between the trolls and elves, which lasted for another century. The humans, sometimes caught in the middle, united and drove the dwindling elves and trolls out, founding Toron on the remains of Tarana. Jaggar retreated to the Troll Mountains, and the elves settled on the island of Lavalor in the east, where they built the beautiful white city of Elvar. A time of stability followed, so the magic wielders of the day convened to build the Wizard's Guild. Its purpose beyond learning and study was to keep the peace.

"Roughly a thousand years after the Great Forget, an elven prince was born named Killian. Morgo arrived, showing him the dark arts and teaching the young elf to remove the Wall to his Power. His eyes went black, and he killed his father, Galal, King Luminor's brother. That was the beginning of the Breaking, the split between the elves into light and dark. Galal was the one who had figured out how to birth the dragons. Killian took the black ones with him, and for a thousand years, the Elf Wars raged. The tides turned when Killian stole the Orb of Power from the Red-Eyed King in the Ancient City. A very brave, noble young wizard stole it back."

Everyone rolled their eyes. Ethrang and the twins laughed out loud.

"What?" Xander said with indignation. "He was also very handsome."

'Ha." The green-robed boy doubled over.

"My goodness. It wasn't that funny," Xander remarked, but there was a glint of amusement in his eye. "Now, where were we? Oh, so this dashing young wizard stole the orb and turned the tide of the war. You know the rest. The question is, which part of these histories would talk about the missing Light Elves four thousand years later? And who would be the author?"

Everyone glanced around, thinking hard.

"I know!" Kristan exclaimed, raising a finger. "Prophecy."

The wizard's brow furrowed. "This room has been scoured for true prophecy long ago. All those documents were taken upstairs. However, old prophecies failing to predict the right Path did end up here. I don't see how they could help."

Thomas raised a finger. "It must be in the writings of an elf. Who better to know than their own people?"

"It's very possible. I agree we should look at elven writings first," the wizard said.

"Perhaps a better question is, where would you try to hide if you were the elves?" Eleanor asked.

"I've asked myself that a million times," Xander mused. "I could never really come up with an answer. Other than somewhere where no one else was."

"The trolls hold the north, and the surrounding mountains are inhospitable," Mary stated. "The Dwarf Kingdom by the Lumber River is occupied, and the Grey Mountains between them and Vanalon are uninhabitable. In the middle are the Great Plains, where someone could be spied on from leagues away. To the southwest lies the Barbarian Forests, and further south are the Swamplands, which have those white demonic creatures. They are impassable." She shuddered. "To the southeast lies Flod and the Marshlands, which get progressively deeper if you try to go further in. That leaves the east, which takes you past Toron to the human fishing city of Halfar. Beyond that, we arrive back in Lavralor, which is where they disappeared in the first place."

"What about underground?" Ethrang asked. "I know in Banfar, if you want to lie low, that's where you go."

Xander shook his head. "I know the elves. They would never live in darkness underground unless, of course, they were the Dark Elves. Even then, they are above ground in caves with access to the mountains. No, the Light Elves like light and trees."

"What if they crossed the ocean?" Chip asked.

"The deep oceans are impassable. The sea monsters there are larger than any ship. No one has ever returned from a crossing."

"They have the orb," Kristan added.

"True," Xander pursed his lips. "I suppose it's possible."

"Couldn't the dragons of old cross the oceans?" asked Chip.

"I'm afraid not. Two of them tried on separate occasions and never came back. Other riders flew far out but had to return when the dragons showed fatigue. It may be possible with the orb, but it does not explain how the whole city disappeared. Even the orb could not float Elvar across the ocean."

"What do you think is on the other side?" Chase asked. Chip could tell the thought of exploring filled his mischievous friend with excitement.

"As far as we know, nothing. Endless water circling the Earth." He blew one last smoke ring. "We have no choice, it seems, but to trust that the prophecy is right. Follow your instinct. Most of the shelves should have similar authors or time periods. Pull out a book or scroll, and if that shelf interests you, delve deeper. If you find something that might help, let the others know."

Everyone nodded. Chase looked glum, likely because the wizard hadn't said there was some far-off mystical land across the ocean. He turned to stare at the overflowing shelves. "I hate reading."

Chip slapped him on the back. "Then find out where the Light Elves are, and you will never have to read again." The tall boy grunted and wandered over to a shelf.

The twins ran off to an empty section, pulling volumes out and whispering excitedly. Chip couldn't tell if they liked reading or solving mysteries. Mary and Eleanor picked a shelf together. She noticed him watching and gave him a wink. He smiled and decided to look at scrolls first, pulling them out with care.

The boy began to read a few lines of each. Most of the initial ones described boring things like the settlement of a village or methods of farming. One shelf detailed the discovery of magic and the populace's distrust of magic wielders, which he found quite interesting. He didn't realize that wizards and mages were initially shunned. Some scrolls on the same shelf talked of villages offering rewards to capture magic wielders and hang them. He scanned the whole library and found a section with the oldest-looking scrolls, gone almost completely yellow. He pulled one out, and it crumbled to dust in his hand.

"Oops, that's not good."

He looked around guiltily, but nobody was watching. For a fleeting moment, the boy worried that he had jeopardized the world by destroying the one document that could save them. He reminded himself of mathematics and the infinitesimal odds of him ruining the exact document needed. Chip decided to try something.

Seizing his magic, he gently sent out a thin haze of red Power to infuse itself in the paper, strengthening it. He once saw Xander imbue a shield when defending Vanalon against the demon hordes. It had temporarily made the shield stronger, allowing the scout to withstand a fireball sent by the Dark Elves. He used the same principle with the paper. Chip sent a thin blanket of magic into all the scrolls on that shelf, which required a surprising amount of concentration. When finished, he pulled another old scroll out. It did not crumble. Amazingly, he could bend it, and it did not break apart. The boy impulsively threw it at the ground, and nothing happened. He looked up to see Chase watching close by with a grin.

"I didn't realize they were that strong," Chase said, roughly pulling a scroll from a nearby shelf and throwing it on the ground. The whole thing disintegrated. His face turned red. "Awkward." Mary was watching and turned up her nose. Ethrang giggled.

"I added magic to mine," Chip explained. The others gathered around. He showed them how he did it. "You put a sliver of magic to infuse it, almost like a mist."

Xander nodded. "That's exactly how we used to do it. In fact, this room has been fortified many times over the years when we held the Guild. Now, its effects have all but worn off. Good job. Keep it up."

Chip strengthened Chase's section for him then pulled another scroll from the old shelf. The words mesmerized him.

"There were incredible lights in the sky, so beautiful. The red colours were dazzling. I could not look away. And then it stopped. Everything seemed different, but I couldn't explain how. The feeling lasted for several weeks. I'm sure there was something before all this, but I cannot remember. I know how to do things, but I don't know where I learned it. I can't remember. The others in the village say the same thing. Now, at the end of my life, I realize something happened to my generation. We feel robbed. We forget what happened before. I have strange dreams of a city, people, and something bad, but I cannot remember what it looked like. We call ourselves the Forgotten Ones. I take comfort in knowing my children born after the event have lived full, rich lives. They remember everything about their life. We feel lost. Farmer Tom, Village of Calgar."

Chip exhaled, running his fingers over the words. He felt strange reading the thoughts of someone who experienced the Great Forget five millennia ago. A living human being had written those words, now long dead. He felt sorrow for the man. He couldn't imagine living a life where half of it was gone. He yearned to know more and discover what happened to these people. What happened to Earth?

He turned to the others and shared the story.

"That's deep," Kristan said, his face serious.

"So sad," Eleanor said solemnly.

Xander sighed. "I read some of those a long time ago. The stories are similar, even among the different races. I hope one day we will have the answers." Chip nodded and continued reading.

They worked for several more hours before the wizard cleared his throat. "That's all for today. Remember where you left off. Tomorrow, we start again."

Chase let out a sigh of relief. The others nodded wearily. It had been a long day. The guard showed them back to their rooms. Chip felt exhausted. They washed up and went to bed.

He dreamed of scrolls, books, and an orb.

9

They woke early and refreshed. All were eager to continue the search, except Chase of course. The tall boy relished physical movement and the outdoors. He did not take well to being cooped up in a dusty room in the bowels of the keep. Chip reminded him how important the mission was, and he nodded reluctantly. They washed up and congregated in front of the impassive guard.

"Uh, do we get breakfast?" Chase asked, giving the troll a hopeful smile.

The guard grunted, "Follow me." He led them back to the dining hall, where other students were filing in from their dormitories. Princess Miriam sat alone at the big table and waved them over, her face lighting up. King Jaggar was not present.

The girls immediately sat on either side of her, and she smiled shyly. Chip did not realize how huge she was. Only a half head shorter than her father, the princess was almost as large, dwarfing most other trolls. Her long hair was neatly combed, and she wore what looked to be a diamond necklace. Chip sat next to Eleanor.

A small selection of food arrived, most unrecognizable, causing Chase's famished smile to wilt. The servers placed huge brown eggs before them in small bowls. Miriam noticed their odd expressions and grabbed an egg.

"Here, you do it like this," she instructed in her high, soft voice. The troll cracked the egg on the table then emptied the yellow and white contents into her bowl. Everything looked tiny in her massive hands. She grabbed the bowl and drank the liquid, slurping the egg yolk in one gulp. The troll princess let out a satisfied sigh then accidentally emitted a loud burp.

"Oh my," she squeaked, covering her mouth and blushing. Mary was able to hide her disgusted look almost immediately. Eleanor gave her a genuine smile. Ethrang, sitting across from them, stifled a laugh. "Pardon me."

"Um, so we eat these raw?" Chase asked dubiously.

"Duh," Kristan said beside him. He cracked his egg, dumped it in the bowl, and guzzled the mixture. After he swallowed, the blond twin's eyes opened wide, and he pursed his lips, clearly trying not to vomit. "It tastes good," he gulped, turning green, "maybe a little...like poop." Everyone stared at him.

"Yes, that 's right," Miriam explained. "These rare eggs are from the Vultura bird. They eat carrion and animal feces. It's a delicacy."

Ethrang cackled. "Hey, I've eaten much worse in Banfar." He cracked an egg in his bowl and slurped it down. "Cool." He grinned, wiping his mouth.

Mary made a face. "I'm allergic to eggs, so I will pass. What is that?" She pointed to a bowl filled with tiny brown things. "Are they moving?"

"Yes," Miriam beamed, pleased at her interest. "They are brown beetles, which are hard to find. The key is to lightly fry the insects to make them crunchy, but you still want them alive. When they are dead, they are poisonous." She poured a generous portion on her plate then grabbed a handful and happily munched on them. The crunching sound was audible. Mary was so shocked that she was unable to look disgusted. Ethrang covered his mouth, turning red with laughter. Thomas elbowed him from the side.

"Uh, my stomach is not doing well today." Mary rubbed her

midsection. "I will have some bread." She reached over and took a slice in front of her.

The troll princess nodded. "I understand. The bread is really good. The cook spoils us by throwing in deer lice. It adds a rich, nutty texture to the dough." Mary's face blanched. Ethrang started tearing up, holding his mouth.

Chase grunted and took a portion of everything except the beetles. The other Protectors passed the bowls around and didn't complain. Chip and Eleanor looked at each other, trying to keep a straight face. Xander watched it all with an amused expression while the weapons master arched an eyebrow. Ultimately, the Blue Wing Leader ate nothing, and the others picked whichever items they could keep down.

Chip observed that the Guild only had about a hundred students. The fact that there were twelve Blues surprised him. They had the same amount as the new Guild, which housed five hundred students. Rafael kept watching them with narrowed eyes.

When everyone finished breakfast, Eleanor looked at the princess. "Would you like to join us in our research today?" she asked.

Miriam's face lit up. "Oh yes, I would like that."

A guard led them straight from the dining hall to the archives room while another took the Protectors upstairs, other than Garth and Chase. A sad look passed across the princess's face when she heard the screams coming from the dungeons below, and she hung her head. Xander lit the lamps again, and everyone returned to the shelf they had been working on the night before. Eleanor described to Miriam what they were seeking. Looking at the troll's hands, Chip decided to sweep each shelf with his magic, strengthening the documents.

The princess watched in fascination. "Such Power," she breathed, and then, seeing everyone staring at her, looked away in embarrassment.

The work was tedious. Chip went through the shelf of the oldest scrolls one by one. The stories were similar, but one intrigued him. It was written by an elf woman who must have been a Teller. "I see the

Great Forget in my dreams, over and over. Sometimes, I remember what was before, but upon awakening, the memories flee. Yet I know one thing. I wasn't an elf. One will find out what caused it long in the future, but the world may break." He shared it with the others, and speculation arose about what the elf woman could have been before the Great Forget, but it was all conjecture.

By the time he finished the shelf, it was late morning, and they broke for lunch. The food this time was no better. The fare consisted of frog legs, sheep's offal, and a strange purple fish filled with tiny bones from a nearby mountain lake. Miriam ate the thing whole, crunching loudly, then picked her teeth clean with a knife. Ethrang covered his mouth.

They resumed their search after lunch. The Protectors went out on the patio to spar and get fresh air. Chip examined several shelves and then picked one with books about the elf tribes uniting to fight the trolls in the early centuries after the Great Forget. He noticed Ethrang picking out scrolls on a shelf next to the weapons master, but he was not fully reading them. Some he skipped entirely.

Garth looked down at the skinny blond boy and stated, "How you do anything is how you do everything."

"Huh?" Ethrang responded.

"You are not doing a thorough job. No matter the size of the task in life, do it well. Make it a habit." The boy still looked confused. "Even if it's making your bed, cleaning up after yourself, or sweeping the floor, do it well. In practice fighting, try as hard as you would in a real fight, and you will perform at your best."

"I can fight well," the boy countered then shrank back when the weapons master turned to him with narrowed eyes. "Not against you, of course, but you know what I mean." Garth didn't break his gaze. "Alright, I get it. How you do anything is how you do everything."

"Good, carry on." The weapons master turned back to his shelf.

Ethrang paused a moment then nodded to himself and looked at each scroll in detail from then on. Chip smiled, remembering that lesson from his early training. He had since made it a habit to try and do his best on whatever task was put before him. Focus was key.

He turned back to his shelf and began reading. The boy learned that the elves were nomadic but soon developed tradition. They were wonderful artists and respected the land. When they met other tribes with pointed ears, they naturally banded together, seeking a permanent settlement. They all possessed magic, which they used to better themselves. The elves wandered the lands for centuries but always felt a pull towards the mountains. Chip suspected it was the lure of the eggs that motivated them.

The trolls already had settlements there but were not numerous in the beginning. The Dim had almost single-handedly wiped them out. Yet as the years passed, they multiplied and built the walled city of Rathgar. The elves sought the sanctuary of the mountains at a time when the trolls had multiplied, and war ensued. The elves were mighty, but the sheer size and number of the trolls gave them an advantage in battle, and they also had mages. Though long-lived, the elves reproduced slowly, as if the Balance had countered their abundant access to magic with a diminished ability to multiply.

The war was bitter and raged for centuries. The elves dwindled, and when King Malkor slew Luminor's father, they were forced to call a truce. The elves retreated south and built Tarana. The trolls held the north. The scroll was created after the last battle with the trolls, written by an elf mage forced to flee the mountains. "Alas, our king is slain, and we are but few. We must retreat south to find a new haven. The call of the mountains is undeniable, and my heart breaks in two to leave its untamed rivers, high gorges, and fresh air. If I could make us disappear, I would. We would seek refuge far from the other races, amongst high trees and pristine lakes. We would build a white city there, and no one would find us. The mountains will forever pull my heart, but what I yearn for the most is to hide ourselves from the world. May Luminor save us." Lucien, Grand Mage.

The boy recounted the story to the others. "It looks like they always wanted to disappear."

"The question is where." Xander said.

"I've got something here," Thomas said, reading from a small scroll. "This section has fragments of prophecies, but they seem wrong." Kristan looked over his twin's shoulder.

Xander nodded. "That shelf holds the Tellings that did not come true."

The blond wizard cleared his voice.

"The boy, the chosen one, is stillborn.

His red eyes will never open.

Demonic creatures will walk the Earth.

The races shall perish.

The non-living thing eats all the Paths.

Even the Forces will fall.

Then all is lost.

The only hope is the Stone.

I See no more."

"Do you mean the orb?" Kristan said, pulling it out of his brother's hand.

"How would I know?" Thomas retorted, trying to take it back. He snatched at it and the scroll tore in two. Both twins looked up wide-eyed.

Xander glared. "Be careful, you fools. All of it forms a part of history. We can be thankful that Prophecy does not speak true. Try to mend it with your magic. Use the principles of healing."

The twins seized their magic as each pressed their half of the page to the other. A blue line formed down the middle, and after several moments, they released their Power. The scroll was one again.

"I think I see a faint line in the middle." Thomas squinted.

"No, it's a crease," Kristan argued. The others turned back to their work.

They read for several more hours. Miriam put a row of books on one of the tables and pulled up a chair that barely seemed to support her weight. Each time she moved, it protested, causing Mary to cringe. No one wanted to tell the massive troll to stop moving, so they continued working, trying to ignore the sounds. Right before dinner, Eleanor spoke up.

"This sounds interesting. My shelf is about the early relationship between the elves and the dwarves. The elves had completed the palace construction in Tarana and invited the Dwarf King, Lumbar, to attend. The king recounts his experience. "The beauty of Tarana is without equal in all the lands. The elves are whimsical, beautiful people who respect nature. They love trees, which dwarves hold dear in our hearts. King Luminor is young yet already holds great wisdom. He has invited our dwarf mages to make pilgrimages to the city to share knowledge. I offered the same in return. The elves will be powerful allies against the trolls and the growing human threat. We signed treaties for our lumber and their wine. I always thought ale was the greatest drink, but their heady wine, with its scents of cedar and leather, is intoxicating. The city is surrounded by manicured vineyards as far as the eye can see. The elves still feel a strange pull for the mountains but desire above all to be left in peace. One day, they will vanish of their own accord, and no one will be able to find them. A young elf Teller named Galador speaks of a time when they will have the means to do so. I hope they will stay during my reign, for I have found a true friend in the elves." King Lumbar.

"It seems they have been planning this for a long time," Mary noted.

Xander nodded. "Indeed, it's a shame Luminor didn't tell Lumbar where they would go. I suppose that would defeat the purpose." He sighed. "Let's break for dinner and continue in the evening."

A wave of fear crossed Miriam's face, and she looked down again.

"What is it?" Eleanor asked with concern.

The princess looked up with haunted eyes. "It's nothing. My father will join us for dinner. I normally don't talk this much."

"Why do you let him control you like that?" Chip asked, keeping his voice level.

"What do you mean? He did this to all his children." She covered her mouth.

"I thought you were his only child. Are there others?" the boy asked, moving closer.

Now the princess looked terrified. "No, I can't talk about that."

"It's alright, Eleanor soothed, coming over to put one hand on hers. The difference in size was almost comical. "Who are the others?" Miriam hesitated, looking around as if the walls had ears.

Mary sat on her other side, giving the princess a sympathetic look. "You are safe with us. We are not going to say anything. We are your friends."

Miriam trembled then slowly nodded. She lowered her voice to a raspy whisper. "He has had many heirs over the years…" She stopped, looking around again. Xander's eyes blazed bright blue and a thin almost imperceptible shield of magic appeared around them all. "There, you can talk freely now, Princess. No one can hear us."

The troll took a deep breath, still distraught. "He controls the children and hurts us if we get out of line. His punishments are severe. Even talking out of turn is cause for a week in the dungeons. When we reach adulthood, he becomes even more controlling. If he senses at all that anyone is plotting against him, he…kills them."

"So where are his other children now?" Eleanor asked, eyes going wide. Chip felt his heart quicken.

The troll princess struggled to form the words. "He killed them all." She burst into tears. There was dead silence in the room. Everyone stared in disbelief. "Except one."

Mary was able to find words. "You mean yourself?"

Miriam shook her head, sobbing. "My brother. He is younger than me."

"Where is he?" Eleanor asked, her eyes wet.

"He is in the dungeons," she answered in anguish, tears rolling down her bark-like skin.

Chase exhaled, red chips in his eyes glinting. "Let's free him."

"No," the weapons master said, his voice cutting through the air like a knife. "You will jeopardize everything. Thinking is more important than fighting." He strode forward to stand before the weeping troll. "Princess Miriam, we will try to help your brother if we can, but not yet. We need to find what we seek first."

She nodded and raised her head, wiping away her tears. It was clear she had suffered her whole life, but resilience showed in her eyes. "He is a monster. My brother, Striker, grew strong. The trolls respected him too much. Though he has no magic, his fighting ability surpassed my father's, so he sent him to the dungeons. To break him."

"What about you?" Chip asked. "Does he see you as a threat?"

Princess Miriam of the trolls looked at him, and her eyes suddenly flared a dazzling blue. "Yes. I am stronger than him. He fears me. The only reason he has not killed me is to use me as a weapon."

"Against who?" Chip asked.

"Against you."

The boy felt a chill crawl up his spine. He stood before her dazzling blue eyes, knowing she could strike him down. Nobody moved. Chip decided not to seize his Power. He looked deep into her eyes and waited.

She released her magic.

"Does he mean to kill us?" Chip asked.

"He is still deciding. My father is an opportunist. He will side with whoever he thinks will win. Jaggar is controlled by vengeance. He hates King Luminor." She looked at Xander. "He also seeks to kill your brother."

The wizard nodded. "That part does not surprise me."

Chip stepped forward. "Will he be bound by his honour? Will Jaggar uphold our agreement?"

Miriam considered. "I am not privy to his secrets. Rafael is his advisor. For now, yes, I think he will uphold his end. If he finds out I've been talking to you…"

There was a loud knock at the door.

Everyone froze. Miriam gasped.

"It's dinnertime," a gruff voice said. Everyone began breathing again.

Xander released the shield around them. "Thank you. We will be outside shortly." The wizard looked at them all, putting a finger to his lips.

They filed out of the room. Chip and Eleanor walked together, giving each other concerned looks. The boy knew they had to find the missing Light Elves before something happened, and a renewed sense of urgency filled him.

King Jaggar sat at the great table, wearing his crown. His face was unreadable. They all took their seats. His eyes lingered on his daughter as she sat beside him. "Somebody sensed magic being used in the archives room. Care to explain?"

"Oh, that," Xander said smoothly, waving it off. "We were using our Power to strengthen…"

"I wasn't talking to you, Xandrostika." He stared at his daughter.

She looked at him with surprise then let out a small smile. "The scrolls are brittle down there. They showed me how to strengthen the paper with our Power. Now they don't tear." He stared at her hard for several more moments then leaned back.

"Did you find anything interesting?"

She acted shyly, looking down, appearing subservient. "I read more about the Dim killing our people. It took centuries for us to recover and build Rathgar. It was quite interesting. We haven't found anything yet as to the location of the Light Elves." She looked up and then down again.

Jaggar grunted then turned to the others. "Don't use magic again. Your purpose here does not require it. I will have a mage accompany the guard to make sure. This is taking longer than I expected, and my patience is wearing thin." He paused, scrutinizing them, then changed the topic. "Today, I had my warriors capture a ten-foot mountain snake. It pairs perfectly with the eel from the lake. I hope you are hungry." This time, Eleanor blanched. She hated eels. Chip glanced at Ethrang, whose lips trembled. At least the boy was smart enough not to laugh when Jaggar was around.

Everyone, for the most part, forced down the food. Chip tried the snake, which surprisingly tasted like chicken, but the skin gave it a rank odour. The eels were cooked whole and placed on the table with heads attached. The boy could not believe how ugly they were. Razor-sharp teeth filled the eels' mouths, surrounded by twisted, gargoyle-looking faces. Mary was having trouble keeping anything down but managed to smile politely. The talk was sparse, consisting of the weather and mountain animals. When finished, Jaggar grabbed his daughter roughly by the neck, whispered something to her, then took his leave.

The guard escorted them back to the archives room, this time in the accompaniment of an old Blue Level mage. He had a thin, ill-favoured look about him. Chip immediately felt a dislike for the troll. When they were all inside, everyone breathed a sigh of relief.

Xander gave them a look of warning. The unspoken message was clear. "Let's get back to work then, shall we?" he said loudly. He lowered his voice. "If you find something, we will gather together and look at it." They all nodded and went back to their shelves. Eleanor gave Princess Miriam a reassuring look, and the troll smiled shyly in silent appreciation.

Chip tried to read as fast as he could without missing anything important. A sense of urgency grew in him to find the missing Light Elves before Jaggar changed his mind. He skimmed through book after book of elven accounts describing battles with the trolls. Some were written from the troll's perspective, but far fewer. They did not seem like a race interested in writing. He thought about their thick fingers trying to hold a pencil and smiled.

One of the few books written by a troll mage recounted an interesting battle. "The elves, desperate to take our lands, tried to attack us from the frozen ice desert west of the troll mountains. It is a cold, desolate place where nothing grows, even in the brief summer. Their strategy was to attack Rathgar from a different direction, but the elves were not used to such freezing temperatures. The wind howls across the ice like a lost soul, sometimes shrieking so loud it can pop your eardrums. I asked the captain from Rathgar to make a bold move and surprise them while they slept. There would be no way for them to hear or see us. A mighty snowstorm was brewing, and that night, it unleashed its fury. We dressed in our thickest furs and trudged across the frozen sand. We put bits of cloth in our ears lest we lose hearing. With my magic, I sensed the elves' location.

"We fought the wind for half the night, which chilled us to the bone, but luckily, we stumbled upon them. The sentries were as surprised to see us as we were to see them. My soldiers struck their elven bodies with small throwing axes before they could flee, but one managed to scream. It was to no avail, for no one could outmatch the wind. The elves were sleeping in reindeer-hide tents, and we fell on them without mercy, almost killing them all. Only one escaped, and I gave chase, but he disappeared in the storm within moments. I knew he would not survive for he only wore underclothes. The elf would die within minutes. Shortly after, I sent my presence out to make sure he was dead and encountered something in the ground further to the west. It was not a life form, but a radius of spent energy surrounded it in a vast ring, encompassing the borders of the ice desert. I had never noticed there was a faint energy to the whole desert before, but being that close to the source made it apparent.

"I wanted to find it, but the storm was intensifying, and I had used my magic to set many tents on fire. I vowed to return and seek the source. We trudged back to Rathgar, exhausted but exhilarated. We had killed many elves. A week later, I returned to the spot when the weather cleared, but the source of the power radius was gone. The ground was still infused with its aftereffects, which explains why nothing grows. An unimaginable Power had been used there long ago. I believe it could be the source of the Great Forget. I have always regretted not seeking it that day when I had the chance. However, I take solace in knowing that the elves suffered a great blow that day, turning the tide of the war." Grand Mage Salazar.

He showed it to the others, who passed it around. Xander stroked his chin in thought. "It has never been verified," he whispered, "but that object could very well be the source of the Great Forget. The fact that nothing grows there, even in summer, lends credibility to the theory. Good work. We will work another hour, then call it for the evening."

They found nothing else that night and retired. The thin troll mage escorting them back had an even deeper scowl than before. He likely was not pleased with how long they had stayed in the archives room. They bade Princess Miriam good night as she exited the stairs at a different level than theirs. The guard and mage did not even acknowledge her.

When the small party arrived in their rooms, they conferred briefly about the day's discoveries and went to bed.

The following two days proved fruitless. They had managed to comb through almost half the archives but found nothing that would indicate the location of the missing Light Elves. A sense of frustration permeated the room. Jaggar was becoming increasingly erratic. He stopped allowing the princess to say anything and frequently lambasted humans and elves. The food seemed to get worse. He kept the so-called delicacies on trays for himself, saying only trolls could appreciate fine cuisine. He delivered an ultimatum on the fifth day.

"I have been a gracious host, providing you with meals fit for a king. I have given you access to the Guild for an unprecedented amount of time, even though you are my people's sworn enemy. The trolls are getting restless. They are even beginning to question my rule."

Xander opened his hands in a placating gesture. "These things take time, High Mage Jaggar. We are trying…"

"Silence, wizard," he bellowed. A few tables over, the Blues began to rise from their seats. "You have two more days to find what you are looking for, and if unsuccessful, we will meet with all my mages in this hall to decide your fate." He rose, whispered something to the princess, and left the table. Chip looked over to see Rafael grinning wickedly. Miriam had her head down.

They decided to all go into the archives room from then on, including the Protecters. Most were not scholars and could not read well, but anything was better than nothing. Miriam arrived late with a swollen eye. Chip could tell she had been crying. They gathered around her once the door shut.

"What happened?" Eleanor whispered to the injured troll.

The princess looked around cautiously. "He wants me to tell him everything we find, but I only give him useless information," she said in a soft voice. "We found nothing in the last two days, so he took his frustrations out on me. It's alright. I am used to it."

Miriam went back to her table and picked up a book. Chip looked at Chase, whose eyes glinted dangerously. He shook his head.

Everyone read with vigour for the remainder of the evening. Although the room was crowded, they worked around each other late into the night. Several of them whispered passages they had found out loud, but it shed no light on the search. Finally, Xander called it. Most of them had a light sheen of sweat from the increased room temperature.

"We start again in the morning. Sleep and renew your energy." The wizard led them out. When he arrived in his room, Chase flopped down and started snoring in moments. Chip rested on his bed, trying to put everything he had learned together. The boy felt he had read something important but couldn't piece it together. Sleep was a long time coming.

The boy awoke to Xander knocking on the door. He opened it groggily, feeling like he had only slept a few minutes. "Let's get back at it," the wizard said, giving him a sympathetic look. Chip took a breath and nodded, then washed, dressed, and left.

Their second last day proved even less fruitful. A Protector named Charlie read a passage, but it only recounted the Light Elves retrieving the three dragon eggs from the trolls. The author, an elf mage, heard King Luminor talk of abandoning Tarana one day to move further east, for he was weary of war. Nothing was written of any other locations the elves might seek.

The lunch was sparse, consisting of bread and beans. It seemed King Jaggar's generosity was at an end. Mary didn't mind, saying she could at least recognize it. The afternoon proved even more disappointing, but at least they were three-quarters of the way through the archives. Jaggar did not show up for dinner, which relieved most of them, but Chip knew his absence spoke volumes. Rafael was peering at them with a half-concealed grin.

They redoubled their efforts that evening despite the group's flagging energy.

"This is much harder than training," Chase muttered. "It feels like my head is going to explode." Some of the other Protectors grunted in agreement.

"I feel like I've learned all the history of the world," Ethrang complained.

The twins looked over. They were the only two that seemed to be enjoying themselves. "What are you talking about?" Kristan said. "Learning is fun." Thomas nodded as if it was obvious. The green-robed boy gave them a funny look and grabbed another book.

Xander pushed them harder that evening, going later than the night before. Ethrang yawned and swayed on his feet. The wizard finally sighed and wiped his brow. "Get a few hours of sleep. I will wake you in the morning." They all nodded.

Chip felt overtired and tossed and turned that night. So much information was in his head that he found relaxing difficult. There was a puzzle that needed to be solved, but he was missing pieces. His frustration grew.

The boy closed his eyes for what seemed like a moment then heard a soft knock on the door. He opened it to find Xander standing there with a sympathetic look. A dim light was streaming through the hallway window. Chip groaned, "Coming."

He pulled on his robes and donned his red cloak. Chase looked refreshed.

"Really?" Chip said.

"What?" His best friend looked confused.

"Never mind."

A bowl of porridge greeted them at the breakfast table and nothing else. The princess was absent.

"What if it's poisoned?" Kristan whispered to no one in particular.

Xander scoffed. "He could have poisoned us ten times over by now. He almost did with his delicacies. No, Jaggar wants to see if we can find out where the elves are and seek vengeance."

"Makes sense." Ethrang sat down and inhaled his bowl. "I like porridge anyway," he said between mouthfuls. They sat down and at least forced themselves to try it.

Mary made a face and pushed it away. "Baby food," she muttered.

They ate in a hurry and immediately asked the guard to take them to the archives room.

"It's the last day," Xander said solemnly. "May you find fortune." He was going to say more then turned and started reading. The others did the same. The tension in the air was palpable. Chip read a shelf devoted to the end of the Retribution Wars between the elves and trolls. The humans who tried to move east were being caught in the middle of the war, slain randomly by trolls. A powerful man emerged to unite the human villages in the west and build an army. He collected all the magic wielders of the land and trained them. He was more powerful than all of them.

His name was Arkan.

Chip blinked in surprise and hurried over to Xander. "Did your father unite the humans to defeat the trolls and elves?"

Xander winked. "He most certainly did."

"Amazing," Chip breathed.

Ethrang was listening in. "Cool."

The wizard thought for a moment. "In fairness, the elves and trolls had dwindled from all those centuries of warfare, but the feat is still impressive. When they created the wizard council, my father was voted in unanimously for his brilliant military mind and unrivalled strength in Power. The elves and trolls were gracious in defeat. Back then, honour meant more than it does now. He was an impressive man. I work under a long shadow."

"He would be proud," Chip said and returned to his shelf.

The morning went by with little progress. They returned to the dining hall for lunch and found the table empty, save for bread and water. The troll students were pointing and laughing. The Protectors looked mad. They liked to eat. Everyone wolfed down one piece of bread with a small glass of water. Chip looked at the group's tired faces, sympathizing with their mounting stress.

"That was a short lunch," Xander quipped. "Let's get back to it."

Everyone knew it was the final afternoon, and if they didn't find anything by dinnertime, something bad was going to happen. All signs pointed to it. They were nearing the end of the archives room by that point. Chip wondered the odds of the answer being in the last book. Or else they had simply missed it. He knew not all books were fully read. Each person had decided if a shelf, time period, or author merited their full attention. They could have made a mistake. The implications were staggering. The boy read as fast as he could, and the afternoon faded.

They were almost out of time.

Everyone felt the pressure and flipped pages madly, faces displaying exhaustion.

"It's almost dinnertime," Xander said. Dark circles ringed his eyes. "May the Creator help us."

Chip was furiously reading a book on the formation of the wizard council when he heard Ethrang giggle. The blond boy stood at the last shelf beside him, reading a short book.

"What is so funny?" he said, his anger rising. "This is no time for jokes."

Ethrang looked up. "Sorry, but this book is a collection of adventure stories from different people, and this elf talks about being the only survivor of a battle with the trolls. He escapes across a frozen desert in his underclothes, picks up this strange object and meets a witch…"

Chip blinked. "I know that story. That object may have created the Great Forget." He grabbed the book. "If I can't find the Light Elves, at least I can learn something about the Great Forget. Where does the story begin?" The blond boy pointed.

"Time is up," Xander said sadly. "Let's stay here until they knock."

Chip read as fast as he could. "My story is one most won't believe. I was part of an elven tribe sent to attack the trolls across the frozen ice desert. It was winter, and a storm raged. The winds howled to the point where we had to stuff bits of cloth in our ears. We figured the trolls would not think someone could be foolish enough to attack from that direction. My tribe, for better or worse, was brave and foolish. We were set upon in the night by a regiment of trolls and a powerful mage. I saw their tents go up in flames, and the screams will forever haunt me. My tent was on the western edge of the encampment. I grabbed my knife and slit the back, rolling out as it caught fire. The other elves inside didn't make it. In my underclothes, I ran barefoot across the frozen wasteland. I looked back to see the troll mage chasing me, but he disappeared in the snow. I felt a strange thing in front of me and ran towards it, unaware whether it was friend or foe.

"In my desperation, knowing I had only moments left before I froze to death, I felt an energy. No, I felt the residue of a great energy. I followed it by feeling, for swirling snow blocked my vision. My feet turned numb, and I staggered but pushed on, following a line of power that I couldn't describe. It led me to a spot on the ground, indecipherable from anything else. I reached down instinctively and found a hole. Clearing the snow away, I dug deep, unearthing something at the bottom. It was round and smooth. I pulled it out, feeling a vibration run through my body. I held it before my eyes, shocked by its beauty.

"It was a see-through ball. The object was so transparent that I would have seen right through it if I had not held it. A warmth rushed through my body, and I ran west with it. I do not know how long I ran, but all thoughts vanished, and morning arrived. Yet I kept running, spurred on by something unseen. The next day passed and the next, and I did not tire or stop, nor did I hunger. The winds died down, and the cold lessened.

"Finally, I reached a forest. A beautiful woman stood at the edge. She smiled and welcomed me with open arms. Her name was Morgeth." Chip's eyes widened, remembering the name from Balor's story about the staff and the cults in Banfar. She was the High Witch of the Secret Caves, whatever that meant.

"You did your best, Chip," Chase was saying, "Let's go face the music."

"Shhh," he responded and continued reading.

"I was smitten. Her beauty was without equal. She said she had been waiting for me. Only a special person could pick up that object. Only someone in dire need. She cautioned that the forest was very dangerous but knew a way through. She led me all day and into the next. Those woods held terrifying creatures, but the object's energy or the woman herself seemed to keep them at bay. When we reached the other side of the forest, there was an enormous meadow with a low hill in the middle. The forest surrounded the whole place in a massive ring. We walked to the hill and went into a cave hidden by rocks and bushes. It led downwards for a long time. We turned down many tunnels and arrived in a large chamber. A circle of white-eyed females surrounded a large stone altar, and they asked me to place the object on it. An older woman said she knew I was coming. She said the Book of Seeing ordained it. I asked her what the object was."

There was a loud knock on the archives door. "Times up," the skinny troll mage's voice rang through. There was an element of glee to it. "Move it!"

Chip frantically tried to find his spot again in the book, then continued.

"The old woman said the object used to be something else, but now it is a..."

The door crashed open. The massive troll guard stood in the entranceway. "Everyone out now."

The Guardian looked down at the page.

"...it is a Seeing Stone. It sees everything. Say a person's name, and it will show you what they are doing. Pick up the stone, and it will lead you to them..."

Someone slammed the book out of his hand. The troll guard stood before him menacingly. "I said move it, boy."

Chip looked up in shock at what he had just read. He broke into a grin.

"Think it's funny, eh boy." The troll reached for his club.

The Guardian smiled broadly. "Now, now. Jaggar wouldn't like you to hurt his guests. Lead the way, kind fellow."

The guard looked at him as if he was daft then bellowed a raucous laugh. "You are right about that, boy. King Jaggar will take care of you." He moved out of the way so Chip could pass. The boy bent down to reach for the book, but the troll stepped on it.

"Last warning," he said with menace.

Chip shrugged as if it didn't matter and walked to the door. The others were waiting for him in the hall. He came up to them with a mischievous grin.

"Well?" Ethrang asked.

Chip nodded. Everyone's face brightened. Xander let out a sigh of relief. The skinny mage looked at them funny then warded the door and locked it.

"I said move it!" The guard started shoving them forward. No one resisted.

They were escorted back to the dining hall.

10

This time, King Jaggar and Princess Miriam stood in the middle of the room. All the students in the Guild were already seated. The Blue Level table eyed them with wolfish grins. Rafael's fangs gleamed.

"Sit," King Jaggar said, pointing at the empty head table. They took their seats. Chip made sure he was facing the king and the rest of the Guild.

"Now, did you find what you were looking for?" Jaggar leaned forward. The room went silent.

"Yes."

The Troll King's eyes widened. For a moment, he was speechless, and then a strange gleam entered his eyes.

"Where are they?"

"Who?" Chip asked innocently.

Jaggar slammed his hand on the table in front of him, causing it to splinter.

"Where are the Light Elves?"

The Guardian stared at the Troll King. The boy knew that if he gave him the answer, their usefulness would end. "That is not part of the bargain."

The king's mouth worked as his face turned red beneath his bark-like skin. "You do not have to tell me. You will show me." Jaggar's eyes blazed a bright blue, and Chip felt a powerful presence enter his mind.

He instantly wrapped it in the Calm. Time slowed as the room disappeared.

The king did not notice the intrusion, likely due to his singular focus on vengeance. Chip scanned his memories, willing the important ones to materialize—the secretive ones.

Suddenly, he saw Jaggar pulling the stone crown off his dead father's head after King Luminor had slain Malkor in front of the gates of Rathgar. The new king screamed for the trolls to attack the elves. They poured out of the gates in vengeance. The basket with the eggs had overturned, and three were still on the ground. Several elf mages tried to pick them up, but Jaggar seized his magic and shot thick lines of blue Power into them, ripping their bodies apart like paper. The trolls inexorably pushed them back, a wall of massive bodies and armour.

The elves fought brilliantly, shimmering blades whirring gracefully through the air with uncanny precision, but the trolls outnumbered them. King Luminor, surrounded by his elven guard, lifted both hands and shot a massive fireball at the Troll King then staggered back, still weary from his fight with Malkor. Jaggar absorbed it in a thick blue shield and then retaliated. His eyes blazed bright as he unleashed all he had at the weakening Elf King. The mages linked and formed a combined shield, repelling the assault as Luminor was rushed back from the fray. Forced to retreat, the elven army did it in an organized fashion, rotating fresh troops to slow the trolls. As they reentered the mountains, the elves used their magic to block the pass with a landslide of boulders and debris. King Jaggar stood on the valley floor in front of the capital city of Rathgar, gazing at the blocked pass.

He vowed vengeance.

Chip flew forward to the memory of a tall, hooded figure standing before the Troll King deep in the bowels of his castle. The room was dark and cold, weakly lit by a torch in the hallway. Three eggs rested in a basket on a small table in the center of the room. Suddenly, red eyes blazed to life under the hood, causing Jaggar to gasp.

"Your allegiance will be rewarded." The voice was strong and deep. "These are the Originals. The rest of the dragons are extinct. I could win the war with these alone, but first, I seek a talisman in an ancient city."

"I want Luminor alive," King Jaggar said, his voice cracking. "That is the bargain."

An evil chuckle sounded from the depths of the hood. "I sense your fear, troll. It is well justified. You will get your vengeance. My uncle will be yours once I have finished with him."

"Keep him alive, Killian." Jaggar shifted uncomfortably.

The red eyes blazed brighter. "Know your place, troll. You will not call me that name again and live."

Jaggar bowed his head quickly. "My apologies."

The hooded figure took a step forward, lifting his head. Chip could almost make out his face. "You will address me properly. Now bow." His voice exuded power.

The King of the Trolls stood for a moment longer then fell to his knees. "My apologies, Master."

Chip flew forward in Jaggar's memories, already sensing him becoming aware. He latched on to a recent one of the king and Rafael standing in the hallway after their first dinner a week ago.

"I despise humans," Raphael spat. "We should have killed them in the council room."

"Soon, my eager advisor," Jaggar grinned. "They cannot win this war. I will not aid my sworn enemies." His grin vanished as a terrible hatred surfaced. "High Wizard Balor will pay for his treachery, but above all I seek King Luminor. I will crush the Elf King with my bare hands and avenge my father. Once these fools find the location of the missing Light Elves, we will destroy them."

King Jaggar wrenched his presence from Chip's mind and staggered back. "How?"

The Guardian of Humanity shouted, filled with anger. "You

betrayed the world long ago, and now you seek to betray us! I will never tell you where the Light Elves are!"

Princess Miriam placed a hand on Jaggar's shoulder. "Father, please stop."

The king threw a vicious elbow to her face. Blood sprayed the floor as she crashed into a table, unmoving. He then lifted his hands towards Chip, eyes blazing.

The Guardian's rage exploded.

Chip shattered his Wall and filled himself with Power. Jaggar unleashed everything he had. The boy formed a solid shield, absorbing the onslaught. Then the Blues stood up and, as one, shot a torrent of fire at him. The combined might of the troll mages staggered him, and he drew deeper of his Power. He saw the student mages stand up, eyes flaring to lend aid.

"Link to him!" cried Xander.

The wizard's eyes blazed as they formed the link. Chip welcomed the extra Power and strengthened his shield, covering them all. Ethrang abruptly vanished. Now, the entire old Guild combined their forces, and he knew they could not hold.

There were simply too many. Troll students at the Yellow, Green, and Brown Levels added their magic. The room became a maelstrom of Power, and the stones in the walls and ceiling began to shake.

Eleanor's eyes glinted with red chips, but he could see her straining. Xander's face was a mask of concentration. Some of the weaker students began to fall over, their magic spent. The Protectors stood behind them all, unable to use their skills. King Jaggar's face was a rictus of hate. He started to grin, sensing victory.

Then Furiosa appeared out of nowhere beside the blue table. The trolls looked at her in terror, some releasing their magic in fear, likely thinking she was back from the dead. She had a green shield around her body. The eight-foot troll grabbed the huge table like a toy and flung it into the Blue Level mages. Rafael tried to turn in time, but the broadside hit him in the face. The Blues collapsed in a tangled heap of furniture and bodies. Jaggar recovered first from the shock, sending a bright stream of fire at Furiosa, but she disappeared into thin air. A moment later, a green-shielded charging buffalo careened into dozens of students and tables, sending people flying like straw.

"He's a shapeshifter," bellowed Jaggar. The buffalo vanished.

Chip saw his opportunity as the Blues scrambled to their feet. Holding both hands together, he shot a massive red fireball at the king. Nothing could escape the speed and fury of the attack. Jaggar turned, grinning wickedly, and lowered his head. The red fireball struck him on the crown with full force. Then it disappeared.

The Troll King stood unscathed.

Chip stared in shock, almost dropping his shield. The crown had saved King Jaggar. An image of Balor holding a staff with runes on it entered his mind, and he realized the crown must be strengthened. What was it made of?

He had no time to formulate an answer, for the Blues were again throwing everything they had at him.

"Run!" shouted Xander. Chip strengthened the red shield while the others made for the door behind them. It was getting harder to maintain the barrier as the students began joining in again, groggily getting to their feet.

The boy backpedalled through the massive doors into the great hall, following the others. It was empty.

Xander was already running to the back doors of the Guild, making for the stone stairs they had climbed a week earlier. He skidded to a halt, and the others nearly collided with him.

"Back!" he shouted. "It's a trap!"

They could see several hundred trolls, weapons drawn, covering the courtyard and stone steps through the open doors. Chip realized with a cold fear that Jaggar had already called reinforcements. He had been planning this all along.

They turned around as the soldiers charged forward through the large entrance. At the same time, mages spilled out of the dining room into the hall. They raised their arms, shooting streams of different coloured fire, depending on their Level. Rafael came out, his face bloody, and formed a blue fireball.

"Follow me!" Xander shouted above the din. Chip reinforced his red shield. The fireball struck it and his Power held, though he was weakening. They raced to the other end of the hall, but several blue mages had already gathered ahead of them.

They were boxed in.

Suddenly, Ethrang appeared out of midair, swooping down in demon wasp form, sending an arcing stream of green fire into the group. They tried to shield themselves, but the shock of seeing a winged demon froze them. The fire singed their flesh, and several robes caught fire. They ran into the walls to put out the flames. Other students who were pouring out of the doors ahead screamed and tried to scramble backwards. One mage held his ground, and blue fire struck the shapeshifter, but he veered off, sustaining a glancing blow. It did not pierce his demon armour. A moment later, Ethrang vanished again.

It created enough of an opening for the small party to make it through the main hall and turn left down a long passage. The sounds of soldiers running followed them, and Chip could feel bursts of magic attack the back of his shield. Keeping the barrier up around that many people was draining, and when they turned another corner into an empty hall, he released his magic. The boy staggered, but Kristan caught him.

"We've got you, Guardian. It's our turn now." The blond twin's face showed focus. Thomas nodded, running on his other side. They did not have to wait long. A knot of soldiers appeared at the end of the hall in front of them, trying to cut them off. They pointed and shouted, running full speed towards them.

The blond twins strode forward and stood side by side, hands raised. Two intense streams of blue fire shot into the group of trolls like a battering ram. The front ones slammed backwards into the others, melting into a gooey ball of flailing limbs. Kristan and Thomas were two of the strongest in the Guild, and their Power was breathtaking.

With the way cleared, the others raced around the burning corpses, following Xander to the right. More shouts rang out as other soldiers spotted them. Chip noticed several young-looking student mages leading the trolls and seized his Power to fling a cushion of air, throwing them off their feet. He did not want to hurt them if he could avoid it.

They reached the end of the hall by the stairwell. "Go down the stairs," Xander ordered as Ethrang materialized to his right.

"I will go last," the skinny blond boy said as they rushed through. They were in the stairwell that gave them access to their dorms and the hall leading to the archives room. The wizard went down at a fast pace. Chip looked back to see Ethrang heat and melt the door and the stones around it with his magic so it wouldn't open. They rushed down two more levels and entered the hall with the large iron door. They could hear banging and yelling from above. Xander's eyes blazed and the locking mechanism melted, allowing him to push through.

"Do you know where you are going?" Ethrang asked, catching up to them. The blond boy had a light sheen of sweat on his face.

"I used to live here, remember?" the old man answered, taking the steps two at a time. They went down three sets of stairs, passing the archives level. Screams and groans reached their ears from the dungeons below. The wizard descended until the screams came from the door they were passing. The stairs continued downwards.

"Xander, wait." Chip turned to the entrance leading to the dungeons. His rage ignited, and he blew the iron door off its hinges. It landed flat a dozen feet down a long hall that stretched into the distance, lit by weak torches. Rows of cells with iron bars lined both sides. The smell of urine and unwashed bodies assaulted them. The boy ignored it.

"They are coming," Eleanor shouted.

"Hold them off," Chip said without turning, raising both arms. His magic turned into two red hands that flew down the hall to the very end, at least one hundred feet. He felt the queen and Mary summon their magic behind him, spraying fire up the stairs, stopping anyone from descending. Concentrating hard, he used the red hands to grab each set of doors and yank the cells open. Cheers erupted up and down the hall as the prisoners realized they were being freed. The boy continued pulling doors open, until finally he reached the front. Trolls staggered out of their cells, covering their eyes. Some looked large and powerful, while others could barely walk. Blue fire rained behind him from the stairwell, but the twins erected a solid shield.

"Will you fight for us?" Chip yelled from the door, eyes blazing red.

"Yes!"

"With pleasure!"

"I've waited so long."

"We are being chased by King Jaggar, his mages, and his soldiers...everybody. We are escaping the fortress. Help us," Chip shouted. He was about to turn away, but a large troll with a heavily muscled body pushed his way to the front.

"I am Striker, Jaggar's son. I do not know who you are, but you have saved us. You have my axe and sword. The others will follow me to the death."

Chip nodded. "Death may very well find all of us, but your swords and axes are most welcome."

"Hurry, Guardian," the twins said as one, faces straining as they held the shield.

"Protectors, offer these trolls a weapon to aid us. Let's move," Garth Stone shouted. He gave Striker his dagger. The troll grabbed it and flipped it into his other hand with ease. It looked like an extension of his arm.

Xander turned and descended the stairs. Eleanor sent a stream of brown fire laced with red up the stairs, which seemed to cause havoc. Muffled screams and thuds sounded and the attack on the twin's shield stopped. They took advantage of the lull and raced after the wizard. Chip made sure all the prisoners made it out. The last one stumbled through the door. He was missing an eye and smelled terrible. His legs were bent at odd angles as if he had been tortured for a long time. The troll smiled crookedly, revealing the few teeth he had left.

"I wait here, human boy. I'm almost dead anyway. I surprise them. Go!" He slipped back into the dim tunnel and waited.

Garth passed him a dagger then urged the rest of them down the stairs. "Let's make his sacrifice worth it." Chip nodded and followed the others.

The group went down several more flights before reaching the bottom. The sounds of footsteps far above started up again. Above it all, a bellow of rage erupted followed by horrifying screams. It was a sound reminiscent of a wounded animal, but one that could still fight. It spoke of endless pain and suffering, of the loss of freedom and life, and the terrible primal need for revenge. The snapping of bones and the thud of bodies was audible, and then there was a flash of light, and the sound ceased. Chip felt a deep rage fester knowing the troll had only experienced a few moments of freedom. He couldn't imagine how long the poor thing had been locked in the dungeons. He gritted his teeth and followed the others through the door at the bottom of the stairs. Needing a vent for his anger, the boy turned and melted the door and stone as Ethrang had done above, buying them a little time.

"This way," Xander called from the front. "We are at the lowest level." It was pitch black other than the ball of light in the wizard's hand. He turned left, then right, and right again down a series of tunnels. "Hmmm. This doesn't look right." He paused, tapping his chin. The sounds of ragged breathing were audible as everyone stopped.

Thomas stared at Kristan with wide eyes. "He is getting old, after all," he whispered. "I hope he remembers soon."

"I heard that," Xander muttered.

"Ha," Ethrang smirked, but even he looked a little fearful. "I hate tunnels. Reminds me of the cults."

"My goodness, go back!" the wizard ordered. "I haven't been here for three thousand years. Pardon my memory. I went right instead of left." Everyone scuttled backwards in mild disarray. "Follow the blue ball of light." Xander levitated his magic ahead of them and the ball whizzed down another tunnel. They raced after it. Banging sounded on the door far behind them at the bottom of the stairs, then the tearing of metal.

The blue light bobbed ahead, turning down branches and cutting corners. The air was cold and stale. Twice more they had to backtrack before the wizard finally whispered, "Here we are."

They arrived at a door that looked completely rusted shut. The wizard used a small amount of magic to loosen the rust then pulled on the handle until the door squeaked open. He gritted his teeth at the sound. Behind them, still a distance away, they could hear the thuds of boots getting closer. They entered a large room with nothing in it but a few faded tapestries.

"This is a dead end," Mary said, steadying her voice.

"That is what it is supposed to look like." Xander walked to the room's far side, where a large tapestry covered the wall. It showed a faded picture of Arkan in his youth, seated at the council table. "Thank you, Father," the wizard whispered before using his magic to set the hanging to the side. Behind it was a blank wall.

"We serve the people," Xander intoned, and suddenly a doorframe emerged etched by the wizard's blue magic. "This wall is featureless unless you know the phrase. Arkan was a military strategist above all else and knew that no fortress would be safe forever." He pushed the stone door with his hands, and it opened into a downward-sloping tunnel. "Don't use your magic until we are further away." The wizard pulled a torch from a rusted sconce and lit it with his finger. The whole thing crumbled in his hand. "That's no good. The tunnel is straight. Walk down it in the dark for now."

The footsteps behind them were getting louder, and voices reached them.

"This way!"

"I sensed their magic."

"It was the wizard." Rafael's voice was unmistakable.

Everyone filed into the tunnel. Chip waited with the other wizards until everyone had passed. As the last troll prisoner went through, Chip could hear footsteps outside the rusted door leading into the room. Xander closed the stone door, and the blue lines vanished. It was pitch-black.

"Let's see how long they take to figure it out," the wizard whispered. A faint dull clang sounded on the other side, indicating the trolls had entered the room.

Chip could hear the prisoners and Protectors up ahead, moving steadily downwards. He followed the noise in the dark but found himself brushing up against a wall. The boy put his hand out and felt slime, instantly regretting it.

Eleanor was close beside him. He reached out instinctively and grabbed her left hand with his clean right one. She squeezed it in reassurance. It seemed that they might have finally lost their pursuers when a knocking sounded far back. They were testing the wall. A few moments later he sensed a great release of magic, and the sound of broken stone reverberated down the tunnel. Looking back, they could see a pinpoint of light at the very end of the tunnel. Then shadows blocked it.

"Run," Garth ordered from the front.

Chip sensed another burst of magic and turned to see a tiny ball of blue light growing larger and larger behind them, speeding down the tunnel.

"It turns right up ahead," Garth called. Everyone turned, the way now lit by the glowing ball behind them. Chip was about to raise a shield and use more of his depleted magic to block the attack, but then they were around the corner. The ball of light had grown into a roiling ball of blue energy that filled the entire tunnel. They ran full speed down the next tunnel to get out of harm's way as it slammed into the wall at the end, creating a crater amidst a shower of stone and flame. A rumble sounded far above them, and dust fell from the ceiling.

"I hate tunnels," Ethrang panted. "Did I mention that?"

"If they keep this up, the whole place is going to come down," Kristan observed.

Xander lit a ball of blue light and shot it ahead, illuminating the way. "It will zigzag now until we reach the bottom. Trolls run fast, so keep up the pace." Some of the prisoners were out of shape, likely locked up for years. These started falling back, breathing hoarsely. Chip slowed down to help.

"Give them a weapon and leave them," Garth ordered, dropping back. "There's nothing we can do." He handed one of the exhausted trolls a dagger and placed him on one of the zigzags after a turn.

"Thank you. Death will set me free," the troll gasped. A strange smile appeared on his cracked lips. His fangs had long been worn away, likely from gnawing on his prison bars.

Chip desperately wanted to stay and send his magic into their pursuers, but he knew the group was almost spent. They needed to conserve it for whatever was ahead. Two other trolls, unable to go on, stayed as well. They held weapons handed to them from the Protectors.

"May the Creator shine on you," Chip said. He turned and continued to run.

It didn't take long for the screams to start. Some were of surprise, so the boy knew they had at least slowed them down. A flash of blue light signalled their end, and he shook his head in pity.

The tunnels seemed endless, and more trolls fell back to make a stand. He had freed at least fifty prisoners, but soon they were down to less than forty. He gritted his teeth and followed the bobbing light. The flashes of magic behind them continued, and then the sound of boots became louder. The trolls were only a few hundred feet behind them. Bellows of anticipation erupted as their pursuers closed in. By the sounds of it, an entire army with many mages were behind them. A weariness engulfed the boy. The lack of sleep in the last few days had taken a toll, and he returned to his training for inspiration.

"Never give up." The one lesson above them all. One time, Garth had added to it. "You can sleep when you're dead." The boy shook his head and carried on.

The end came swiftly. The sound of pursuit had intensified until he knew they were around the corner. He could hear hungry whines and the sounds of the trolls gnashing their teeth. They all turned to make a final stand.

"It's here!" Xander called from up ahead where the tunnel ended against a flat wall. "Hold them off while I try to remember the phrase. I forgot there were two."

The twins turned around in disbelief. Kristan stepped forward. "Forget the phrase. Stand back."

"I don't really recommend that..." Xander started to say, but a flaming blue fireball shot out of Kristan's hands. Chip knew he was linked to Thomas, so the effect was impressive. Their combined magic flew into the stone with stunning force, causing an explosion of rock blasting outwards onto what appeared to be the base of the cliff. A giant hole appeared. He looked out onto the meadow they had climbed the stairs from at the base of the cliffs. A rush of cold but fresh air wafted in.

Then the cracking of stone sounded, and chunks of rock began falling from the ceiling.

"Run!" cried the twins. Everyone made a mad dash for the hole

Chip could make out the troll's bodies running the final stretch behind them. The mages had let their soldiers go ahead. Grunts and bellows of fear started replacing the trolls' rage-filled faces. Loud cracking sounds came from the stone as more rocks fell.

The boy dropped his hands and ran for his life, bringing up the rear.

Chip managed to leap through the hole as a troll grabbed the back of his red cloak. A resounding thud sounded behind him, and he turned to see a large rock had crushed the soldier's head, pinning him to the ground. Then the whole entrance collapsed. A knot of soldiers were trying to clamber through, but they were completely crushed. Chip felt someone yank him back.

"Sorry about that," Thomas said in his ear.

"Yes, it might not have been the best idea, but it worked out in the end, right?" Kristan smiled weakly. Chip stared at him.

The boy turned around to see that the evening sun was beginning to set over the meadow.

"Watch out!"

A group of trolls were pouring out of the stairwell half a league south of their location.

"Use magic only if you must, and even then, short bursts," Xander instructed. "We must conserve it to give ourselves a chance to escape. Jaggar probably thinks we are still in the Guild. The trolls and magic wielders who do know where we are remain trapped in the tunnel, so we are safe for the moment. Use your weapons."

"You don't have to ask me twice," Striker said, twirling the dagger in his fingers. The weapons master threw him an axe, and he easily caught the handle, holding a weapon in each hand. His size was impressive, rivalling Jaggar's. The other troll prisoners spread out, faces eager to take vengeance on their captors. Garth and the Protectors drew their swords.

"Finally," said Chase, pulling out his blade. "Beats the archives room."

They had no more time to think. The trolls were upon them. The savage brutes ran full speed, bellowing war cries, brandishing all manner of weapons. Most had cudgels, but many preferred the axe or short sword. Some swung maces or iron-studded clubs, fangs gleaming in the evening sun.

The Protectors took the front, finally in their element. After a week of confinement in the Guild and stuffed in a cramped archives room, they could unleash their frustration. Bulch pulled out his club with a grin, taller than most trolls. Carvor, Hunter, and Sheldor formed a line, swords at the ready. The rest of them fanned out, protecting the wizards. The troll prisoners ran out to meet the soldiers with Striker leading the charge, faces full of fury that needed venting.

The clang of metal sounded, and bodies thudded with sickening force. Screams of pain and anger replaced bellows. The front line held, but the trolls' savagery was frightening. Chip understood why they invoked fear. It was not only their size, but each of them had been fighting since birth. They were formidable enemies.

Yet the Protectors were the best in the world, trained with all fighting techniques considered. If there was one weakness the trolls had, it was that they all fought the same way, always on the offense. The Protectors used that to their advantage, allowing the trolls to overextend or rush past them then coming in from the side with deadly accuracy. Carvor used his sword like a scythe, dodging the direct attack then cutting trolls' heads almost clean off from an angle. Sheldor and Hunter ducked the attacks and took advantage of the enemy's exposed underbelly, spilling troll guts all over the meadow. Bulch took the direct approach, which his size and reach allowed, simply smashing skulls before any weapon could reach him.

Striker seemed possessed. The Troll Prince, betrayed by his father and people, showed cold, unforgiving vengeance. Axe and dagger moved in blurs of speed as he dodged and pirouetted, chopping off limbs and dealing death blows at will. At one point, a cluster of trolls surrounded him, and he disappeared, only to emerge as they fell one by one until only he was standing. Garth Stone went to lend aid, but there was no need. The weapons master nodded to him, and he returned the gesture, two warriors acknowledging the other in battle.

They had repelled the initial assault, but now more trolls were spilling out from the stairs. Explosions came from the tunnel behind them, and chunks of rock started flying outward. The mages were trying to get out. Chip had hoped the collapsed entrance had crushed them, but he knew to prepare for the worst.

"Make for the plain!" Xander yelled. "If we can get to the front lines we—" The wizard stopped, eyes going wide. "May the Creator help us." A dark smudge appeared in the pass leading to the plain. It materialized into a mass of trolls running full speed towards them.

"Oh dear," Elayne said.

"It looks like they brought their whole army from the front lines," Chase said, cleaning his bloody sword. Another explosion sounded behind them, and the makings of a small hole appeared in the cliff. The mages would be out soon.

"Head north!" Xander shouted. "It's our only hope of..." The wizard's eyes widened in disbelief. Another army of trolls began filing out of the mountains from the north, breaking into a run as the soldiers spied the enemy. They were coming from Rathgar. King Jaggar must have summoned them when the party had arrived.

The humans were trapped.

For a moment, Chip stood in an oasis of calm. Trolls ran from the stairs, fanged mouths open, screaming for blood. An army approached them from the south, blocking their escape. To the side, mages and soldiers were about to emerge from the base of the cliff. Their only hope was to flee north, but another army blocked that escape route. He knew they would be overrun before they left the meadow. He sent his presence out to find the unicorns, but they were long gone, possibly even eaten.

Chip felt a cold fear.

Standing in the middle of an approaching maelstrom of destruction and death, he felt all alone. He was a lost little boy again, surrounded by darkness. Even the light of the sun was disappearing as the meadow darkened before the inevitable onslaught. His friends would all be slain in front of him. There was only darkness and death.

Chip Oathbinder was afraid.

Memories of Miss Stern shutting him in the cold storage room while the bugs and rats crawled over him surfaced. He had been brought before King Barton weak and sick, as lonely a boy as there ever was. Nobody wanted him. They sought to banish him so he could die on the One Road all alone. Then, incredibly, he had made friends and saw that he might have a life as a common soldier. It was beyond his wildest dreams. When people started caring about him, he couldn't believe it at first. He latched on to them, and they became his world. As the years passed, the bond with his friends strengthened. He had experienced unbelievable adventures, heartaches, and true love.

And now they were all going to die.

He was scared.

The unfairness of everything struck him hard. All their battles, victories, and sacrifices would amount to nothing. The boy sighed, closing his eyes.

Despite it all, he would fight to the end. He had given his word.

The Guardian tossed the negative thoughts aside and faced his enemies. He would talk to himself and not listen. Life was not fair, and it never would be.

Courage was being afraid but doing it anyway.

The boy stayed his fear as the enemy closed in on all sides, keeping calm to make the proper decision, and then Chip seized his magic.

The Guardian turned to the wizard with blazing eyes. "We retreat north towards Rathgar then west across the frozen desert. There is something I need to find."

Xander was about to protest, but he saw the grim resilience in the boy's eyes, and he nodded.

Garth Stone put his hand on the boy's shoulder. "We will follow you."

The trolls from the stairs were almost upon them.

Chip turned and unleashed a red swath of fire into the ones in front, incinerating them. The trolls behind stopped their advance to wait for the flames to diminish. The boy turned to the cliff wall as the mages and soldiers started spilling out. He raised his hands.

"No, let me," Eleanor said, stepping in front of him.

"Use mine as well," Mary offered, standing beside her.

The Queen of Vanalon linked with the Blue Wing Leader and raised her arms. The mages' eyes blazed with Power, but it was too late. A mixture of brown, blue, and red-laced magic shot from the queen's hands, striking the cliff above them, creating a massive landslide. The falling rock crushed many trolls, but the mages dove forwards, escaping the worst of it. Eleanor moved her hands and scooped out the earth under their feet, creating a massive hole the mages helplessly fell into. She then dropped the raised earth back into the hole, burying them alive.

"Watch out!" cried Thomas, pointing up.

A massive blue fireball hurtled towards them from the cliffs above. King Jaggar stood with several blue mages, grinning with glee. Princess Miriam was beside him, looking down. Chip glanced right, then stepped forward. The troll army in the pass had reached the meadow.

The boy swung his arms to the side, deflecting the massive ball of blue energy into the approaching trolls. It streaked across the meadow in a blazing blue arc, causing the soldiers to skid to a stop, trying to move out of the way. When it struck, the ball burst apart, decimating the front line. He sent another streak of red fire at the trolls from the stairs and then turned to the others.

"Run!"

They headed north, moving at an angle to try and bypass the army from Rathgar. The trolls immediately spread out, covering the top of the meadow. Behind them, Jaggar was using his magic to pull the mages out of the dirt at the base of the cliff wall. Soon, they would be freed and give chase. The trolls from the stairs and the pass had joined, close on their heels. Chip knew they did not have much time.

"Head northwest!" he yelled, but then his voice failed. The size of the northern army was not several hundred but several thousand, and they had more mages. Knowing it was impossible, he pushed on anyway. The boy brushed all fear aside and let his rage take over. Then they were at the front lines of the Rathgaran army. The trolls bunched up, waiting for them.

The boy raised his hands and sent a massive fireball straight ahead. It cleared a wide swath for hundreds of feet. Trolls flew through the air, body parts landing on their comrades. The mages retaliated immediately, sending different-coloured magic streams from splayed fingers. Xander formed a shield while the twins counterattacked, sending wicked ropes of blue magic hurtling towards them. The mages had no choice but to form their own shield. Even so, many Lower Level wielders flew backwards or caught on fire.

"Behind us!" Garth pointed. The trolls had caught up. Now they were completely surrounded.

A Giant Eagle suddenly materialized in front of the southern army, sending green fire into the front ranks. The eagle swooped across the line and held them at bay.

"Move forward!" Chip shouted. But the trolls had already closed ranks and began pressing in.

They all attacked at once.

The Protectors and trolls from the prison fought valiantly but began to fall. Garth and Chase stood back-to-back, slicing and dicing until a mound of bodies formed around them. The twins climbed up the mound then spun around and unleashed blue fire in a wide circle, causing the enemy to balk. Ethrang turned into Furiosa, decapitating trolls then vanishing and reappearing an instant later somewhere else, causing mayhem. Eleanor turned with blazing eyes, lifting mounds of dirt that threw trolls high in the air to land on their comrades. Bones snapped and faces impaled on each other's weapons as the enemy soldiers flew madly about.

Striker was a blur of motion, fighting alongside the remaining prisoners. Xander formed a shield around those who needed it each time a mage tried to throw a fireball or spray fire at the group.

Yet it was not enough.

Hunter went down first, his head caved in by a troll cudgel, and then a short sword pierced Sheldor in the stomach, causing him to double over and stagger back. Bulch was surrounded, staying alive by pure savagery, but his multiple wounds were adding up. The sheer number of trolls pushed Garth and Chase into an ever-tightening circle. They became defensive, parrying death blows, but eventually some would get through.

The troll prisoners looked exhausted and began falling one by one. A mage shot green fire into Thomas's back, and he flew off the mound of bodies. Kristan screamed and leapt down to help his brother, but the blond twin was smoking on the ground with his eyes closed. Eleanor and Mary had almost spent their magic and desperately held on to a wavering shield. Furiosa was bleeding from several wounds and forced to turn into a Giant Eagle to try and escape, but the shapeshifter couldn't fly right and crashed into the middle of the troll army, disappearing.

Chip sent out a final wave of fire, his Power nearly spent, then screamed in frustration. He wrapped everyone in a red shield and waited for his magic to run out.

It was the end.

THE DARK ELF Hagatha stood at the side of the pass behind a rock outcropping gazing at the Troll Kingdom. The setting sun shimmered off her stark white hair. She patted her speed demon's neck. The creatures had carried them across the Great Plains in less than a week with their abnormally long legs. They could run all day, stopping only occasionally for a drink of water or to kill something and lap up its blood. She preferred to consider them the offspring between a horse and a wolf. They had the characteristics of both. Her mount's tongue wagged between its fangs after a full day of running. It sniffed the air and pawed the ground restlessly. It would need to feed soon.

The thin, skeletal woman surveyed the spectacle before her. Two troll armies were converging on the hapless humans trapped in the middle of the meadow before the old Wizard's Guild. She smiled in satisfaction. It looked like King Jaggar would do the work for them. The Dark Elf would bring the heads back as a courtesy to her Master. He could mount them in the throne room until they shrivelled to desiccated husks before his eyes. Even their skulls would eventually turn to dust over the millennia as the Age of Demons flourished.

She sighed, allowing herself the small emotion of satisfaction. Hagatha rarely indulged in any form of pleasure. Long ago, she had realized that emotions were the weakness of all races. She had watched as countless of her brethren fell prey to the insidious lure of emotion. They were controlled by pain and pleasure whether they realized it or not. Every thought and every desire served to satisfy a craving or to avoid pain. The end goal was what? Happiness? Joy? Power?

Hagatha almost laughed out loud, but that would have been a disgusting display of emotion. She needed to look no further than her son, Bashan, to see what a vile, despicable thing one could become when they catered to every whim and desire.

A small amount of bile rose in her throat at the thought of someone seeking pleasure for its own sake. Still, they were male, so she couldn't blame them. She had nurtured Killian and Bashan as best she could, knowing they would fall prey to their indulgences. It was in their nature. The only thing she could teach them was to avoid the truly pathetic emotions such as sympathy, love, and kindness. She taught them to embrace narcissism, for it could achieve true power. Under her and Morgo's guidance, they had nurtured the two young elves by strengthening the emotions that mattered to achieve power and control, while punishing them for displaying any weaker ones, especially love. She felt her stomach stir in disgust at that vile feeling. When Killian had shown kindness and love to a white unicorn, she had killed it.

Only loyalty mattered, not love.

She would have killed Bashan herself for his disloyalty. And she wouldn't have felt a thing.

A sound behind her brought the Inner Circle Elf out of her reverie. Six male trolls were running across the plain, pointing at them. They were likely stragglers to the main army already in the field. They drew their weapons, intent on killing them. Trolls were such savage brutes, but again, it was to be expected.

Hagatha looked at Blade, seated on the speed demon next to her. "Deal with them."

The weapons expert bowed his head without a word and dismounted in one fluid motion. She watched him draw two crossed swords from his back. She respected the Dark Elf, for out of all the males she ever knew, he displayed the least emotion. Yet Blade still took pleasure in his craft, but that was his nature. She conceded he was loyal to a fault, and that earned her respect.

Blade was as dangerous an elf as she had ever met, save for her Master. At first, she had resisted the idea of imbuing a Yellow Level elf with that much Power, but Killian was clever and saw the value. Her only concern was disloyalty. What if he turned? He could likely resist even Killian's magic for a short period of time. His skin had hardened to a shield, capable of stopping almost anything. Even if injured, he could heal himself almost instantly. Blade truly was the perfect weapon.

Hagatha watched him glide a few paces towards the advancing trolls, and then he took his stance, remaining motionless, coiled muscles ready to spring forward into breathtaking action. The first troll ran at him with an overhand strike of its battle axe. Blade remained frozen, discerning the exact moment when the troll had committed to the attack and then unleashed. The troll's axe met air as Blade slid beside it, quicker than thought, and chopped both its hands off, still attached to the weapon. The other five arrived at the same time. Blade did not pause. Both swords whirled in the air, slicing and chopping with unmatched precision. The Dark Elf moved through them like a wraith, the eye unable to catch his full outline as he blurred through his patterns to perfection. Three thousand years of training had created the ultimate killer.

In moments, it was over. All six trolls were in pieces on the hard ground.

Blade smoothly leapt back on his speed demon, calm and collected. "Do we assist, Mistress?" He nodded towards the battlefield. "The Protector in black fights well. I would like to end his life."

She watched as the wizards and Protectors valiantly tried to fend off the troll army. The boy used his red magic to great effect, but they were terribly outnumbered. Still, she could feel his Power from here. Impressive. "No, we will watch from a distance. I still do not know King Jaggar's loyalty to our just cause. His attack on the humans is promising. I may let the troll live and serve us until our enemies are dead, and then I will destroy him for his disloyalty all those years ago. Disloyalty is unforgivable. For now, let us watch the red-eyed boy die."

Hagatha almost smiled but caught herself. Emotions were for the weak.

11

A hum sounded.

Standing with his red cloak in the center of the battle, Chip pushed through his grief and rage. The hum was familiar. Then a presence entered his mind.

Redmane!

The boy turned around to find the source of his connection and saw them. A white spearhead with a red tip was coming down the slope of the western mountain. The humming sound increased, and then the thunder of hooves.

The unicorns were here.

The red horse led them down the smooth slope, moving at speeds unmatched by any land animal. Their horns gleamed in the last rays of the setting sun as they galloped in a blur of motion straight into the troll army. The soldiers and mages started shouting and pointing. The entire army turned to face this new threat. Chip felt their magic. It encapsulated the small herd with shimmering energy. Hundreds of trolls stood between the beleaguered group and the horses. All the boy could do was watch.

Redmane led the charge without slowing. The unicorns sliced into the trolls like a giant spear, opening an unstoppable growing wedge. Their magic went through bodies, armour, and weapons alike. Some trolls, unfortunate enough to be in their direct path, were sliced in two. Onwards came the magnificent animals, splitting the army open like a rotten melon.

"Gather together!" Chip yelled, feeling a surge of hope in a world of despair. The Protectors pulled their injured towards the boy. The surviving troll prisoners, including Striker, staggered back to join them. The trolls had stopped fighting, watching in awe as their comrades split apart by what seemed an unstoppable force.

Redmane arrived in front of the Guardian. His presence urged the boy to mount quickly. Already, the trolls were getting over their shock, replaced by a hunger to eat horse meat. Several ran at them with raised weapons.

Chip enlarged his red shield to include the unicorns and staggered at the effort. "Get on! Double up if you must." Kristan threw his unconscious brother over a white unicorn then leapt behind him. Garth and Carvor picked Sheldor up and grunted as they heaved him on another one. Blood dripped onto the unicorn's white coat. Everyone scrambled up, exhausted.

"Don't let them get away!" Several mages yelled, raising their hands. The trolls moved in, but the red shield burned them. They screamed as the weight of the soldiers in the back pressed them forward, melting their bodies. Chip sat on Redmane, trying to get the horse to turn around, but the unicorn showed him in images that there were too many behind them. Thousands of trolls were still coming through the pass from Rathgar. The horse pointed northeast. It had the least amount of trolls between them and freedom. He felt Xander and the others buttress his failing shield as the mages unleashed their magic. The boy showed the horse he understood.

Chip felt his strength buckle as he squeezed his knees into the horse's ribs. Redmane's horn glowed and hummed as he leapt forward, pushing through the trolls. The boy looked around desperately for Ethrang, but the blond boy was gone. A heavy pang of grief weighed his heart but he pushed on. They began picking up speed as the horses gained momentum. Thankfully, some trolls leapt out of the way as self-preservation overrode their desire to kill.

They were almost through when Chip's magic gave out.

Rafael had arrived on the eastern edge of the battlefield and shot a blistering blue fireball straight into the side of one of the unicorns in the back, piercing the weakening shield. No one was able to stop it in time. Chip wasn't sure if anyone had the strength. The horse went down with two troll prisoners on its back, screaming. Within moments, the troll army had killed the prisoners and covered the unicorn with their fangs, tearing into its flesh. Chip raised his arm to do something, but he had nothing left. Redmane neighed shrilly in consternation, but they could not stop.

Finally, they were through the trolls, galloping across the northeastern part of the meadow into a tight pass not well travelled. The sun had set, and the stars were beginning to glow. The temperature continued to drop. The mountains ahead looked treacherous, and he prayed there was a way through. The soldiers were giving chase behind them, but the unicorns gained ground easily.

The boy breathed in the fresh air, thankful the trolls were gone. The others looked drained, and he felt a pang of loss to see how few prisoners remained. The Protectors had lost two members as well. His mind turned again to Ethrang, and tears filled his eyes. He would miss the skinny blond boy.

Something slammed into his back and grasped his waist.

Chip turned in a panic, knowing he was defenceless.

"It's about time you dropped the shield, Guardian."

"Ethrang!" he shouted. "You're alive!" He looked at the blond orphan. The boy's hair was matted with blood, and he looked terrible, but his face held a broad grin. The others took up the cheer.

"Welcome back," Kristan yelled. Thomas was sitting up now, looking around bleary-eyed. "I would heal you, but I used it all on this lout here."

"I saw you fall into the troll army. How did you manage to get out?" Chip asked in amazement.

"I broke my arm when a troll hit Furiosa in the elbow with a mace. I tried to fly away, but it didn't work with a broken wing. The soldiers tried to get me when I landed, but I turned into a bug for a while, which eased the pain somewhat. Bugs still feel pain, you know. I waited for them to lose interest then shifted into a regular troll, walked up to a Yellow Level troll mage, and asked him to heal my arm. He did, and then I punched him in the face and flew here as a sparrow. I couldn't land because of the shield, but then I guess you ran out of Power, so I thought I'd drop in." He smiled.

"Well done, lad." Xander called from the right. The wizard looked tired, but he sat straight.

"Can you try to heal Sheldor?" Chip asked. "I think we are all out of Power."

"Already done," Eleanor called from the back. "He will make it."

"So where are we going?" Ethrang asked. "I'm a little weak, but I could scout ahead a bit to find a path."

"That would be splendid," the wizard said.

"Wait," Mary said, pulling up beside Redmane. She reached out and touched Ethrang's head, healing his wounds. The blond boy blushed, causing the twins to chuckle. Mary gave them a scathing look, then returned to ride alongside the queen.

"Uh, thanks," Ethrang said then shot into the air as a Giant Eagle and soared northeast through the narrow pass.

They rode at a dizzying pace to create distance between themselves and the trolls, but the terrain and darkness forced the unicorns to slow down. Before they followed the mountain's curve, Chip took one last look at the meadow behind him and saw lights far in the distance merging together to give chase. The armies had joined in pursuit. They would not give up. The companions wouldn't be safe until they left the Stone Kingdom.

Ethrang arrived a while later, landing gracefully on the back of Redmane. The horse didn't seem to mind. Chip almost jumped out of his skin again, but he didn't mind either. He was happy the boy was alive. Xander and Garth leaned over to hear.

"It is hard to see even with my eagle eyes, but this trail becomes less travelled as you head northeast and gets rocky and jagged. There is no way to the west until you pass this mountain range on the left. For now, you must follow the trail northeast. You have put a good distance between yourselves and the trolls, but we need more before we stop and rest. Up ahead is a valley, followed by another meadow. I recommend you gallop at unicorn speed through them." He grinned. "I might catnap on your back Guardian. Being Furiosa takes a surprising amount of energy."

"No problem. How did you touch her live body to be able to shapeshift into her form? She was burnt to a crisp," Chip asked.

"I got there in time. She was still alive when I touched her foot. Then it stopped twitching. Female trolls are tough." Ethrang yawned. "So where are the Light Elves? I assume you found the answer in that last book."

The others gathered closer as they rode, and soon everyone was looking at him with bated breath.

"Um, well, you see… I didn't find out exactly where they are yet." Their faces dropped. Xander stared at him in disbelief, and Garth arched an eyebrow. "But I now know how to find them," he finished quickly. Their faces perked up. The twins nodded to each other as if there was no doubt.

"Ahem," Xander waited. Chip gave him a blank look. "My goodness boy how do we find them?"

"Oh, that's easy." Chip waved. "We only have to walk through a forest which leads to a cave and then retrieve the Seeing Stone. That will take us right to them." The wizard looked at him as if he had three heads. Ethrang stifled a laugh in Chip's cloak. Even the twins were waiting for him to elaborate.

"Oh, alright. I will tell you the whole story." Chip recounted the tale of the elf fleeing from the trolls in the ice desert. When he said Morgeth's name, Xander's eyes narrowed. "An older woman told the elf it was a Seeing Stone that could show you what someone was doing if you spoke their name and take you to them if you pick it up. So there you have it. All we have to do is grab the Seeing Stone and find King Luminor," Chip finished. The others nodded, but Xander's face was stark white.

"Dear Creator," the wizard breathed. "You speak of Darkwood and the Secret Caves." The old man exhaled, eyes blinking in disbelief.

"Sounds pretty easy," Ethrang commented. "Then again, I have heard tales of Darkwood. People use it to scare children."

"It's worse than any nightmare," the wizard warned. "No one has made it through in three thousand years. Many have tried but never returned. The witches came to Banfar after the barrier to herald the return of the Demon King. My brother drove them out but allowed Morgeth to live in exchange for a powerful staff. It was always rumoured they came from the Darkwood area. The witches follow a book named The Book of Seeing, and it sounds like its origins are long before the Breaking or the rise of the Demon King. Millennia ago, several powerful magic wielders made it through Darkwood. My father was one of them. This was before he united the humans. He writes of a cave system in a meadow surrounded by a deadly forest. Arkan found the caves empty but spoke of a powerful magic residue. He coined the place 'The Secret Caves.' When my brother drove Morgeth out of Banfar over a millennia later, she claimed the title 'High Witch of the Secret Caves.' He put no stock in it at the time, thinking her a harmless but beautiful zealot, but now it makes sense. Since that time, Darkwood has become much more dangerous. Terrible things have spawned in there over the millennia. We will talk more about this later."

They arrived at the dark valley that Ethrang had spied from the air. Chip urged Redmane to increase his speed over the open ground, and the horse responded. They rode low over their mounts as the cold wind whistled by. The stone mountains stood on either side like black specters, funnelling them down a dark corridor lit faintly by the bright stars above. There was an eeriness to the landscape that began to permeate his senses. It was a cold, harsh land. He remembered King Jaggar's description of some of the nasty creatures inhabiting these mountains that ended up as so-called delicacies on his dinner plate. Chip shuddered, and a weariness enveloped him.

They could not speak anymore due to their speed and wind noise, so he focused on the land ahead. He felt a small thud on his back, which was Ethrang's head, as the boy nodded off. He pressed his elbows around the orphan's arms, which were clasped around his waist so he wouldn't fall off. He marvelled that someone could fall asleep riding at full speed on a unicorn, but then the rhythmic hum of the hooves started making his eyelids go heavy. Chip shook his head to refocus.

Things had looked so promising when they made a pact with the Troll King in the council room. He should have realized it was too easy. Trolls and men had been fighting for a thousand years. Jaggar's hatred of Balor and Luminor had never died. If anything, it had festered and strengthened over the millennia. Now, the entire troll nation was after them, and they were headed in the wrong direction.

The boy sighed. Again, things looked impossible, but there was always hope. The man with the silver hair said he was not strong enough to fight the forces of darkness by himself, but he was not alone. He took solace in knowing that his companions were still with him. He glanced back, making a count of who had made it out. Nine Protectors, including Garth and Chase remained, many double mounted with the surviving troll prisoners. Striker rode the last unicorn in the back, his massive form silhouetted between the dark mountains. Chip couldn't imagine the troll's trials under his father's reign. Yet instead of folding, he persevered and became stronger. He was a valuable asset in their fight. The boy made a prayer to the Creator for the fallen then hardened himself for the road ahead.

They reached the edge of the meadow and slowed.

"Let's continue riding for a few more hours then set a watch and grab some shut-eye," Xander said. "The trolls are fast runners and will continue coming. We need a good buffer between us and them. Follow this trail northeast towards the end of this mountain range. Keep your eyes open. I have been to Rathgar before and have some knowledge of the mountains. They are dangerous."

Chip nodded and urged Redmane down a narrow trail leading north. The route was rocky and twisted, slowing the unicorns. Even so, they were nimble and graceful, finding footing despite the conditions. For several hours, they progressed until the wizard pulled up beside him. "If you see a cave, rocky overhang, or anything that might protect us from the wind, let's stop and rest."

Chip agreed, thankful that he would have a chance to sleep. He was tired to the bone after days of staying up late trying to find the missing Light Elves to the chase and battle that followed. The barren, windswept slopes on either side seemed to provide no reprieve from the steady wind, but then he spied a cleft in the rock ahead.

The boy signalled the wizard. Xander nodded, and they turned the unicorns towards the opening. It turned out to be more of a large double-sided overhang, but it was enough to provide them with a respite from the bitter wind. Everyone except Chase and Garth seemed drained from the ordeal. They still had some belongings in the packs left on the unicorns and pulled out whatever clothes and blankets they could find, spreading them around. The horses went to graze on the meagre bushes.

Ethrang did not wake up, so Chip hailed Bulch. "Can you put him over there on that blanket?" The giant Protector nodded, picked the orphan up as if he were a piece of clothing, and set him down gently. The skinny boy groaned once and started snoring.

"Should I make a small fire?" Thomas asked with a hopeful look. The blond twin shivered under his cloak.

"No," Garth replied. "The light and smoke would draw them to our exact location. The Protectors will set a rotating watch. Share a blanket if you need to." Everyone nodded, saying little. Eleanor nestled up to Chip, and he wrapped her in his blanket, then lent hers to Striker.

"Don't need it," the big troll said, grinning. "Our bark-like skin keeps us warm. Further north is a different story. Give it to him." He pointed at Thomas, who accepted it with gratitude. Everyone settled in, huddled together at the back of the cleft. Eleanore rested her head on Chip's shoulder, snuggling close. The boy finally relaxed as a soothing warmth overtook him. He could see the silhouette of the Protector taking watch at the entrance to the overhang. By his hulking form, he recognized Sheldor, happy that the man had survived his injuries.

He looked up at the stars, finding beauty in the darkness. The sound of the incessant wind pulled his thoughts apart, and he drifted off, finally able to let go.

"They're here!"

Chip opened his eyes, heart racing. Dawn was breaking. An explosion sounded to their right, and a shower of rocks fell into the cleft. He frantically broke through his Wall and felt relief that some Power had returned.

"Grab your weapons and belongings. They snuck up behind a rocky outcropping," Carvor yelled. Another explosion sounded, and several massive rocks fell from the mountain above them. Chip reached up and sent his Power out, stopping their fall. The top of a large boulder ruffled Chase's hair.

"That was close, thanks." His best friend pulled his sword out and ran to the cleft entrance. Chip flung the stones sideways around the cleft and heard several bellows of pain.

Several trolls had arrived, and the clang of weapons rang out. The other Protectors formed a ring at the front.

"Summon the unicorns!" Xander yelled. Chip was already sending his presence out. He found Redmane nearby to the north. The majestic horse was already on his way, leading the herd.

Chip shouted to the former troll prisoners. "Load the horses while we hold them off." They grunted in agreement and began picking up the blankets and other items. The boy ran to the front with the other wizards. Ethrang leapt into the air, morphing into a sparrow, and sped around the corner. More trolls spilled into the cleft entrance. Chip arrived to see several mages about to unleash more magic. Some looked young, so he summoned a cushion of air and flung it at them, slamming the troll mages backwards into the soldiers, where they crumpled to the ground.

The trail had narrowed so that only six abreast could come simultaneously. As far as the eyes could see, the entire trail was filled with columns of trolls. Interspersed throughout were mages with eyes blazing. The Protectors, led by Garth and Chase, were engaging the ones in front, slicing and hacking them to pieces. The ones behind snarled and gnashed their teeth, pushing their comrades forward, eager to enter the fray. Their movement was forcing the Protectors to retreat by sheer force of numbers. The unicorns arrived, and the troll prisoners ran to load them up. They needed more time.

"Let's return the favour, Guardian," Kristan said, his eyes shining a wicked blue. The blond twin unleashed a thick stream of blue fire straight into the mountain behind the front lines. There was an immense crack as an entire rock sheet slid down the slope, crushing at least fifty trolls.

"I could have helped," Thomas said.

"That was for what they did to you," Kristan replied, eyes blazing.

There remained a couple dozen trolls trapped on their side who fought savagely, grinning even as they died. Ethrang appeared out of thin air as the demon wasp, raking his claws across several necks. Striker was there to help, dagger and axe whirring in his hands.

"Let's finish them," Mary said, wrinkling her nose at the smell. She raised her hands.

"No," Xander instructed. "We must save our magic. You never know when you will need it." The Blue Wing Leader nodded.

With the rest of the army blocked by the landslide, the Protectors became dealers of death to the remaining trolls. Garth, Chase, and Striker took half out by themselves. The rest of them were cut down in short order. As they turned to leave, a loud explosion sounded, and the landslide began to shift.

"They are breaking through with their magic," the wizard warned. "Mount up."

They all ran to the unicorns as more explosions sounded. The trolls would not take long to get through. The companions leapt onto their horses, and Redmane took off without a prompt. Ethrang sat behind Chase. Chip led the way as the path narrowed and the mountains closed in, becoming rocky and uneven. Despite their unmatched speed on open ground, the loose rock hamstrung the unicorns. Redmane sensed the urgency, taking risks to increase his speed.

A short while later the red unicorn slipped on a small, loose stone and his leg sank into a hole, getting wedged tight. His forward momentum caused his leg to break in two and he went down. Chip landed hard in front of the screaming animal, somersaulting onto his back. The boy scrambled up and seized his magic, pushing the rocks apart around Redmane's broken leg and then setting the animal down gently. The other unicorns neighed shrilly, likely sharing his pain through the bond. A loud crash erupted behind them and then the sound of running feet increased.

"They are coming," Xander said grimly.

Chip sent his magic into the injured animal, pulling the bones back together and fusing them even stronger than before. One of its tendons had snapped in half and he reattached it. The sounds of stomping feet became louder.

"Uh, you might want to hurry up," Chase said, offering a weak smile.

"Done," Chip grimaced, absorbing the poor animal's pain. He leapt back onto the red unicorn as shouts rang out behind them. Despite the danger, Redmane continued maintaining a solid pace, doing his best. The trail got even worse up ahead, and the shouts sounded closer. Chip sensed magic, and a ball of green fire suddenly shot towards them from a mass of dark figures in the distance.

"I got it," Mary yelled, forming a blue shield behind the last troll prisoner who brought up the rear, absorbing the ball. The troll nodded thanks, thumping his chest as a sign of respect. Mary looked taken aback for a moment, then turned around.

"You won't like what's up ahead." Kristan pointed. The mountains narrowed further to form tall cliffs on either side. The trail turned into uneven stepping stones, causing further difficulty for the horses.

They entered the gap and were immediately forced to go single-file. Darkness surrounded them, further reducing their speed. A small vertical opening one hundred feet above provided scant light. Xander shot a glowing ball ahead of them so the struggling animals could see. Even so, the footing was treacherous. Chip knew trolls ran full speed and that these obstacles would not impede them nearly as much.

A vicious ice-cold wind assaulted the group as it whistled through the gap. Shouts rang out behind them, much closer now. Chip held on tight as the horse bobbed to make progress. He could not see an opening to the other side. For a frightening moment, he realized the cliffs might wedge them in entirely until the walls touched their sides. A feeling of claustrophobia swept over him as he relived the Dim reaching for his ankle in Cave Mountain. His anxiety began peaking as the walls began to narrow up ahead. The trolls had almost caught up to them. He could hear their war cries as they drew weapons. The boy's mind raced to quell his anxiety, and then the weapons master's voice rang through, "Bring it on. Kill me. Do your worst." He repeated the phrases over and over, and then his anxiety, which was really a fear of death or pain, decreased as he accepted the end, even encouraged it. His heart rate slowed, and he moved forward, able to think again. Then his worst fears actually materialized.

Up ahead was a wall.

The two cliffs ran straight into it. They were in a dead-end tunnel.

"That's no good," Ethrang muttered behind Chase.

"They are here," shouted a troll prisoner from the back. The wizards at the front tried to use their magic, but everyone was in the way. "Somebody help—" He never finished his sentence. Chip raised his head to see the troll pulled off his horse by multiple hands, and then his unicorn went down too.

"Ethrang," Chip yelled. "Do something!"

The blond boy leapt into the air and spun around as a small falcon. Beating his wings, the shapeshifter hovered and shot green fire into the trolls behind them. Bellows of pain erupted but the sounds of pursuit did not diminish. Chip gritted his teeth at the dying screams of the unicorn. He felt Redmane's pain through the bond.

"Here, link with me and use my Power," Chip shouted. "Blast them to oblivion."

A moment later, the falcon shot two thick cords of red-green Power out of its claws, arcing over them to smash into the oncoming trolls. Chip raised his head to see a red ribbon of destruction course through the two cliffs behind them as bodies exploded in showers of blood or burst into flames. For a moment, a blast of heat reached them from the aftermath, and then there was dead silence. He peeked again to see a long line of gore and fire stretching as far as he could see. Then a mournful ice-cold wind returned.

A thought suddenly struck him. *Where was the wind coming from?*

Ethrang abruptly appeared behind Chase. "Now that's what I call Power!"

"Shhh," Chip said. "The wind must be coming from somewhere."

He urged Redmane forward to the stone wall in front of them and gasped. The tunnel continued to the right. The opening couldn't be seen from farther back.

"There's an opening," he called to the others. Sheldor, now at the very back, let out an explosive sigh. Chip could not blame him. He turned Redmane to the right, and the gap continued a short way before turning left again. From there, he could see a faint vertical line of light ahead of them.

There was a way out. He smiled, saying a silent prayer to the Creator, and urged the unicorn through. The steps were uneven and filled with holes, but Xander's light provided guidance. They still could not hear sounds of pursuit. He imagined it would take a while to remove all the bodies. A pang of sadness filled him at the thought of losing another unicorn, and he patted Redmane's neck in sympathy. The beautiful horse bowed his head once, white horn dipping to the ground.

Finally, they exited the narrow cliffs, and a white world greeted them.

A blanket of snow covered everything, and the wind was more pronounced. The mountain ranges on both sides had sheer rock walls with snow caps. At least the range on the left ended farther ahead. That was where they needed to be to head west towards Rathgar.

"This is not good," Chase stated the obvious.

"The unicorns cannot even see the trail, and it will be slippery." Chip clenched his jaw. "Wait." He seized his Power and shot a thin stream of red fire, melting the snow. He continued until his Power strained, but the path was clear for a good league. "Let's go."

They followed the uneven trail for a while, and then Eleanor called out, "This will take too long at this pace. We need to slow them down further."

She moved away from the group and turned her mount in a circle. Her unicorn faced the gap between the two cliffs. Taking a deep breath, Eleanor's eyes blazed a rich brown with flecks of red. The Queen of Vanalon released her magic in arcing swipes, slicing massive shards of rock off the sides of the cliff. They slowly slid down then plummeted to the bottom of the gap, blocking it. She had a dissatisfied look and then lifted her hands again. No fire came out this time, but the rocks on both sides of the cliff began to shake and rumble. As the noise quieted, she shot small bursts of brownish-red fire into the walls. Everyone watched as the stone on both sides began to crumble inwards. She had destabilized the rocks and now only needed to nudge them. Then a deep rumble sounded as the cliffs caved in on each other with the sound of a thunderclap. The gap was completely gone.

Satisfied, the queen turned around. Everyone was staring at her with mouths agape.

"That should do it." Kristan nodded to his brother.

"Wish I could do that," Thomas mused.

"Oh, it wasn't that hard. You must be one with the rock and..." She looked at their confused faces. "Um, never mind. I guess being a Brown has its advantages."

"Especially if you have red in it," Chase quipped. She turned her nose up at him and moved beside Mary. They immediately started whispering.

Xander smiled. "My goodness, that should buy us some time. Alright, lead the way, lad."

Chip urged Redmane forward. They took turns clearing the snow so the animals could pick their footing, but it was tedious. He thought they would reach the end of the range on the left by nightfall, but they were still a ways away. Ethrang had taken a quick scouting trip by air saying there was a monstrous meadow at the end of the range with a clear passage west. On the right up ahead was the only grove of trees for leagues. He could not find any caves or rocky overhangs, so they decided to camp in the thicket. The sun was beginning to set, and the air grew noticeably colder. The north wind was a constant annoyance. More than anything, they were hungry. Earlier in the day, they had eaten some salted meat and mouldy cheese left in one of the packs, but it was gone in moments.

"I have not seen a single animal," Chase commented. "How does anything survive out here?"

Garth pointed to rabbit tracks in the snow on the other side of the trees. "You have to know where to look." Chase grinned sheepishly.

"I can send my presence out in a small radius and see what I find," Thomas offered. The weapons master nodded for him to proceed. It took some searching, but in the end the twins found two rabbits in a hole under the snow, pulling them out with their Power. Garth skinned them while the other Protectors built a fire using fallen branches. As the sun set, they ate roasted rabbit, which didn't amount to much given the number or people, but Chip savoured each tiny morsel. At least it appeased his hunger for the time being. Lacking water, they ate the snow around them, letting it melt in their mouths.

"A wizard did a study on this once, and for the time being, it will give us liquid, but the energy used to stuff it in our mouths and melt it is more than the tiny bit of water it releases. So eventually it will dehydrate us." Ethrang gave him a doubtful look then shrugged and ate some more.

They talked a little about better days and said prayers to the

Creator for those who fell. Nine Protectors and an equal number of troll prisoners remained. The temperature continued to drop, so they piled more branches on the fire. Secrecy was not a concern since the trolls would find them with or without a fire. It was more important to stay warm and get rest. Chip had a feeling the days ahead would not be pleasant. They were going further into inhospitable land without food, water, or proper clothing. He knew the unicorns were not suited to such a climate, but their magic would sustain them up to a point. He could already sense their energy flagging as the temperature plummeted. They had rooted up hardy bushes beneath the snow to eat, but they were truly at home in temperate grasslands and forests. The herd stayed close to the trees, using it as a shield against the wind. They settled down beside one another to keep warm.

The snow around the fire had melted away, so everyone set down their cloaks and covered themselves with blankets. Many had to share. The Protectors insisted on taking watch, claiming it was their duty. No one argued. Eleanor snuggled close, and Chip put his arm around her, feeling comforted. The heat of the fire soothed him, and his mind drifted back to when he was a young boy sitting on Auntie Clare's lap, listening to her soft voice as she read him a story in front of a crackling fire. He fell asleep with a smile.

A ROAR SHATTERED the night's silence. Chip opened his eyes to see a hand covered in white fur yank Eleanor away from him. She screamed as it dragged her. The snow was falling so thick he was having trouble seeing. He leapt up with eyes blazing and threw balls of red light into the thicket of trees. What he saw chilled him to the bone. Huge white apes were dragging the women away and beating sleeping bodies with their massive fists. More roars sounded. Chip needed no more fuel for his rage. He blasted the ones closest to him with bursts of red-hot magic, setting them on fire. They roared in pain and went running into the snow. He looked around for Eleanor and Mary, but they were gone. Screaming her name, Chip ran into the swirling snow.

A massive body charged into him with devastating speed. He put up a red shield, but the impact sent him hurtling back into the trees. He broke several branches before landing hard against a trunk. White spots flashed in his head, and his magic wavered. His ribs felt caved in. A monstrous white ape roared in his face with foot-long fangs. It beat its chest, then lifted both hands to end his life.

A massive human jumped in its way, taking both hammer fists to his shoulders. It was Bulch. He sank to his knees as both his collar bones cracked from the impact. The ape lifted its arms again, and somehow the huge Protector jumped to his feet and kicked the beast in its stomach. The ape staggered backwards for a moment then beat its chest twice before delivering a roundhouse hook to the side of Bulch's head. The big man toppled sideways, unconscious. It roared again and ran on all fours at Chip, who now was ready.

And his rage knew no bounds.

Eleanor had been taken from him. He would have his retribution. He stood up and formed a massive red shield, infusing his body with Power, rooting him to the ground. The ape slammed into him with unbelievable savagery, but he didn't move. Instead, its body melted onto him. He grabbed its neck and twisted, sending magic to strengthen his hand. Its neck broke instantly, and he burned it to ash. His fury became uncontrollable, and then something snapped in his mind, a hidden reservoir of Power that had been inaccessible.

The boy filled himself with more magic and screamed in frustration. He managed to barely regain a semblance of control, Chip sent his presence out, searching for the queen. A blue flash of light appeared in the distance, and he recognized it as Mary. He sped towards the light with unnatural speed, using his magic to propel him. Ropes of red fire coursed around his body. He vaguely remembered someone else who looked like that.

All thoughts vanished as he came upon the Blue Wing Leader being thumped by three snow apes at the same time. She was trying to maintain a blue shield, but the hammer fists were starting to get through. He seized them all with one immense red hand and squeezed. Their ribcages and limbs broke into a bloody mess, and he tossed the crumpled bodies aside. Chip saw the unicorns standing in a circle, fending off the apes with hoofs and horns.

"Where is she?" he demanded. His voice sounded off, deeper than usual.

Mary weakly pointed to the slope of the nearest mountain. He ran through the snow, a red blur streaking across a white carpet. He saw a flurry of movement and arrived to find the queen lying unconscious, blood running from her ear. Four apes surrounded her, each holding one of her limbs. They were going to tear her apart and eat her. Afraid to strike Eleanor with his magic, he froze them in place with his Power, surrounding them with condensed air. Chip walked up, his concern for her reducing his rage. He ended their lives by shooting a red line of fire into each of their hearts. He released the condensed air and pushed them all away to fall on their backs, eyes staring vacantly at the swirling snowflakes.

Chip knelt quickly and sent the shield around her. He cradled Eleanor's head, feeling a large lump behind her right ear. "No, no, no," he whispered. Flashes of her lying dead in his arms in the Brown Wing of the Wizard's Guild shot through his mind. He sent his magic into her, assessing the damage. She was barely breathing. He saw that her skull had fractured, causing her brain to swell. Chip felt relief flood him, knowing he could heal her. He started to send his magic out, but something was wrong with him. Blood leaked out of his mouth, and his vision blurred.

He suddenly realized he was the one dying.

The Wall in his mind appeared and disappeared. He was losing his grip on the Power. He knew he could save her but couldn't focus his magic. Chip looked down to see one of his ribs sticking out. His thoughts began to jumble, and his heart felt funny.

It wasn't supposed to end like this.

12

"It is the risk of having Power, and no human has ever had Power like him," Xander was saying.

"He was not himself. His voice even changed," Mary added.

"He was a force of nature. He took out eight of them in the blink of an eye," Ethrang said in awe. "Look, he's waking up."

Chip opened his eyes. Everyone was gathered around him. A flood of memories rushed by. "Eleanor! Is she..."

"I'm right here," the queen said, bending over him, her eyes full of concern. He realized his head was in her lap.

He breathed a sigh of relief. His right side still hurt, and he felt it to see if his rib stuck out.

"Don't worry, we healed you. Mostly. None of us are Yellows. It took all of us. You were right on the verge..." Kristan patted his shoulder.

"Glad you're back," Thomas added.

Xander stepped forward. "Do you remember what happened?"

Chip sat up, ignoring the dull pain in his side. "I was trying to find Eleanor. This ape attacked me, and then Bulch... Is he alright?"

"Bulch good," the big man said, stepping into his view with a smile. "They heal me."

"Thank you. I didn't think you could survive a right hook from a snow ape." Chip grinned.

"I have hard head."

The boy continued, "After Bulch held the ape off me, I could stand, and then a rage enveloped me, and I had trouble thinking anymore. I only wanted to find Eleanor. My Power...expanded. It has done that before, but this time it felt different, as if it was controlling me. My only thought was to find her, and the longer it took, the more my rage increased. Does that make sense?"

"It makes perfect sense," the wizard said. "You are not the first to lose control of the Power. Some people even remove their Wall, and we know what happens to them." He studied the boy. "You have been able to control your magic admirably so far. Today, it got the best of you. You must understand the gift you have is a double-edged sword. Anger is what breaks through our Wall. The problem is that it is a negative emotion. Only through calmness can we think clearly. The paradox is that you must maintain your anger to use Power. Yet, if you don't learn to control it, magic can consume you. It can control you just like the negative emotion of anger can make people do bad things. Nobody has ever had Power like yours, Chip. Today, your magic increased, and you couldn't control it, due to unfettered rage. You have also repeatedly used magic for the last two days on little food and sleep. Not to mention watching someone you love dearly being dragged away. You only reduced your anger when you found her and felt a positive emotion again. I am starting to see why it is so vital she lives, why the powers that be let her live. Eleanor keeps you rooted and calm. She brings out your positive emotions like love, kindness, and sympathy. She is a balance to the rage."

Chip nodded. "I understand. I will work on controlling my Power. Calmness is mastery."

"There is something else," Striker said, stepping forward. The muscular troll looked around. Dawn had arrived. "I am familiar with these mountains, though few tread this far northeast. Those apes never hunt in packs. They are solitary. The snow ape waits until a winter storm hits and then attacks, usually at night. We will occasionally find a troll's remains the next day, if at all. They particularly like females. Tonight proved that again. Maybe the meat is softer. I do not know. What I do know is that a pack of twenty is unheard of. We killed sixteen of them, and the rest ran off. I believe somebody sent them or had control over them. How, I know not."

Xander's eyes narrowed. "Do you know anyone with the power to control animals?"

Striker nodded. "There are rumours. Only one troll, who prefers to be a man, may have that power."

"Barko," Chip said.

"Yes." Striker looked surprised that the boy knew the name. "But why is he trying to hunt you?"

"Good question," Xander said. "I wish we had the time to find the answers. Barko has a lot to be accountable for. He has shaped the history of the world. He made Morgo and the Creator knows who else."

"Why don't we pay him a visit and ask him?" Ethrang asked with a mischievous grin.

Striker looked at the skinny blond boy. "There are predators in these mountains that could snap you in half or drink all the blood out of your body. Yet nothing is more dangerous than Barko."

Xander nodded. "We are also going the other way to find the Light Elves. One day, he will answer for his crimes."

"Did we lose anyone?" Chip asked, afraid to hear the answer.

Striker glanced at him, and his face softened. "Protector Jansen on watch lost his life. Another troll prisoner perished as well. The rest of us suffered some form of injury. A single snow ape can wreak havoc. To fight twenty and live is a story on its own."

"Weapons Master, I see movement." Carvor pointed south. They had a long view of the trail in the morning light, showing a black speck moving towards them. The trolls had broken through.

"Let's go," Garth ordered. "Everyone mount up." They picked up their belongings and approached the unicorns, who were huddled to the side.

Chip walked up to Redmane and patted his neck. He sent his

presence into the horse's mind, seeing the fear still there from the night's event. Interestingly, the unicorns displayed concern for him, not only themselves. They felt he was part of the bond. He hugged the magnificent animal. "Thank you for everything." Redmane let out a melodic neigh in response.

They mounted and continued down the trail. The snow had stopped, but the path was even more obscured, forcing them to use their magic to clear the way. It did not require a lot of Power, but they were still drained from the night's events. For the first time, Chip felt an apprehension about using his magic. His last use of it made him feel invincible. His fury was such that he ignored a nearly mortal wound. The boy vowed to control his rage so he could make proper decisions. Perhaps that was one of the darknesses that little Han said he would face. Chip sighed. He would know soon enough.

They continued at the fastest pace they could for the rest of the morning. The black speck behind them had grown to a large dark blob that extended back as far as the eye could see. Chip knew they were running out of time. If they could reach the vast meadow before the trolls caught up, they could speed away and lose their pursuers for good. He looked to his left as they passed the last mountain before the range ended. They were almost there.

Dark clouds were amassing in the north and west, seeming to converge on their spot. The wind began to pick up in strength, a harbinger of the storm to come. He felt more hunger pangs and still felt weary, but he could do nothing about it. Chip pushed the thoughts out of his head. Worrying about something that was beyond his control was foolish. He focused on the task ahead.

The mountains finally opened, and a vast round meadow emerged. The path completely levelled out with no more stones, only dirt. It was flat all the way across. They did not need to clear the snow anymore. He looked behind him to see the trolls much closer, running full speed towards them. The sounds of war cries reached their ears. He urged Redmane forward and the horse increased his speed to a full gallop. The dark clouds had moved closer, and a wicked wind whistled across the empty space. Chip didn't care. They had made it. A sense of wildness imbued him as he bonded with the horse, and his spirits lifted. He rode low over Redmane's neck, the wind whipping through his hair. The last hill disappeared on the left, and he turned the unicorn to follow the curve to freedom, eyes taking in the beautiful vista. Chip's breath caught in his throat.

A massive troll army filled the western part of the meadow.

He stared in disbelief. Redmane slowed down and whinnied in fear. This army was at least as large as the combined forces behind them. The others pulled up, everyone digesting the implications.

They were trapped.

"How many of them are there?" Ethrang asked, for once looking afraid.

Striker moved his mount forward. "All of them."

"What do you mean?" the blond boy looked over.

"There are about five thousand trolls in front of us. The rest of the Rathgaran army. Behind us, the two joined armies form another five thousand. My father is taking no chances." His face grew grim.

Chip felt his anger surge. They had been so close to freedom. He remembered his lessons and sought the Calm, but his eyes smouldered.

Xander cursed. Ethrang's eyes widened. The epithet caused even the weapons master to glance over.

"I have to admit we may be outnumbered," Chase commented. The others stared at him. He cleared his throat awkwardly.

"How did they get here so fast?" Chip asked.

"Mountain hawk," Striker replied. "They sent a message as soon as we escaped north. The main troll army resides in Rathgar, and they immediately marched east to intercept us. If they had arrived any sooner, we would have been sandwiched back there between the mountains with no chance of escape. There is always a positive to any negative." Garth looked over, nodding in agreement.

Chip sighed. "Always another challenge. No one said it would be easy. Very well, what do we do now?"

War cries erupted from both armies as they charged.

Striker looked at the group. "We run. East is our only option. I know a trail leading into the mountains, but you won't like where it leads."

"Uh, we may want to hurry up," Chase said, pointing. "They have a lot of mages. Bits of colour had lit up in the main army as the troll magic wielders seized their Power."

Chip turned Redmane and gave him a gentle nudge. The unicorn shot forward, streaking across the meadow heading east. He slowed to allow Striker to catch up, indicating the troll should lead the way to the trail. The Troll Prince acknowledged the gesture and veered slightly left towards a small cleft in the eastern mountains.

"Look out!" Kristan shouted.

Several massive fireballs were whizzing in their direction. They were multicoloured, indicating the mages had linked.

Everyone seized their Power, but the fireballs arced over them or to the sides.

"They don't have very good aim," Chase laughed.

Chip watched as the great balls of roiling energy struck the meadow to the front and sides. Suddenly, great holes appeared before them, and plumes of water and ice exploded skyward.

"It's not a meadow—it's a lake!" screamed Ethrang.

The unicorns skidded to a halt as open areas of water appeared around them. Striker was able to maneuver between two holes and escape to the other side, but Redmane slid on a tilting ice sheet straight into the water.

They both went fully under, and Chip experienced an ice cold like no other. He almost involuntarily tried to suck in air but knew it would be instant death. His hold on the Power disappeared as fear and shock swept over him. For an eternal moment, he was paralyzed. The boy floated in a dark world of ice and death, forcing himself not to breathe with all his strength. He had never experienced such cold.

Yet he had. He alone had experienced the coldness of Death.

And he had not given up.

Nor would he now. The boy forced his muscles to work and kicked with Redmane. His head finally reached the surface, but he hit something hard.

It was ice!

The lake current had carried them past the hole, and now they were trapped under a thick sheet of ice. A wave of fear such as he had never known struck him and his lungs burned. He needed to break his Wall. He needed his magic. He opened his eyes to see a white immovable wall of ice above him. Redmane was kicking frantically. If he died, all the unicorns would die. Chip had never felt so scared. For once, he needed to find his rage. For once, it would be useful and necessary. He needed to find something that would break through his immobilizing fear. He was about to die.

Eleanor.

She is in danger.

The image of her dying ignited his rage. The Guardian broke through his fear, broke through his Wall, and filled himself with a tidal wave of Power.

Chip reached up and sent red fire in a wide circle, liquifying the ice and heating the water around him. His head broke the surface, and he sucked in life-giving air. He raised the struggling unicorn out of the water, levitating him to solid ice. The boy turned around, red eyes blazing, treading warm water. He surveyed the scene, using as much calm as he could muster to soothe his rage. Three other unicorns and riders were flailing in the water. He reached out and pulled them into the air, sending warmth and heat into their bodies. He carried them to solid ice. More fireballs were coming, and he swept his hand sideways, knocking them far off course.

"Kristan is under the water!" Thomas screamed behind him.

Chip sent his presence down and located the body of the blond twin and his unicorn. The horse was already dead, but Kristan's heart held a faint beat. And then it stopped.

He reached down with his Power and pulled his frozen body from the bottom. The boy paused and decided to pull the dead unicorn up as well. He believed there was always a chance. Lifting their cold bodies out of the water, he infused them with heat then pulled the icy water out of their lungs. Chip sent his magic into their chests and restarted their hearts. One of the tests in the Guild was to restart a pig's heart. He was well-versed in the real thing.

Kristan suddenly gasped for air, breathing in short, rapid breaths. Incredibly, the unicorn breathed in life and opened its eyes. The coldness of the water had preserved it. There was always hope.

He set them down to the side then swatted a new series of fireballs out of the way. Deflecting their magic required much less energy than absorbing them. He was tiring though. The water began to drop in temperature.

"Uh, can someone pull me out?" he called.

"My goodness, I never thought you would ask." Chip felt blue Power surround him as Xander pulled him up and out, drying his clothes at the same time. The boy landed on his feet and looked around. Everyone was staring at him with a mixture of awe and respect. The unicorns took a knee.

"Thank you," Kristan and Thomas said together, their eyes wet.

Chip waved it off. "You aren't getting off that easy. We have more work to do." He gripped Kristan's shoulder then turned to the trolls charging across the lake from both sides. "We need to move."

"Guardian," Striker said, pointing to the east. The troll had never called him that before. "The trail goes straight up. The unicorns cannot come."

Chip turned to look at Redmane, his heart quickening. He sent his presence into the unicorn's mind. The horse already understood. "Remove all the packs." Everyone took all their meagre belongings off the animals. "Go now," he said out loud, sending the horse images. "We will shield you as best we can. Cut through them and run free. Thank you."

All the unicorns neighed and reared on their hind legs in homage. Then they dashed off, Redmane leading the way. The horses skirted the open water, running on the side of the lake where there was dirt, forming a spearhead. The others watched in amazement as the unicorns became a blur of speed and power. Chip felt a hum as their magic formed a natural shield around them.

"Link with me," he commanded, eyes focused on the herd. The

mages in the troll army were already turning to the animals, eyes blazing. Everyone linked without question.

The Guardian combined his Power with theirs and threw his magic out to strengthen the shield around the unicorns. Fireballs erupted from the mages, streaking towards the herd. The army spread out to block them. This time, the magic was aimed directly at the horses since they ran on shore instead of the ice.

The fireballs struck the shield repeatedly. Chip gritted his teeth as the distance increased. A wall of trolls had gathered on the shore, trying to block their escape.

Redmane reached them without slowing.

Even from this distance, Chip watched as the unicorns ploughed through the army as if they were paper. Trolls flew into the air as the wedge separated them. Just as it looked like they would make it through, a flash of blue erupted, and the weakening shield failed at the back. A unicorn went down, and the trolls swarmed over it with their gleaming fangs. A ripple passed through the herd, but they continued, finally breaking through to the other side. Chip withdrew their combined Power, unable to assist anymore, but he knew they were safe through the bond. Seventeen had made it to the other side.

The unicorns were running free.

The trolls turned back to the fleeing humans, breaking into a full charge.

"We must go," Striker urged.

They all ran into the cleft and began ascending a steep trail. Snow covered everything, but they picked their way up the rocky steps. The giant troll led the way. A few more fireballs came hurtling towards them, but Chip deflected them down into the approaching trolls, causing havoc. The companions continued climbing, pushing their weary bodies to the limit. They had no choice. It took an hour for them to crest the pass, and when they stopped on a rocky promontory to look back, the entire troll army had gathered at the base of the eastern mountains, funnelling into the cleft.

King Jaggar stood in the center go the army, wearing his stone crown. Their eyes met and the giant troll shook his fist in the air. The rest of the army noticed the gesture and raised a thunderous war cry. The sound of ten thousand trolls screaming made the boy shudder, but he lifted his chin in defiance. To his left, far behind the army, Chip noticed two figures standing stock still, watching the events unfold. One had long white hair, and the other was dressed in green. He could not make out their features. Xander noticed them too.

"Who are they?" Chip asked, still catching his breath from the climb.

"Dark Elves," Xander spat. "The Demon King's reach is long."

Even as he said it, the dark clouds covered the midday sun, dimming the world. Han's foretelling rang in his mind. A darkness was coming.

"Eleanor, do you have enough strength to slow them down?" the wizard asked, turning to the queen.

"Yes." Her eyes blazed brown, red chips glinting. Everyone stepped back. The queen pointed downwards, and a low rumble began to sound. The trolls climbing below looked around with narrowed eyes. The stones on the side of the gap began to shake. This time, they fell on their own accord as they were already loose. Great sheets of rock and boulders caved into the narrow pass, cascading down the mountain like a river made of rock. Screams erupted from below, but they extinguished as immense quantities of rubble buried the climbers. She lowered her hands.

"Yup, that should slow them down awhile," Chase noted.

"Let's make use of this reprieve," the wizard said. He turned to Jaggar's son. "Did you know that was a lake?"

"I thought everyone did." Striker spread his hands. "Who told you it was a meadow?"

All eyes turned to Ethrang. The skinny blond boy shrugged. "Looked like a meadow to me." The twins grinned.

"I thought it was a meadow too," Xander confessed. All eyes turned to him. The wizard grimaced. "My goodness, I may have come this way, but it was millennia ago. An old man can be forgiven for a lapse in memory." He cleared his throat. "Alright, lead the way."

Striker nodded, and they began descending into a narrow valley.

Jagged mountains rose all around them. They made their way across a rocky ridge in the valley's center, the only part not covered with snow. The wind picked up, whistling down the slopes. The skies looked ominous. On the other side, a faint trail appeared between two mountains. They stopped to eat more snow, barely satiating their thirst, then ascended the trail. At that moment, the dark clouds decided to release their cargo, and huge snowflakes began to settle around them. The wind steadily increased as they climbed.

"Where are we going anyway?" Chase asked the troll.

Striker didn't turn around. "This trail leads to Barko's cave."

The others stared after him.

"Looks like we will be paying him a visit after all," Chase said cheerily.

"Yes, it has been a long time coming." Xander's face hardened. "I would like to have a word with that creature."

"It would be easier if ten thousand trolls weren't chasing us, but who's counting?" Chase asked no one in particular. When no one answered, he shrugged and continued up the trail.

Chip shook his head. They ascended for the better part of the afternoon. The wind strengthened, infiltrating his clothing and numbing the boy to the bone. The snow started coming down heavier, beginning to whip sideways. At least it was at their backs. The trail narrowed and fell away on one side. Chip remembered his ordeal in Fang Pass, where he almost fell off the side of the mountain in the wind and rain. At least they didn't have horses this time. They hugged the curve of the mountain, the wind trying its best to pull them off. Everyone had their hood on, pulled tight against the elements. The rocky ledge became increasingly slippery. Sheldor fell first, his body sailing into the open chasm below. Chip broke through his Wall, seizing the flailing Protector and floating him back on the ledge. The big man tried to say thanks, but no one could hear above the howling wind. Ethrang fell off twice, but each time turned into a sparrow and flitted back with a grin.

At the apex of their climb, there was a small indent in the rock face, almost large enough to be a cave. Two mountain goats were hiding in the back and immediately charged. Striker had his axe out in a moment and clobbered both in the head, moving with uncanny speed. He slit their throats to let the blood drain, then threw a carcass over each shoulder. "Dinner," he barked over the wind then continued down the trail. Everyone looked at each other wide-eyed. Even Ethrang was speechless for once, not that Chip could hear him anyway.

The storm intensified but the effects finally decreased when they reached the bottom as the sun began to set. They were in a narrow valley out of the elements.

"Do we make a fire and eat our supper?" Striker asked. "I could try and find some bushes. There are no trees around here. Only stone and snow."

The wizard shook his head. "Not necessary, plus we don't have the time. I will take care of it." He deftly levitated the two carcasses and skinned them at the same time with his magic. Chip was amazed at his dexterity. The old man looked back. "It only takes about a thousand years of practice to do this." He expertly roasted the meat with his Power, then detached it from the bone, removing ligaments and tendons. He gave the final product a light sear, then floated a generous piece to everyone.

Chip chewed each morsel, savouring the flavours.

"It's good," Chase said, chewing happily. "I think slow cooking it would make it even better."

The wizard gave him a withering look. "We don't have time for that."

"Or even some salt..." Chase began. Xander stared at him. "Never mind, it's great. Best I ever had. May I have another?" Ethrang giggled. The wizard shook his head and floated another piece over.

"Do we continue through the night," Thomas asked, wiping his mouth.

Striker looked around. "Normally, no. Things come out at night. But with the entire troll nation on our tail, I recommend we keep moving. We will need a few hours of sleep at some point, but we must create distance. Keep your eyes open. If things go right, we will reach Barko's cave by midday tomorrow."

Chase was going to make another quip but then thought better of it. They ate quickly and proceeded across the valley. The sun had nearly set, reducing visibility and causing the temperature to plummet. They pulled their cloaks tighter and plodded on. The snow would not relent. The dark trail wound upwards again, and they crested a rise to feel the full force of the wind.

In front of them, an immense mountain bear pawed the ground. It studied them impassively, the wind howling as the snow swirled. The beast rose on its hind legs and roared in challenge. The twins' eyes blazed blue, and the creature paused. Then it sank slowly to all fours and wandered away. It had decided there were easier meals. Ethrang laughed, and they carried on, pulling their cloaks tight.

The trail became clogged with snow, slowing progress considerably. Chip felt fatigued, but he focused on putting one foot in front of the other. As the storm passed over, the wind started to come straight at them, nearly pushing them back at points. The snow was more than two feet deep in spots. They managed to make it around two more mountains before a dark shadow filled the night sky.

"That's Hawk Mountain," Striker yelled. "We must climb halfway up it to reach a large plateau that leads to Barko's cave. Let's camp in this valley and get some shut-eye. There is a fissure in the rock ahead that will provide shelter. You may have to use your magic to remove the snow."

Xander shook his head. "We are too close to Barko to use our Power. He will sense it. If we have to lie on snow, so be it." The troll grunted, and they descended into a shallow valley where Striker led them to a fissure in the rocks. It was half full of snow. They crawled in, laid their cloaks out, and shared the blankets. Chip couldn't remember feeling so tired. One of the Protectors took watch, sitting at the entrance. The sound of the storm faded as he lay with Eleanor. He fell asleep in moments.

13

"He's dead."

Chip opened his eyes to see the weapons master staring grimly at the corpse of the Protector resting in the fissure's entrance. "What did you see?"

The troll prisoner next to the body was trembling. "First, I heard something drinking. I looked over to see a black shape on the Protector's chest. It looked at me with yellow eyes. I pulled my club out and it slunk off, then I woke you."

Garth grunted. "His name was Jeb." He peered at the corpse. The young man's throat had been slashed, and the blood drained from his body. The sun was beginning to break over the mountains.

Striker stood beside him, head bowed. "There are stories of a creature that does this. It has yellow eyes and drinks blood. Nobody knows what it is. Perhaps another gift from Barko."

"Weapons Master!" Carvor pointed down the trail. "I see torches. The trolls are coming."

"Everyone up. Pack your things. We need to go. They are only a few hours behind us." Garth sighed. Even he looked tired.

Chip felt like he hadn't slept at all. His muscles were sore from the previous day's hike, and his body did not want to move. "I have no choice," he muttered, repeating the phrase in his head. What the brain could do was amazing if it knew it had no choice. He stood up, pulling Eleanor to her feet. A grim resolve began to build in him as he thought of where the trail was leading them. How Barko had altered history could not be understated. If he was going to die in these forsaken mountains, then Barko was coming with him.

Everyone stepped around the dead body as they left the fissure. Eleanor gasped at the man's face. A deep gash on his throat ran from ear to ear, and his skin had shrunken and shrivelled around his facial bones. His eyeballs were missing. The face staring at them with empty eye sockets, leeched of blood, was almost unrecognizable. Chip shuddered and urged her forward.

The sun rising in the east illuminated the landscape but would soon be obscured by the dark clouds overhead. Everything was snow and stone. Jagged mountains surrounded them. In the distance, the trolls were running down the trail, a black line that continued growing as they rounded a smaller mountain. Chip turned to see that the trail ahead had disappeared, covered with several feet of snow. The clouds had cleared in the west but hunkered over Hawk Mountain as if daring them to approach. The size of the monolith was impressive. He could see that halfway up it levelled off into a large plateau before climbing again to the peak. It looked like a single piece of dark stone, brooding over its lesser siblings. For a moment, the boy thought he saw a black figure on the plateau, but it disappeared.

"We cannot see the trail, but I know the way," Striker said. "My father took me here once when I was a lad. I had to wait outside the cave while he consulted with Barko. The creature is a hermit, willing to bargain with those seeking him. The whole place reeks of evil. Be wary."

"I wonder what bargains your father has made with that creature," Xander mused. "Let's find out."

They began hiking up the long slope to the base of the giant mountain. It was arduous work. Striker took the brunt of it, pushing his massive legs through the snow, making it less difficult for the others. Chip realized that the troll army would have a much easier time running down a cleared trail. It would not take them long to catch up.

The small party reached the mountain base by late morning, brows wet with exertion despite the freezing temperatures. They paused to take a breather, looking up at the steep climb to the plateau. Behind them, the trolls were coming out of the valley with the fissure. They were running out of time.

The weapons master looked at their exhausted faces. "Dig deep, my friends. It is always darkest before the dawn. There is a saying that the Creator will only give us what we can handle. I don't know what awaits us at the top, but we will face it together. If you feel you can't go on, I assure you that you have lots left." He gave Chip a wink.

"Um, what if you run out of what's left?" Ethrang asked, causing Mary to roll her eyes. He noticed her look and blushed.

The weapons master turned to him, putting his hand on the skinny boy's chest. "This will feel like there's nothing left to give." He then tapped Ethrang's forehead with the tip of his finger. "But up here never runs out. Up here is the only one that can choose to give up. Don't give yourself that option." He turned and indicated that Striker should continue. The blond orphan seemed to digest the information, then grinned.

"Cool."

If they thought the climb to the base was challenging, the snow-covered, almost vertical trail was downright treacherous. It took until midafternoon to get halfway up before they all stopped, panting while hugging the slope. Looking back, they could see the trolls had arrived at the base of Hawk Mountain. Their speed was unnerving. Without slowing, the soldiers sprinted up the trail. Chip prayed to the Creator that they would make it before the trolls caught up. Their war cries grew in volume, bellows and chants intertwining to form a symphony of destruction.

The boy looked up at the dark, roiling clouds crowning the peak of the massive formation. He felt vulnerable, hanging exposed halfway up the base. With the plateau extending out, Chip felt like an ant climbing the shins of a seated stone giant waiting to snatch him up. An icy wind blew across the slope, screaming for them to give up. He would not do that. He had no choice.

They continued climbing, the wind increasing in ferocity. His hands and feet felt numb. He often had to reach forward and grab a piece of icy rock to stabilize himself. Chip realized he couldn't feel the rocks anymore. He pushed on.

They seemed to be making decent headway, and then Ethrang slipped ahead of him, sliding off a stone. The blond boy flailed his arms for a moment then flew backwards. Chip remembered the wizard's warning not to use their Power. He desperately wedged his foot on a rock below and braced for the impact. The boy caught the skinny orphan around the waist, but the force pushed him back. He teetered on the edge, straining to stay upright, but the momentum was too great, and they both fell back. Chip tried to seize his magic despite the wizard's warning, but he panicked, thinking of tumbling end over end down the mountain.

A massive hand suddenly pushed into his back, holding them both up. Then he was upright again, able to set the blond boy back on his feet. Behind him, Bulch grunted.

"I here. No problem."

Chip let out a sigh of relief. "Thank you again." The huge man grinned and slapped him on the back, knocking him into Ethrang.

"I was about to turn into an eagle, but the wizard said not to use magic. I figured you would catch me anyway, Guardian." He tried to grin, but a gust of wind almost knocked him off again.

Chip stared at him.

"They're halfway up!" Striker called from the front. "We need to hurry."

Chip looked down to see the trolls making good headway up the trail. He gasped at the column of soldiers snaking through the mountains as far as the eye could see. For a moment, he realized they were hopelessly trapped, but he dashed the thought. There was always a way. He had to figure it out.

It took until late afternoon when they finally crested the top. The trolls were not far behind. Before them was a massive plateau leading to a single giant cave at the base of the second tier. Thunder rumbled in the dark clouds overhead as if in warning. The wind whipped about in a frenzy, swirling odd piles of snow across the sheet of dark rock. Despite the winter storms, the snow could not accumulate here long enough before the wind swept it down the slopes. The black cave opening looked like a giant cyclops, staring at them from a stone face. The second tier shot up to dizzying heights before ending in a pointed peak. Hawks flew around the top, under the dark clouds, justifying its namesake.

"They have almost caught up," Striker shouted above the wind. We need to make it to the cave before they arrive." Everyone nodded, still panting from the recent exertion. "We must run."

They sucked in deep breaths and ran across the massive sheet of stone. The wind buffeted them mercilessly, a maelstrom of air and bits of snow. A blaze of lightning streaked across the clouds, followed by a jarring peal of thunder. All the elements seemed at work as they dashed to the dark opening. Even as he ran, Chip felt something in the air, in the very stone around him. It was a pall of evil, giving him goosebumps not caused by the icy wind. There was a malevolent presence permeating the entire plateau, and it emanated from the cave.

They only made it halfway to the cave before the trolls crested the slope and spilled out onto the plateau behind them. Screams of glee rang out as the soldiers gave chase. Chip looked back and felt relief to see there were no mages. The ones in front were the hardy foot soldiers built for this sort of thing. The mages would be coming though. He could be sure of that.

The final sprint was exhausting. The war cries rang out behind them, and they could hear the pounding of feet. Chip was exhausted, his body beginning to give up. An image of the weapons master tapping Ethrang's forehead surfaced, and he forced himself to keep moving. There was no choice. Then the giant cave was before them, a stone ramp leading up to a flat area before the entrance. He glanced back to see the trolls right on their heels, reaching for them. The group ran up the ramp into the cave's entrance and then spun around, pulling out their weapons.

The trolls, as one, skidded to a stop in front of the ramp, snarling and gnashing their teeth. Only a couple dozen feet separated them. They milled around, brandishing their weapons and beating their chests. Their ranks began to swell as more trolls arrived, but they did not press forward. The whole plateau was visible from the cave's entrance, and they watched with alarm as a dark wave of bodies began to spread out onto the immense rock sheet.

An insane cackle sounded behind them. "Don't worry. They cannot enter here. Come."

Everyone turned, trying to find the source of the high voice. They moved further into the cave, weapons ready. The darkness receded, revealing a large chamber with a straight-backed stone chair in the middle. Resting on the seat was an ugly creature leering at them. Torches lined the walls.

"Welcome, I am Barko. I have eagerly awaited your arrival. Do not fear. They cannot enter. I have made bargains forbidding it." The thing was not quite troll nor human. It had an ill-favoured mix of the worst traits. Patches of wispy white hair hung limp, framing a face with bits of bark-like skin hanging off the cheekbones and nose of a human. Half-grown fangs jutted from its mouth, which opened in a loud, high-pitched cackle. Its arms and legs were skinny, with dark patches of troll skin fused with pale white human flesh. Barko only wore a loincloth. It was then Chip realized the cave was warm, and the feeling began to return to his numb fingers. An unnatural, rank wind flowed towards them, its source hidden in the darkness at the back of the cavern.

"Like what you see?" Barko tittered, spreading his limbs in grotesque poses. Mary looked like she was going to vomit. He stopped and leaned forward, his face taking on a greedy look. "Did you come to make a bargain?"

Xander stepped forward, eyes narrowed. "No, we came to hand out justice for your crimes against the world." His tone was menacing, barely containing a deep-seated rage. Chip had never seen him like that.

The half-troll looked at him in surprise for a moment then started shrieking with laughter, flailing his skinny arms and legs. Abruptly, he stopped, and his eyes grew cunning. "You are not in a position to make threats, Orb Stealer. I could snap my fingers, and the trolls would pour in here and tear you apart. I am the only one who can save you. Let's make a bargain." He grinned, showing missing teeth.

"We can find a way out of here ourselves." The wizard's eyes blazed bright blue.

Barko wagged a finger. "Oh no, you can't. Only I know a way. For three thousand years, you have been the voice of reason. Are you going to throw it all away now? Are you going to let your anger get the better of you? Your decisions can change the world. Or at least you think they can." He half-heartedly covered his mouth to hide a smug smile. "If your brother can make a bargain, why can't you?"

Xander recoiled, searching the troll's face. "You lie."

"Do I? After Balor helped erect the barrier, he came to see me. You were supposed to be the next High Wizard, Xandrostika, but you are stubborn like your father, unwilling to seek a bargain. Jaggar and Balor wanted the position for themselves, so I made two bargains." He cackled, rubbing his hands. "I told Jaggar he would have to wait but gave him the old Guild in the meantime. The Troll King attacked the fortress three millennia ago, according to my instructions. Balor resisted at first, not wanting to give up the fortress, but I promised him a new Guild much grander than he could ever imagine. His greed is commendable."

The wizard stared at the creature with smouldering eyes. "And what did you get in return?"

"Me? Why, I got to be...me!" he chortled. "For many years, I was a man. Their Power sustained the transformation for a long time, and when I stared at my refection in the pool below, I was human. Now, look at me." He ran his fingers up and down his hideous body. "I need a bargain. And you need a bargain."

Chip stepped forward, incredulous. "You created Morgo which

changed the world, creating the rise of the Demon King. Are you telling me you did it for looks?"

"Ah, the red-eyed boy." Barko leaned back, appraising him. "I care not for consequences. The Balance takes care of that. I do know that you wouldn't have been born without me and my so-called meddling with history. You humans always complain about your parents' fallacies but don't realize that if your parents were perfect, you wouldn't exist. So ungrateful. What I would give to be born a human…" He drifted off, and then his eyes refocused. "Are you so sure the world would be different if I did not bargain with Morgo? Do you think no other so-called evil would have arisen? More importantly, how do you know I had any free will?" He leaned forward, eyes haunted. "I didn't ask to be born this way, to have this…need. I should have been born a human, not a troll. The powers that be made a mistake. I don't do it for others to look at me. I gaze into the pool and see my beautiful face for me." He had a desperate look in his eyes, stroking his wispy hair. "Right now, I am not so pretty, but I will be. Make a bargain, Chosen One, and I will show you the way out of this. I always keep my bargains."

The boy stared into the face of madness. He looked at his friends. Most were shaking their heads, but the twins and Ethrang held up their hands as if it was at least worth considering. Mary had a contemplative look on her face, weighing the options.

Striker turned to Chip. "I have no love for this creature. He has made many bargains with my father, likely keeping him in power all these years. For all I know, he has instructed Jaggar to kill his heirs. The only good thing about this thing before us is that it always keeps a bargain."

"Always." Barko held up his hand then cackled again, unable to maintain a straight face.

Chip considered. "What do you want?"

The wizard tried to intervene. "I think we can find our own way…"

"I need a little of your Power to make me human again. That's all, and then I will show you the way out. They will not be able to find you." The half-troll waited expectantly, trembling.

The Guardian stepped forward. "If I do this, I want you to know I will come back one day and kill you."

Barko stared for a moment in complete shock then shrieked with laughter, slapping his bony knees. Suddenly, he stopped mid-laugh. "I don't see you winning, red-eyed boy. Killian has grown too strong. Morgo was...creative. He accomplished things with the true Force that even I could not fathom." He cocked his head. "Do you know why some demon babies are born with white eyes?" Chip shook his head.

"Not even Killian knows, but I do. It's their souls leaking into their bodies. Morgo taught the Demon King to drink the white-eyed ones' magic, but he was also ingesting their spirit essences. That is why he is so powerful. By tearing down the Wall to their magic all those millennia ago, the Dark Elves blurred the lines of Power and soul. One day, all the demon offspring will be born with white eyes. It's already started. They will have Power but no soul. Once their body dies, it will be forever. When the Demon King realizes his children have no soul, he will wail for eternity. So you see, the Balance really does have a sense of humour."

"What about all the good people who will die in the meantime?" Chip retorted.

"Good?" Barko shrieked again. "Please."

"What about the Dim?"

The half-troll stopped laughing. For the first time, he looked uncertain. "One of you must destroy it. Either you or Killian. It matters not to me." He suddenly looked at the pouch with the dragon egg. "Careful not to lose that. Be prepared to sacrifice it when Killian proves stronger. You see, it matters not which dragon dies, for the power and knowledge go into the remaining one. I would smash it right now if I could be sure that Killian would use his dragon to destroy the Dim instead of taking over the world. He is mad, you see. Sometimes, I wonder if I'm the only normal one." He erupted in hysterics, laughing at his own twisted humour. Then he stopped again. "How come no one ever knows when they've gone mad?" He giggled mischievously, hiding his mouth.

Ethrang laughed out loud.

Barko turned his gaze to the skinny orphan. His eyes narrowed then widened. He fell from the stone chair onto his knees. "You are worshipped above all, shapeshifter." His eyes grew wet. "You are what I dream to be. With your abilities, I would be…happy. Able to take any shape I wish. No more bargains."

Ethrang gave him a strange look. "You should be happy with whatever shape you are."

The half-troll sprang to his feet, dancing madly. "Ha, the Balance is funny. A shapeshifter who doesn't care what shape he is." He doubled over in laughter, skinny body convulsing with mirth. Finally, he wiped his eyes and sat back down. "Now, where were we? Oh yes, do you accept the bargain?" He extended a skeletal hand covered with patches of bark-like skin.

Chip looked at the others. Half of them shrugged and nodded. The others shook their heads. Finally, he looked at Xander.

"This decision could change the world," the wizard said softly. "I leave it to you."

Prophecy ran through the boy's mind. Tellings of darkness, betrayal, and impossible choices struggled for dominance. Then he made a decision. "I create my own Path."

The Guardian walked forward and shook Barko's hand. "Deal. Don't forget what I said earlier." The half-troll leapt up and clapped his hands together with glee. "Oh, how I love a bargain. Come, come with me." He scurried to the back of the cavern, waving for them to follow.

A large tunnel led downwards. Barko grabbed a lit torch off the wall and hurried ahead of them, dancing excitedly. There were openings on either side of the tunnel, but he kept going straight until they arrived in a vast chamber. Stalactites comprised the ceiling above, and to the sides were several rough-hewn doorways leading into darkness.

Chip felt an instant revulsion for the room. The ominous feeling he experienced hiking up the mountain was magnified. This was the source of his discomfort. In the center of the chamber was a waist-high round stone well. Barlo walked up to the well, holding the torch high, urging them to look in. With trepidation, the boy peered over the wall to see a pool of water perfectly reflecting the torch's light and the faces of those looking in. With a start, he realized that Barko's eyes in the reflection looked like dark orbs of infinity. It was the eyes of Death.

He snapped his head up to see the half-troll grinning at him. "Don't look in the water too long, or you will start seeing things." He ran to the wall and placed the torch in a sconce. At the back of the well, three stone steps led up to the top. Barko scampered up them, grinning madly, then lowered himself into the water. It went up to his waist.

"I'm not sure…" Chip mumbled, still unnerved by the vision.

Barko's face turned deadly serious. "A bargain is a bargain."

Chip looked at him and nodded. He had given his word. "What do you want me to do?"

The half- troll broke into a broad smile, displaying his short fangs. "Slowly feed your Power into the water. I will be muttering some phrases. Don't stop until I tell you, or it will pull you in. Begin."

The boy was about to ask what he meant by that, but a sense of urgency filled him, and he wanted to get it over with and leave the room. Chip seized his Power, eyes blazing. Barko looked at him enraptured, like a small child watching a wondrous thing.

The boy fed a steady stream of red magic into the water. It started swirling. With his senses extended, Chip realized there were tiny runes carved into the floor and walls of the well. They flared to life, and the water began to blacken. He knew this didn't feel right at all and realized he had made the wrong decision. His anger flared, but he controlled it, focusing on the task. The water continued turning darker until it absorbed all light. The others stepped back, clearly feeling a malevolence enter the room. The Protectors gripped their sword hilts, eyes alert.

Barko let out a small gasp, face radiating joy and sank under the water. He emerged a moment later, covered in a layer of darkness, and then his body began to morph. The half-troll contorted and spasmed, skin bubbling then reforming. He arched his back and then stood up straight. The blackness disappeared into his skin, and a newly formed young man stared at them.

"Release your Power," he said in a deep, rich voice. He had a smooth face and midnight-coloured hair. Chip cut off his magic to the well and stepped back. Barko looked eerily similar to Death when that Force entered his mind at the Wizard's Guild. The eyes were dark, but at least they were not pools of infinity. The resemblance still frightened him.

The nearly naked man stepped out and descended the stairs. He turned and approached the well wall to look in. Chip realized with another start that the water had turned crystal clear again. Barko leaned over and looked at his reflection.

"Ahhh." He smiled, showing a full row of gleaming white human teeth. The boy recoiled, seeing the eyes of infinity in the reflection. Barko looked up and smiled at him. "This will last me a very long time." He stepped backwards into the corner of the room. "Thank you."

"Take us out of here," Chip demanded. "Fulfill your oath."

Barko looked at him with genuine sadness. "Dear boy, I'm afraid I cannot do that. For five thousand years, I have lived this miserable existence. I witnessed the Great Forget. I've seen and shaped history. Long I studied the dark arts, experimenting, questioning, refining...I eventually found a Force, the real power. I nurtured it, coaxed it, until it developed an awareness."

Chip's blood went cold. Barko smiled.

"Morgo was an eager student, and I set him on a course that would change history, even destiny. The Demon King is a product of our instruction and dedication, a loved child, if you will, nurtured to become a manifestation of this awareness. For now, it resides in me, thanks to your special kind of magic. The man with the silver hair cannot help you anymore. He knows what will happen if he interferes. Don't look so afraid. I'm still Barko, sort of." He let out a deep, rich laugh. "But I'm afraid for the first time ever, I must do something that truly hurts me. You see, the only threat to me is not you or the Demon King. It is the Dim. The truth is Killian has a much better chance of destroying it than you. And that is why I must break our bargain."

Chip was betrayed.

The boy's rage ignited. He unleashed a blistering stream of red Power at Barko, incinerating him. When the fire cleared, he gasped. Barko had wrapped himself in a shield of black energy. Essentially, he was covered in Death. He emerged unscathed.

"My pets!" Barko called. "Come out and play!"

Suddenly, a stream of white apes poured out of the opening on one side of the cavern. A group of black, muscular cats with large fangs and yellow eyes slinked in from the other side. A massive mountain bear lumbered down the tunnel behind them.

They all attacked at once.

"Form a ring," shouted Garth as the Protectors drew their swords. The wizards' eyes blazed to life. Chip turned to lend aid. Barko's deep laugh echoed above all.

The fanged cats leapt with a blur of motion. Two former prisoners went down with feline jaws clamped tight on their throats. A dozen apes ran into the melee, swinging wildly. The wizards shot concentrated bursts of fire lest they strike one of their own. Everyone wrapped themselves in a shield, but two apes barreled into the twins, knocking them off their feet. Ignoring their singed fur, they began pounding Kristan and Thomas with massive fists.

Ethrang, wrapped in a green shield, morphed into a brown tiger, scattering the smaller, yellow-eyed cats. His speed was unmatched as the shapeshifter slashed throats and tore out jugulars. Two cats leapt on him, trying to sink their fangs in his back but the shield held. He shook them off and gored their bellies. The twins set both apes on fire, sending them running into the walls. They slid down the stone, bellows silenced. Bulch swung his club with bone-crushing force, cracking white ape heads open. The bear tore into another prisoner, then confronted Eleanor and Mary, roaring on its hind legs. They linked and sent a blistering stream of mulitcoloured Power into its chest that burst out the beast's back in a spray of flesh and bone. A massive snake came out of nowhere, biting Chase's leg.

"Ow!" he cried, hacking down on its neck, eventually severing the head. More animals came out, and Chip decided that his best course of action was to shield everyone.

"Yes, use your Power, boy," Barko called, laughing. "Use it all up."

The Guardian paused then reluctantly pulled his magic back. Xander had always told him to conserve. "Use your shields," he yelled. He looked at Barko, whose face changed to one of hate. Chip pulled his sword and entered the fray, shielding himself only. There was a short period of frenzied fighting, and then everyone looked around. All the animals were dead. Three prisoners and one Protector named Todd had died. Chip clenched his jaw. Only seven Protectors and four prisoners remained.

"That's better," Barko gloated. "How much more can you withstand before your Power runs out? Oh, Jaggar," he boomed in a deep voice. "They are all yours as promised."

Trolls suddenly filled the openings on the sides of the cavern, hefting various weapons as they grunted in anticipation. King Jaggar strolled down the tunnel, a broad grin on his face. Princess Miriam followed with her head down. A score of mages surrounded them, eyes blazing.

"You are trapped." Barko smiled. "How does it feel looking Death in the eye?" He let out a deep laugh.

Chip's rage exploded. He lifted his arms, but Barko was waiting for it. Black energy shot out of the newly formed man's fingers, surrounding the boy.

Chip frantically strengthened his shield, but an icy coldness began to seep through.

"I can only hold him," Barko shouted. "Deal with the others."

"My pleasure. Princess, are you ready?" King Jaggar looked to his left, but Miriam shook her head. "You can watch them die then," he said, shoving her hard into the wall. He lifted both arms. The mages followed suit.

"Link with me," Eleanor yelled.

A torrent of fire shot from the mage's hands simultaneously. Everyone gathered behind Eleanor as she created a massive shield. The impact sent the group of wizards staggering back, but the shield held. Everyone's face strained, trying to maintain the barrier as more mages added their fire.

The Guardian stood wrapped in an icy darkness that slowly compressed his body. He knew he couldn't fight the darkness.

It was Death.

Han's Telling rang in his mind. "A darkness will descend on you that you cannot defeat. You will be betrayed."

Chip shook with rage, pulling in more Power, desperately trying to stave off the blackness. He shivered as the cold chilled him to the bone. His strength began to ebb. The boy looked at his friends through the dark shield. They stood huddled with Eleanor in the front, fighting off a blistering attack. The shield began to waver and buckle. He had to do something. Chip remembered being in the icy grip of Death on the other side of the Divide, finally seeing the preciousness of life and the value of himself.

I'm enough.

The thought rang hollow now. If he was enough, he could save them. He wasn't enough. He was worthless. A complete failure. His choice to make the bargain would cause all their deaths. He was to blame. It was all his fault. Anguish filled him as the cold closed in. He drew in more Power but knew he was running out. He looked at his friends and saw Mary falter. She sank to the ground, out of Power. The shield buckled.

King Jaggar let out a loud laugh. Ethrang suddenly disappeared into a sparrow and flew to the side, unleashing a stream of bright green fire into the mages. They screamed as their robes caught fire, causing the attack to weaken. They turned to incinerate him, but he flitted back behind the shield, reappearing to lend his Power. Chip could tell by his face that the blond orphan had given everything he had.

The unfairness of it all rang through his mind. Death was cheating. It shouldn't be like this. It wasn't fair. Negative thoughts rushed into his mind as the coldness of Death began to shut down his body. He looked over and saw the weapons master turn to him. Their eyes met. The message was clear.

Don't give up.

He forced himself to remember the lessons.

Talk to yourself, don't listen.

Change your negative thoughts.

Everything is a challenge.

Chip looked at his teacher, and he was a young boy again, absorbing life's lessons. When he began training all those years ago, he could not believe there was something on the other side of his pain. The pain of being an orphan, of being ostracized for his red eyes, of spending years oppressed by Miss Stern. He had found meaning and a purpose. People cared about him. It took him a long time but through their guidance he had learned to care about himself.

Now he needed to apply those lessons.

The Guardian, wrapped in the icy embrace of Death, nodded to the weapons master.

There is always a way.

He pulled in a little more of his dwindling Power to buy himself precious time and focused his thoughts. Magic wouldn't work. His sword wouldn't work. He touched the dragon egg. Deep down, he knew she would not awaken. Starlight had made it clear she would only awaken in the presence of the Light Elves. He reached down below the egg and felt the sheath of the unicorn horn.

It could go through anything.

He remembered the dragon egg humming in the presence of the unicorns, suggesting their magic was similar. Starlight had fended off Death, at least temporarily, to allow him to escape through the Divide. The unicorns used their horns to cleave through an entire army when forming a spearhead.

Could the unicorn horn go through Death?

Only one way to find out. Chip grasped the hilt and pulled the horn free. It immediately began humming in his hand. Using his remaining strength, he pointed the horn at the shield of Death and pushed.

It separated.

He sliced up and down, creating an opening as the darkness recoiled and the boy slipped through. Barko gasped, staggering backwards. Chip wrapped his body with Power and sped towards him, holding the horn extended. The troll-turned-man desperately formed a dark shield, but the boy did not slow.

The Guardian plunged the unicorn horn through the darkness to the hilt in Barko's chest. "I told you I would kill you." His voice was full of Power.

Barko's eyes widened in horror, and then for a brief moment Chip stared into the black eyes of infinity before the darkness fled.

The man who looked like Death gave a shrill scream and morphed back into an troll. His skin turned bark-like and wrinkled, pulling taut over his skeletal features. Barko's midnight hair turned white and fell out. His body shrivelled and, with a last high-pitched cry, sank to the ground dead, looking like a five-thousand-year-old troll.

Chip Oathbinder turned with eyes blazing. Red coils of Power wrapped around his body. The wizards crouched low, trying to hold up their failing shield. King Jaggar's face turned from victory to fear. The boy extended his Power, quick as thought, and pulled the crown off the king's head, throwing it to the side. The mages beside him were weakened, so Chip reached out with red hands and slammed them into the walls. The king grabbed his daughter and yanked her in front of him, using the princess as a shield.

"Back!" he shouted. "Move it!"

Jaggar retreated down the tunnel, dragging his daughter with him. The trolls in the side openings did not know what to do. Chip looked at them with blazing eyes, and they ran away. The boy turned to his companions.

"Go get 'em, Guardian." Ethrang was exhausted but gave him a weak smile.

"Take down that monster," Eleanor managed, a sheen of sweat on her face.

"Remember, control," Xander said, looking dishevelled.

The weapons master gave him a nod. The twins weakly held up their hands.

Striker walked over and picked up the crown. He stepped aside to let the boy stride through, and then everyone followed.

King Jaggar stood with Raphael and several other mages on the flat area in front of the cave entrance. He held Miriam in front of him. Below them, ten thousand trolls filled the plateau. The dark clouds overhead were dispersing. Chip walked up to the entrance, roiling with Power, yet he knew he had little left. It had taken much of his magic to fend off Death. The others stopped behind him, equally drained.

"You cannot defeat my entire army," Jaggar said. "Surrender, and I will let you live. Striker, bring me my crown. I will reinstate you as my heir. You have my word."

The prince walked forward. "Release my sister first." Jaggar grinned and pushed his daughter roughly to the side. Striker walked up to the king but at the last moment turned and placed the crown on Miriam's head.

Different emotions played across Jaggar's face, and then he nodded, smiling. "I abdicate in favour of my daughter. I deserve this. Will you ever forgive me, son?" He walked up with open arms. Striker stood rigid as his father embraced him. Jaggar suddenly squeezed the back of the prince's neck and drove a long dagger to the hilt in his son's stomach."

Rafael smiled in appreciation.

Miriam screamed as her brother sank to the floor.

Jaggar raised his hand to strike her.

That was the opening Chip needed. He summoned the last of his Power and was about to release it, but Miriam's eyes suddenly blazed the brightest blue he had ever seen.

"No," she said, holding out her hand, freezing the king's motion. "I am the queen now." She flung Jaggar high into the air. He screamed, flailing madly, making a feeble attempt to form a shield. With both hands, Miriam released a blue fireball at her father the size of Furiosa. For a moment the Troll King absorbed it, face contorting in expressions of anger, shock, and finally fear. Then he simply disintegrated in all directions. Tiny bits of his flesh and bone floated down, but a gust of wind came, and then Jaggar was no more.

The entire army stared at her without moving.

Raphael stepped forward, outrage on his face. "You are not my Queen. I should be..."

Miriam lifted him into the air even as he tried to form a shield. She levitated him over the army, breaking through his magic with ease. "This is what happens to traitors." She filled Rafael with a thick cord of blazing blue Power and spread her hands. Pieces of him flew everywhere. "Does anyone else disagree with me being queen?" She amplified her voice with magic. The trolls glanced at each other then shrugged and looked forward. She stared at the mages, and they quickly bowed their heads.

Nobody made a sound.

Queen Miriam turned to her brother, sending healing magic into his stomach, absorbing his pain. She lifted him to his feet. "Feel like being a general?"

"Why not?" Striker said. "Beats being in prison."

The queen held her brother's hand and turned to the trolls. Her eyes blazed a stunning blue, and her voice shook with Power. "My father has abdicated the throne and named me queen. He has made bargains with Barko, a practitioner of the dark arts, making deals to keep himself in power that included killing his heirs. We have all lived under his tyranny for far too long. My brother, Striker, who many of you know and respect, stands with me, heralding a new era. I name him general. If any of you don't like it, feel free to challenge him in combat and see what happens." The trolls snickered amongst themselves and nodded, thumping their chests.

"To all the mages, I bring in a new era of learning and knowledge. You will be taught with honour and respect. Jaggar has ruled us for millennia, training us in the way of war. I cannot change the past.

What I can do is change who we are fighting against. Long ago, humans, trolls, elves, and dwarves fought against a common enemy. That enemy has returned, stronger than ever, but so are we. The demons are coming, and we must be ready. Do you want to fight!" The trolls bashed their chests, bellowing out war cries.

"Come forward, Guardian of Humanity," the Troll Queen beckoned the boy. Chip strode up, eyes still blazing, surveying the troll nation. She asked the others to stand with him. Some of the trolls started jeering.

Queen Miriam held up her hand. "This is the Guardian of Humanity, Chip Oathbinder, the red-eyed boy wizard. He is the balance to the Demon King. For the last few days, we have attacked and pursued them across our nation. They came in peace, and we broke our accord. My father betrayed his Honour Oath." The trolls looked at each other, anger on their faces. "Yes, it's true. Chip's Protector defeated Furiosa, and Jaggar reneged on our alliance." Grumbles sounded throughout the throng. They were clearly angry at their former king.

"I now reinstate our alliance with the humans. The war is over between us. I know you think of them as the enemy, but you also value a skilled opponent. We fought them for days, yet they are still here. We must value their fighting prowess. Show respect!" The trolls nodded grudgingly and thumped their chests. "Now we have a new enemy. I ask for allegiance to your new queen. My brother and I will lead you to victory! Now kneel!"

Queen Miriam stood overlooking the plateau, eyes blazing. The trolls looked at each other. There were still a few grumbles but many more nods. Striker took a knee, and others joined until the whole army kneeled before their new queen.

"I swear fealty to Queen Miriam," Striker shouted.

"I swear fealty to Queen Miriam," the trolls echoed as one.

"Now rise. I have your oath of allegiance. I expect your unwavering loyalty. Jaggar has sullied our name. I want honour to mean something again. I want trolls to be respected throughout the lands." She turned to Chip. "Tell me what you need. How can we help you?"

The boy stepped forward, red eyes blazing. "I ask for you to bend a knee to me." Gasps could be heard from the mages. "I want your allegiance. I want to be the Guardian of the Races." Queen Miriam looked at him for a long time then finally nodded.

She turned to her people. "It looks like your honour and oath will be tested already. I hold you to it. Chip Oathbinder will lead us against the Demon King in the Last Battle. It will come at winter's end. We will be ready. He is now the Guardian of the Races and has asked us to swear allegiance to him. He has earned the right. In reparations for our broken oath, I accept." The trolls began to grumble. "In return, we get Northbane."

She winked at Chip. He looked surprised for a moment then nodded. The trolls began bellowing approval.

Miriam turned to the boy and kneeled. The army followed suit.

"I swear fealty to Chip Oathbinder, Guardian of the Races," the Troll Queen shouted.

"I swear fealty to Chip Oathbinder, Guardian of the Races," the entire troll nation thundered.

"Does this count in the prophecy when they said three kings must kneel?" Chase whispered to his best friend.

Chip turned. "It counts to me."

Loud cheers erupted amongst the trolls. A gust of wind caught Chip's crimson cloak, and the boy with red eyes stood straight and proud. The trolls began thumping their chests, still kneeling before the Guardian.

The boy looked westward, knowing he had a dangerous journey ahead. Darkwood and the Secret Caves held the key to the missing Light Elves. He now knew how to find them. Ten thousand trolls kneeled before him. He was building an army against the darkness. A ray of sun finally broke through the clouds, illuminating him.

Chip Oathbinder raised his chin, red cloak billowing in the wind, and faced his destiny.

END OF VOLUME SIX

. . .

IF YOU ENJOYED READING THIS, please leave a review on Amazon. It would be greatly appreciated.

Please visit my website: www.terryironwood.com

Type your email address at the bottom of the page to be notified of my next book launch and other important news. I do not send a regular newsletter.

I have added a free short story prequel called "Weapons Master" in the upper right corner of my website. It is Garth Stone's backstory.

The Orphan's Quest audiobook with special effects by the renowned narrator Nigel Peever is now available on Audible.

Volume Seven: Light Seeker – End of December 2024.

I hope you enjoyed Volume 6: Stone Kingdom. Be sure to look out for Volume 7: Light Seeker and the exciting conclusion in Volume 8: Last Battle.

The Great Forget Fantasy Series:
Volume 1: Orphan's Quest
Volume 2: Defenders of Hope
Volume 3: A Dim World
Volume 4: Guardian
Volume 5: Wizard's Guild
Volume 6: Stone Kingdom
Volume 7: Light Seeker (End of December 2024)
Volume 8: Last Battle (Early March 2025)

ACKNOWLEDGEMENTS

I offer my heartfelt thanks to my family and friends, who provided invaluable support, wisdom, and encouragement. You know who you are. I especially want to mention Kevin C., Steve S., and Ward C., who went above and beyond.

I am delighted to work with my editor, Jason Letts from Imbue Editing, who continues to improve my writing.

Last, and certainly not least, I wish to thank an orphan, Chip, for taking me on his quest.

Many thanks,

Terry Ironwood

ABOUT THE AUTHOR

Terry Ironwood resides with his family. He holds multiple university degrees and is interested in the science of self-improvement. He is equally fascinated with physics and spirituality. Terry believes in an 'attitude of gratitude' and is grateful he can write full-time. His dream is to help others reach their full potential.

Printed in Dunstable, United Kingdom